Bones to Pick

Books by Carolyn Haines

Hallowed Bones

Crossed Bones

Splintered Bones

Buried Bones

Them Bones

———

Summer of the Redeemers

Touched

———

Penumbra

Judas Burning

<u>Non-fiction</u>

My Mother's Witness:

The Peggy Morgan Story

Bones to Pick

Carolyn Haines

KENSINGTON BOOKS

KENSINGTON BOOKS are published by

Kensington Publishing Corp.
850 Third Avenue
New York, NY 10022

ISBN 13: 978-0-7582-1090-6
ISBN 10: 0-7582-1090-6

Printed in the United States of America

1

Dahlia House is haunted. No big revelation for those who know me and my family, but on this cold November morning, as I sit and watch the sun gild the harvested cotton fields with a false show of gold, I am acutely aware of the specters of the past. I suppose in one way or another, we are all haunted, though some of us more than others.

In my haste to get to a predawn murder scene, I accidentally picked up my mother's car coat from the hook by the back door. Standing over the body of a dead twenty-three-year-old woman, I inhaled my mother's scent from the folds of her coat. I heard the words she told me when I was ten, grieving the death of a pet. "Death comes to all of us, Sarah Booth. It is nothing to fear or despair of, merely another journey, like birth. It is the cycle of life."

I hated those words then, and I've come to despise them. My mother and father died two years later, victims of a tragic car wreck. It's an irony that now I make my living with death as my employer. I investigate deaths that are not accidental or natural. I'm an amateur authority on murder, and there's no doubt in my mind that Quentin McGee met murder most foul in the bog of a cotton field.

Sometime during the hours of the harvest moon, some-one overpowered Quentin and held her face in the rich gumbo of Delta soil until she suffocated. It was a cruel and gruesome death, and I'm still shaken by it. So I sit on the front porch of Dahlia House with a cold wind cutting into me and stare at my riding boots, coated in a three-inch layer of mud, and I remember my mother with a bone-deep longing.

"Sarah Booth Delaney, what are you doin' mopin' out here on the front porch like your best friend has run off with your man?"

It was the voice of Jitty, my resident haint and vocal sub-conscious. I turned to look at her and did a double take. She was wearing a floor-length gown of gold silk with a bodice cut low enough to show the tops of her nipples. If that weren't enough, her hair was hidden beneath a pow-dered wig of white curls, and her normally bronzed skin was so pale that a beauty mark stood out in sharp contrast near her mouth. "Where the hell are you going?" I asked.

Jitty stepped closer, and I watched the fluid movement of the dress with awe. She frowned as she spoke. "That's not the question of the moment. What I want to know is where have you been? It's a scandal, you sitting out here in the dawn, covered in mud. You look like a participant in a bad reality show."

The story of my life. I was merely dirty, but I was the one who had to give an explanation. "A young woman, Quentin McGee, was murdered last night. Gordon Walters wanted me to see the crime scene before the body was moved."

"Sarah Booth, you're never gonna catch a man unless you get enough sleep to keep the bags out from under your eyes."

I stood up and faced Jitty. She would never have bags. She was dead. "What's the story behind that getup? I pre-fer the flapper look."

"I'm way over the Roaring Twenties. I'm headed to a ball."

"I hope everyone else is going in costume, too."

"Sarah Booth, this is the new me. I yearn for a time where there were social conventions. We need rules, structure . . . finesse! It's time people learned there are choices and consequences."

"Let them eat cake!" I thought I was funny, but Jitty gave me a look that would curdle milk.

"Look around. Our country is crumbling on its foundations. When there are no rules, nothing is valued."

"And you think it was better when a king ruled on a whim? Let me just point out that you look French and dressed for the guillotine." Jitty hopped decades and demeanors like commuters hop trains. One month she was a Cosmo girl, and the next a novice for martyrdom. Today she was getting on my nerves.

"There has to be a ruling class. Even the Republicans know that."

I made a chopping motion with my hand. "I hope you picked out a nice basket." I wondered if it was Jitty or me who was remembering history incorrectly. I didn't have time to discuss it. I saw Tinkie's forest green Cadillac pulling down the long drive between the bare sycamore trees.

Sweetie Pie, my noble hound, was underneath one of the rockers on the front porch, and I heard her tail begin to thud a Latin dance rhythm when she saw Tinkie's car. Sweetie rose, yawned, and trotted past me to the lawn to wait for Chablis, Tinkie's dust mop of a canine.

The Cadillac stopped, and Chablis was deposited out the driver's door before Tinkie stepped out. Even though it was just past six in the morning, Tinkie looked like she'd stepped out of the pages of *Country Gentry*. She wore an umber corduroy skirt and expensive boots that combined both the stables and chic.

"Is it true? Someone murdered Quentin McGee?" She headed toward me at full tilt.

I nodded. "It was a terrible scene."

She came and put her arm around me. Though she was a good seven inches shorter than me, her compassion was never vertically limited. "Come inside and I'll fix us both a Bloody Mary. We can have a little libation on a cold Sunday morning."

She hustled me inside and back to the kitchen. Once I was seated, she prepared two spicy Bloody Marys and put one in my hand. "When I got your message, I was curious as to why Gordon Walters came and got you." She pierced me with her blue gaze.

She had a point. Gordon was acting sheriff of Sunflower County because the elected sheriff, Coleman Peters, had taken an extended leave of absence to take his insane-slash-pregnant wife to a head-shrinking obstetrician. "I think Gordon was covering his bases. He's figuring, what would Coleman do?"

"This could work to our advantage."

I felt Tinkie's sharp gaze on me. She was waiting for my reaction, but I refused to give her one. Only the previous month I'd been in the wretched position of having to choose between my love for Coleman, the sheriff, and my potential love for the wealthy and handsome Hamilton Garrett V. I'd made a muddle of all of it and lost my chance with Hamilton. I'd never really had a chance with Coleman. He was married, and crazy wife or not, he felt obligated to honor that commitment. Tinkie was watching to see if I was backsliding on my vow to keep Coleman out of my heart.

"Having Gordon roust me out at four in the morning could work to our advantage—*if* you think freezing your butt off in a cotton field is a good thing. We don't have a client in this case."

"But we could have, and you're on the case from the

very beginning." Tinkie went to the refrigerator and got out bacon, eggs, heavy whipping cream, and bread. "I'm starving, and I'm sure Oscar has gone on to The Club for an early breakfast with Harold and the boys. I think they're going to play a round of golf. That means we have all morning to figure out what happened to Quentin McGee." She pushed the ingredients toward me, eyebrows arching.

Obediently, I began mixing the batter for French toast, Tinkie's favorite.

Tinkie perched on the edge of her chair. "I hear there was quite a fracas at the bookstore yesterday. Quentin's book has everyone talking, and when she went to her afternoon signing, there were no books to be had. Someone bought all of them and burned them in the alley behind Booking It."

That was a juicy tidbit indeed. "That must be some book," I said. "The title, *King Cotton Bleeds*, was enough to make me steer clear of it."

"Quentin named names. Along with washing some mighty dirty laundry, she even pointed out who has and who doesn't have a legitimate claim to belong to the United Daughters of the Confederacy."

"Do you actually think that matters today?" Tinkie was my touchstone in the world of high society and blue-blood pedigrees.

"You bet it matters. The book has been selling like hotcakes."

"Quentin was so young." I thought about what I'd witnessed. "Why would she want to write such a book? Gordon was saying that she dissed her own family."

"And everyone else in the Delta." Tinkie handed me the cream. "The McGee family is a prominent part of the book, and I'll bet they're howling. If you're looking for motive, that would be the first place to go."

"It still bewilders me." I got up and put the bacon on to fry.

"When Booking It gets more books, I'm going to buy a copy for you," Tinkie said. "I haven't had a chance to read mine all the way through, but Quentin did a good job of digging up dirt."

While the bacon popped in the pan, I turned to face her. "Now that pisses me off. There comes a time when the past has to be laid to rest. Dragging it up over and over again isn't fair."

She began to soak slices of bread in the batter. "I guess—"

The ringing of the telephone interrupted her. I picked up the receiver on the table as I returned to the bacon. "Hello."

"Sarah Booth Delaney?" The voice on the other end was male, cultured, and high class.

"Speaking."

"This is Humphrey Tatum." A slight pause. "Of Tatum's Corner."

I knew the location, and I gathered this had to be a member of the founding family. "What can I do for you?" I didn't add, "At six forty-five in the morning."

"My sister, Allison Tatum, has been charged with murder in the death of Quentin McGee. I'd like to hire you to represent Al. She's going to need all the help she can get."

I put my hand over the receiver and signaled Tinkie to pick up the extension in the other room. "Hold for a moment while my partner picks up." When I heard Tinkie on the line, I asked him to repeat everything and then said, "Mr. Tatum, why don't you come around to Dahlia House? I think it would be better if we spoke in person. Say eight o'clock?"

"I'll be there."

Tinkie washed the dishes while I showered and dressed. When I came back downstairs, she'd spruced up our office. I thought, not for the first time, how Tinkie Bellcase

Richmond, wealthy and spoiled Daddy's Girl, would never have been my first choice for a partner in a PI agency, and how wrong I would have been. In the year we'd worked together, Tinkie had saved my life more than once, and she was the most loyal, constant friend a woman could ask for.

"Are you okay?" she asked as she handed me the recorder she'd set up with a new tape and batteries.

"I'm better than okay. You're the best, Tinkie."

She blushed becomingly, then gave me a sidelong glance. "You aren't going to be able to sweet-talk me into going to that surgeon."

Tinkie's breast lump was a serious bone of contention. I sighed. "I'm not going to try that tactic. I'm going to drug you, tie you up, and take you there. You're going to have that lump biopsied."

She shook her head. "Not necessary."

Now wasn't the time for a full-tilt head-to-head with Tinkie. For someone who could be as pliable as licorice in the hands of a man, she was more stubborn than a mule. Before I could tackle her need to have her lump seen to, a silver gray Jaguar pulled up in front of the house. "Here's our client." An exceedingly handsome Humphrey Tatum it was, too.

We watched as he took note of the glazed glass that read DELANEY DETECTIVE AGENCY and listed our names as investigators. He swept into the room on a hint of interesting cologne.

"Ladies," he said, nodding at both of us, "I put my sister's fate in your hands."

He was tall and lean, with corn-tassel hair and eyes a blue so pale they looked colorless at first. His skin was bronzed, as if he spent time under a sun unhampered by humidity and haze. The image that came to mind was Apollo.

"What is the exact charge against Allison?" I asked as I showed him a chair.

He sat with grace, taking in the office. "Murder One. Deputy Walters said there were footprints at the murder scene that matched Al's shoes."

I remembered the scene vividly. There had been clear prints around the bog where Quentin was killed. I'd thought it was strange, because the obvious presumption was that the murderer had been careless enough to leave such vital evidence. As if he or she had wanted to be caught. "What does Allison have to say about that?"

"She said she didn't wear those shoes last night. Someone must have taken them from her closet. They were found, covered in mud, on a small back porch at The Gardens B&B, where she was staying."

I didn't have to glance at Tinkie to see how she was reacting to that flimsy excuse. "Does Allison have an alibi?"

He shook his head. "She was alone, reading a book."

"What is Quentin and Allison's relationship?" Tinkie asked, cutting to the chase.

"They were lovers," Humphrey said, without batting an eye. "Both families were scandalized by the idea of Lezzielous, of course, but Al never cared about anyone but herself. In fact, she and Quentin were planning some big wedding." He actually rolled his eyes.

Tinkie leaned forward. "Sounds to me like both Allison and Quentin did their utmost to piss off their families." She gave it a ten-beat pause. "That makes me wonder why."

Her implication was clear, and Humphrey smiled. "Quite clever, but why would I be hiring a private investigator if I wanted Al to go to prison? She's two-thirds of the way there without my help."

He had a point, and I decided to try another tack. "Who do you think might want to murder Quentin?"

"Pick up a copy of *King Cotton Bleeds*. I'd say there are at least a hundred people who have motive. A good number of them were at the local bookstore yesterday, so a lot of them were in town."

Humphrey wasn't only handsome; he was smart. "Good leads," I said.

"Just to be sure we're all on the same page," Tinkie said, "where were you last night?"

Humphrey's smile was charming. "Patti Tierce." He reached across my desk and picked up a pen and wrote a number. "Call her. I think she'll remember our evening together quite vividly." He reached into the side pocket of his coat and brought out a checkbook and began to scribble.

He rose and put the check in front of me. It was made out for ten thousand dollars. "I hope that will suffice."

"For the first week," Tinkie said as she saw him to the door. "We'll be in touch."

When he was gone, I arched an eyebrow at her and waited for an explanation. Tinkie was the classiest broad I knew, and she never acted rudely, or seldom ever.

"Humphrey dated Eleanor Hinton."

I remembered Eleanor, though I'd lost touch with her when she moved to Vicksburg. She was a pretty girl who grew into a pretty woman, yet she couldn't hang on to a man. Or at least that's how the Cult of Daddy's Girls would diagnose it. She'd never made it to the altar, sort of like me, so she was offically out of the DG Club. "So?"

"He tied her up to the bed in some kind of sexual fantasy game. He put on a Superman costume and was going to leap from a tree into her second-floor bedroom window and *rescue* her."

"That's outrageous, and if I were Eleanor, I wouldn't have repeated all of this."

"It gets worse. He fell and struck his head and was knocked unconscious. One of the neighbors had to call 911." Tinkie walked around her desk, her boots clicking on the parquet floor. "The fire rescue squad had to untie Eleanor." She shook her head. "Eleanor was so humiliated, she had to move out of town."

It wasn't the kind of rumor one was likely to live down, I supposed. "So why blame Humphrey? She obviously signed on for the game."

"He never called her or even apologized. Once the rumors got out, he was too busy fielding all the date offers he got from curious women."

I had to laugh. "Isn't that the way it always works. The guy gets all the glory, and the woman wears the scarlet *A*."

"He's one of the most eligible bachelors in Mississippi, Sarah Booth, yet I can't try to fix any of my friends up with him!" She put her hands on her hips and stared at me. "Although, he might be perfect for you. Both of you are a little off."

Her insult was good-natured, and I took it as such. "It's almost nine o'clock. We've already had breakfast. Maybe we should head over to the jail to see Allison."

"Then we can go out to The Club for a mimosa," Tinkie said. "I'm sure we'll run into some people who will be more than willing to talk about Quentin's book."

As Tinkie and I drove into Zinnia, I noticed several county prisoners in their green-and-white uniforms, planting poinsettias around the Bradford pear trees that marked Main Street. Tiny white fairy lights were already woven around the trunks and through the branches. Christmas would soon be upon us, a fact that left me depressed and melancholy.

"I'm going to give Oscar a call," Tinkie said as she whipped out her new cell phone, a flip device with a suede carrying case. It matched her purse and boots. "I'm more than a little curious about the McGee and Tatum family finances."

Tinkie had come to realize that most murders were about money. Money could buy sex and power, among other things.

"Good idea."

She pulled into a parking space along the empty court-house square. I got out and walked up the courthouse steps and down the hall to the sheriff's department. It was going to be difficult to go in there and not see Coleman at his desk. He'd become such a big part of my life, both pro-fessional and personal. Since he'd taken an unpaid leave of absence and left for Jackson with Connie, I hadn't heard a word from him and didn't expect to. Whether it was vanity or deluded fantasy, I believed that it had cost Coleman a lot to walk away from a possible future with me and stick with his psycho wife. But I respected his decision. Coleman wasn't a man who gave his word lightly.

My footsteps sounded hollow on the linoleum, and Deputy Walters met me with a carefully blank expression. "I hear you're working for the Tatums," he said.

Word did travel fast in a small town. "Humphrey hired us. Can we see Allison? Tinkie's right behind me."

He unlocked the door to the jail and escorted me be-tween two rows of cells. Only a few weeks before, Sweetie Pie had been incarcerated on trumped-up charges of bit-ing. Coleman and Gordon had been good to her. I could see that Gordon had done what he could to make Allison comfortable. She had four pillows and three blankets, though the temperature was comfortable. She was a pretty young woman with her brother's Nordic coloring and a petite but athletic figure.

"Who are you?" she asked, rising to her feet. She came to the bars and grasped them to get a better look at me.

"This is Ms. Delaney," Gordon said. "She's your private investigator. She was also at the crime scene and saw your footprints clear as day."

I didn't dispute Gordon but merely waited until he was gone. While I was waiting, I took Allison's measure. Her hair was cut in a chin-length bob, and her blue eyes were without make-up. She didn't need any. Her long eyelashes were thick and dark, and her complexion as smooth as a child's, except for three angry-looking scratch marks across her left cheek.

"Why did my brother hire you? He hates me," Allison said.

"Why does he hate you?"

She sighed. "I messed up his life. Quentin fell in love with me, instead of him."

That was something to ponder, but I filed it away and got down to the basics. "Where were you last night, Allison?"

"Quentin and I had a fight." She spoke softly and looked down, blinking her eyes rapidly. Her fingers drifted up to her cheek. When she looked back up at me, tears hung in her lashes. "We'd had a terrible fight. The first book was a tremendous success. Her publisher had already gone back to print another twenty thousand copies, and the book had only been out for a week. Quentin said she was going to write a second book. I didn't want her to."

A good investigator learns there are always multiple ways to bend a motive. Allison had just handed me a gold-plated one. But somehow, I believed her when she said she'd had an argument with Quentin. That was a far cry from a desire to murder her. "So you argued. Where and when?"

"We were having dinner at The Club. Several people overheard us. Quentin got rather loud." She frowned. "That was about eight o'clock last night."

"What happened after that?"

"Quentin stormed out of The Club. By the time I got the car from the valet, she'd disappeared. That was the last time I saw her." She wiped at her cheek. "I really loved her. I hate that we parted with angry words."

"Where did you go?"

"I drove around Zinnia for a while. Then I drove to Tatum's Corner. I was so close to home, I thought I might see Mom and Dad."

This was good news. "Did you see them?"

She shook her head. "No. I didn't stop. There were things in Quentin's book that only I could have told her. I felt like a Judas, so I didn't stop." When she looked into my eyes, there wasn't a hint of self-pity in her gaze. "Quentin and I both believed that people who built their lives on lies should be exposed. That's what her book was about. Somewhere along the way, I guess I lost the taste for unadulterated truth. We hurt a lot of people."

"Which brings me to a logical question. Who would want to hurt Quentin?"

Allison's eyes filled, but she didn't cry. "Who wouldn't? Everyone hated us. I told Quentin that I just wanted to live our lives together. We could have moved to New York or London. We could have gone somewhere we'd be accepted, but she said we weren't going to run away. We were going to rub their noses in it."

I'd learned one thing from Lawrence Ambrose, a truly famous literary figure who'd been murdered last Christmas: People will do a whole lot to keep their secrets out of print. "Can you give me some specific names?"

"Lots of people were angry about the book. Yesterday afternoon at the book signing, Umbria, Quentin's sister, was saying horrible things. I think she bought all the books and burned them."

I'd already planned to visit the McGee family members. "Anyone else?"

"For the past six months someone had been sending Quentin threatening notes."

I gripped the bars and leaned closer. "Who?"

"They were anonymous. I thought they were creepy, but

Quentin just laughed about it. She said we were getting someone's goat, and the book hadn't even come out yet."

"Do you have any of those notes? Did she keep them?"

"I'm not certain," Allison said. "Quentin might have saved them. You could look through her things at the B&B or maybe at our cottage in Oxford."

2

Tinkie was sitting on the courthouse steps when I finished my interview with Allison. To my surprise, my partner was deep in a phone conversation with someone who must have been distraught.

"There's no point in making yourself sick," Tinkie said, and I knew she was talking to a man. In a well-trained Daddy's Girl, there's a tone that both soothes and strokes the ego of a MWP—Male With Potential. There was a pause and Tinkie continued. "Nothing can change it now. Sarah Booth and I will check it out, and I'm sure we'll find everything is okay." She looked up and blew her sun-glitzed bangs off her forehead in a gesture of impatience, but there wasn't a hint of it in her voice. "I'm certain Sarah Booth doesn't think any such thing. She's always had great admiration for you."

I arched my left eyebrow—the only one I could arch after months of practice—as she hung up the phone.

"I'm sorry I didn't get into the jail to interview Allison, but I knew you had it covered, and I thought it best to talk to Harold out here."

"Harold? What's wrong with him?" Tinkie was only half

right. When Harold had tried to buy my affections with a four-carat diamond, I hadn't felt very warmly toward him, but he'd proved himself a good friend in the last eight months.

"He's worried."

"Is it about that book?"

"Partly, but there's something else. He's in a real dither." She patted the step, and I took a seat beside her on the cold cement slab. The courthouse square was lined with white oaks, their limbs all bare. In one tree a murder of crows hunkered down against the wind. It was a bleak and dismal day.

"What's wrong with Harold?" The faintest tingle in my thumb let me know that my appendage hadn't totally forgotten Harold and his attentions. I reminded myself that Harold Erkwell was the president of the Bank of Zinnia, the bank Tinkie's father owned and where her husband was chairman of the board of directors. I'd seen Harold in a fit of passion but never in a dither.

"He had a run-in with Quentin McGee last night. Gordon has already been out to question him."

"It's Allison who's locked up. Why is Harold worried?"

"He doesn't believe Allison killed Quentin, and once she's released, he thinks he may be the prime suspect."

"Why in the world would he think that?"

"Because he threatened to kill Quentin in front of about eight people at The Club."

My mouth made a silent little O. "That doesn't sound like Harold."

"He'd been drinking. I gather he just broke up with Rachel Gaudel and was upset. Then that ass Marcus Kline started teasing him about the book and some dirt on the Erkwell family. About that time, Quentin bumped into him and spilled her drink all over him. That was the last straw."

Harold normally was the most levelheaded person I'd

ever met. It was hard to visualize him making rash death threats. "Did Harold say what time this happened?"

"After nine and before ten, but he couldn't be more exact. He knows that because Rachel left at nine, and Harold said he went home around ten."

That time frame put Harold talking to Quentin *after* Allison had left The Club. "Did Oscar have any information on the financial scene?" My butt was freezing off, so I stood and offered Tinkie my hand. She grasped it and rose.

"He just said we'd better cash that check first thing in the morning and see if it clears."

"Damn." I turned to face her. "I thought the Tatums were the wealthiest family in Crystal County."

"That was before 2000. A lot has changed in this country."

That was a vast understatement. "What about the Mc-Gees?" I asked.

"Seems that Franklin and Caledonia McGee had much better financial advice. They bought low and sold high. They're one of the wealthiest families in the Southeast."

"One thing about this case, we have plenty of suspects."

"Most of them are Oscar's friends." Tinkie started toward the Cadillac. "Want to go check out a few leads at The Club?"

"I think we should forgo the champagne and see what we can find at The Gardens."

Tinkie sighed. "Harold is at The Club, and I think he could use a dose of your humor."

"I'll catch him later today," I promised as we got in the Cadillac and headed the few blocks to the bed-and-breakfast run by one of the matrons of Sunflower County.

When we pulled down the shell driveway, Tinkie slowed. Live oaks lined the way, some with magnificent limbs that crossed over the roadway and touched the ground on the other side. The place hadn't been named The Gardens without reason.

Unfortunately, the owner of the place, Gertrude Stromm, bore no resemblance to the bounty and generous beauty of her establishment. Her pinched face held eyes that shifted left and right, as if she might miss some social faux pas. I'd heard from several people who'd spent the night at the B&B that she served breakfast at seven. If you were late, you didn't eat. It was only the beauty of the place that kept her in business.

"Mrs. Stromm," Tinkie said as she stepped up to the front door. "It's good to see you. Oscar sends his regards."

"You're here to poke your nose into that terrible business with Quentin McGee." She said this to me, not Tinkie.

"Allison Tatum has asked us to pick up some things from her room," I said smoothly. In the sunlight Gertrude's red-tinted hair looked like tiny copper wires bent at the ends.

"You'll need a court order to get in there," she said.

"No, we don't," Tinkie said evenly. "Allison needs a change of clothes, and we're going to get it for her. We've been hired by her brother, Humphrey, to help her out."

"The sheriff's department has already sent someone here, tromping mud all over my polished floors. I won't have this. I'm going to pack up all of their things and have them removed from the premises."

"How far in advance did Quentin pay the room?" I asked.

"That doesn't matter one bit. I don't have to have snoops and cops disturbing my other guests."

"Mrs. Stromm, it looks as if you're going to need a new roof here before long."

Tinkie's observation was out of the blue, and it stopped both me and Gertrude in our tracks. It took only a few seconds for the meaning to register on each of us.

"How dare you!" Mrs. Stromm was honestly shocked.

"It's very easy." Tinkie laughed charmingly. "This is called business. Now we'd like to see Allison's room, please."

The B&B was run like an old-time hotel, with a registration book on the front counter and pigeonholes behind the desk, where keys with large room numbers attached were kept. Gertrude got the key to Room 18. "Just follow me." She started to stomp away, but I stopped her.

"Who stays at the registration desk?"

"I do. I have to check and be sure the people who stop by are quality folk. If I'd had any idea about Quentin McGee, I would never have rented her or her *friend* a room."

I didn't doubt that for an instant, but it wasn't my point. "So when you're overseeing lunch or the gardens, who stays at the front desk?"

She frowned, and her cool gray eyes grew even icier. "What are you implying?"

"Is the desk left unattended?"

"Perhaps."

It was as much as I was going to get out of her without thumbscrews, but it was enough to tell me that anyone could have picked up a key and gone into Allison's room to steal her shoes. This was a point in our favor.

The hallway was long and dark. The floor was polished pine with dark beaded board wainscoting edging the walls. The upper half was wallpapered with hunting scenes. Not my idea of great décor, but it was part of the planter tradition.

When we got to Number 18, Gertrude unlocked the door and pushed it open. "I've made an inventory of every single thing in the room that belongs to me. If one thing is missing, I'll have both of you in a jail cell beside your *client*."

"Do you think you'll go with shingles again or perhaps steel?" Tinkie's face was a careful blank.

Gertrude made a sound like a dog choking on a bone and stomped down the hallway, leaving us alone.

"Oscar would never hold up a loan on our account," I said to Tinkie.

"Of course not, but she doesn't know that. You take the dresser, and I'll take the suitcases."

The only interesting thing I found in the dresser drawers was a choice in undies—white lace thongs. Tinkie hit the mother load when she went through Quentin's brown travel valise. She held the note out to me, satisfaction in her eyes. She read it aloud. *"You're going to pay for dragging your family's name through the mud."*

It was short, sweet, to the point, and virtually untraceable. Even I could tell it was printed on a laser printer. I held the note gingerly and finally dropped it into a plastic bag that had once held panty hose. "We'll take this to Col—Gordon." My correction had come too late. Tinkie gave me a look.

"Coleman probably won't come back to Sunflower County, Sarah Booth." There was no malice in her tone.

"I know. Just a hard habit to break." In more ways than one. "Let's take this to Gordon. He's going to be testy because we found something and he didn't, but we knew what to look for."

She nodded. "This is very good in Allison's defense."

"Allison could have planted the note," I pointed out, "but we can hope to find others in Oxford."

"And we can hope that Gordon has some technology that can trace these notes," Tinkie said. "Or fingerprints."

Always the optimist, I thought. That's why I loved Tinkie so. "Let's get out of here. I'm afraid if I stay much longer, the Wicked Witch of the West will try to steal my dog."

We were laughing as we opened the door.

Gertrude Stromm blocked the doorway. "I heard Quentin and Allison arguing," she said. "It was ugly. That young woman killed her friend, and I'm going to testify to that." She spun around and stormed back down the hallway. When she was at the end, she wheeled to face us. "For your information, Miss Sarah Booth Delaney, I don't like dogs, or cats, or any other animal."

"What a surprise," I replied, feigning shock.

Holding my second Bloody Mary of the day, I sat down at my desk to make a few notes on the Allison Tatum case. Tinkie had gone on to The Club to see her husband, and to see what new suspects she could dig up. The truth was, Tinkie would be able to function better without me tagging along. Zinnia was a small town, and everyone knew I didn't have enough money to be a member of The Club. Since returning to Zinnia the year before—an unsuccessful actress trying to save her family home from the bulldozer—my economic woes were in the public domain. My presence would be a distraction.

And I had other fish to fry. My hand reached out to pick up the phone.

"Don't you dare call that married man," Jitty said.

I looked up to find her gazing at me from behind a domino. "I have a right to call Coleman when I need some professional advice."

"You *need* to remember he's chosen to honor his marital obligation. If he wanted you, he'd be right here at your side."

Jitty had a way of making her point. Coleman could have divorced his loony wife and stayed in Sunflower County, but he hadn't. He'd left his job, his career, and me. All for Connie. And for his child—the child she'd deliberately conceived to hold him. I had to keep that in mind. This was all about Connie's pregnancy, and it was the choice he should have made.

I withdrew my hand and picked up my pen. "Okay, you've emotionally bludgeoned me into submission."

Jitty moved toward me on the soft rustle of petticoats

and silk. "No Delaney woman has ever been desperate enough to go chasin' after a married man."

I was sufficiently shamed; no witty retort came to my rescue.

"Why don't you call Hamilton Garrett V?" she asked.

I considered it but knew I wouldn't. I'd treated Hamilton shabbily. I had my reasons, just like Coleman had his, but in the long run, it wouldn't make a difference to Hamilton. I'd chosen and he'd lost, or at least it would seem that way to him. After all, I'd left him in an airport waiting for me while I ran off to help Coleman. No, it was better to let Hamilton alone.

"There are other fish in the sea," Jitty said.

"I prefer pork."

"Your palate will change." There was a hint of softness in her tone.

I examined her outfit, complete with sumptuous jewels and what appeared to be ermine on the collar. "You're advocating an era when members of the court slept with whomever they chose, married or not, *willing* or not. It was a time without morals or decency. That's what brought on the French Revolution."

"Change is inevitable."

I rolled my eyes. "You're a walking advertisement for excess and out-of-control consumerism. I'm just glad no one else can see you!"

"Jealous?"

I pushed back my chair and got up. "When the guillotine drops, don't come crying to me."

She was laughing softly as I walked up to my room for my riding boots. In less than ten minutes, I had Reveler saddled and Sweetie Pie circling my legs with eager anticipation. I mounted, and we set off at a trot across the cotton fields. Soon the picked plants would be disked under, and the ground would be prepared for next year's crop.

There was something about farming that kept a person connected to the soil, and I felt myself relax as I thought about the passing of the seasons. I'd started my career as a PI last fall. In that short time I'd saved Dahlia House from the developers, found a stray dog that turned out to be a real treasure, obtained the best partner in the world, and been gifted with a horse from my friend Lee McBride. All in all, romantic train wrecks aside, it had been a good year. I had to put aside my longing for Coleman and my regrets about Hamilton. I was where I was supposed to be.

Reveler's long trot was a pleasure to ride. The wind whipped my hair across my face, and my ears were numb with cold, but it was pure bliss. Sweetie Pie bounded along beside me as we rode the edges of the fields. We could cover miles without running into a single vehicle.

The land spread out before me, a flat vista of wealth. The Mississippi Delta is some of the richest land in the world. Top soil eight feet deep. I could not imagine ever leaving it again, not even for Hamilton Garrett V.

We made a circle of the surrounding properties, and then I turned back to Dahlia House as early nightfall was drifting over me. It was only about four, but the cloud cover blocked the light. I wanted to get home before it got too dark to see.

Reveler eagerly took the canter, and I pushed aside all my negative thoughts and feelings and gave myself to the ride. When I trotted down the drive of Dahlia House, I saw a strange red Porsche in front of the house.

Slipping off Reveler's bridle, I walked him cool and left him grazing on the front lawn while I crept up the steps and into my front parlor. My mind was focused on who would enter my house without permission, and it was with relief that I found Harold sitting on Aunt Loulane's horse-hair sofa, sipping a Scotch.

"I knew you were riding, so I made myself at home," he said.

"I need to take care of Reveler." I waved him to follow me. "New car?"

"Rachel encouraged me to get it. I'm selling it tomorrow as soon as the dealership opens."

"Nice color."

"I think I want a truck."

I burst out laughing. Harold was one of the most refined men I knew. He was a gourmet cook and a banker who kept a Haviland china service in his office at the bank. "Keep the Porsche. It suits you better."

"Maybe. Maybe not."

The worry in his eyes troubled me. Harold wasn't paranoid, and he didn't go around looking for something to obsess over. He occasionally paid me a visit, but not often. Perhaps it had been due to his involvement with Rachel, or perhaps it was my involvement with Coleman. It didn't matter; I was glad to see him.

I led Reveler to the barn by his mane, and Harold unsaddled him while I cleaned his hooves and poured up his ration of grain. We worked in companionable silence, but he'd come to talk with me about something important. I'd learned the art of waiting for the talkee to bring it to me.

"Allison Tatum didn't kill Quentin McGee," he said.

I could hear the comb running through Reveler's mane as he worked. "I know. I think she was framed." I walked around and put my hand on Harold's arm and gave it a gentle squeeze. "But I know you didn't kill her, either, Harold."

His smile was warm. "Thank you, Sarah Booth."

"Thanks aren't necessary. I know you wouldn't harm anyone. Once Tinkie and I investigate further, we should have some viable suspects."

"I was so angry with her," he said.

I hugged him lightly. "If that were a crime, we'd all be in jail. Hey, I'm sorry about Rachel."

"Me, too. She's a great woman. I was just never comfortable with all those French hairdressers. And she wanted to travel, something I'm not free to do."

I could see on his face that he'd cared for the eccentric businesswoman who'd built an empire of beauty salons staffed by handsome French stylists. It was a mecca of Daddy's Girl fantasies—the sensual touch of a sexy, foreign man without guilt or repercussions. Rachel was a genius.

He sighed. "Just think, if I'd gone to Paris with her like she asked, I wouldn't be in this predicament."

"You aren't in a predicament," I pointed out. "No one has accused you of anything. Just wait and don't borrow trouble." Aunt Loulane's words were out of my mouth before I could bite them back.

"I can just see your aunt," he said, and this time his smile was real. "I think of you sometimes, living here alone."

"But I'm not alone," I answered. Harold's concern was one thing. His pity was another. "I have Sweetie and Reveler." And Jitty, but I wasn't about to admit to a haint.

"Let me take you to dinner, Sarah Booth."

"Okay, but let me go inside and clean up." I didn't have to look down at my stained breeches and muddy boots to know I needed a little feminine care.

"Perfect. I'll pick you up in forty-five minutes?" He waited for me to calculate the time allotment for cleaning up.

I nodded. "Where are we going?"

"It's going to be a surprise."

3

Highway 1, which topped the thirty-foot levee on the Mississippi River, was the perfect place to open up the Porsche. The road was one of my favorites. On the west side were the river breaks, small sloughs, and swamps, where wildlife flourished. On the east side were pastures filled with grazing cattle. Sometimes the pastures included part of the road. Harold left a whirlwind of leaves behind as we flew through the night. It was perfect November weather, cold with a hint of ice in the crackle of the leaves. With the top down, the wind was freezing, but also invigorating. It brought the first flush of color to Harold's pale cheeks. As we left the levee and hit the interstate to Memphis, I watched Harold's profile. He had begun to relax. I was glad, because I'd never seen him so tense.

"What's wrong, Harold? Did you have to evict some little old lady on a Sunday?"

He smiled. "You give me too much credit, Sarah Booth. You think I might worry about someone else's plight. It's my own neck I'm concerned about."

For all his bravado, Harold was a kind man. There were several elderly matrons around town who owed their homes to his gentle intervention in banking rules. "Right, Harold, I know how hard-hearted you are."

He slowed the car enough so that he could really look at me. "Why didn't we make a couple, Sarah Booth?"

It was a hard question to answer. When I'd first met Harold, with his plan to raze Dahlia House and build a shopping mall, I had good reason to dislike him. Then, things had changed. Antipathy had turned into attraction. Yet we'd never followed through. Why? I still couldn't say.

"You're just hurting over Rachel," I said, touching his arm gently. "And you know what a muddle I made of my romantic life. I have no answers for either of us."

"Coleman Peters." He said the name as if it were the title of a book.

I wisely said nothing as he pressed the accelerator and sped us through the night to a small, expensive Memphis restaurant called The French Connection.

The food was good, the wine excellent, and the crème brûlée to die for. Throughout the meal, we talked about my past cases, Oscar's reaction to Tinkie's involvement in the private investigation business, and the passing of the year.

"Will you be making fruitcakes this year?" he asked.

"Tradition, Harold. It rules my life." I'd had enough wine to believe I was witty, and I was rewarded with his bold laugh. Several patrons of the restaurant turned to look at us, and not without envy.

We ordered coffee, and I watched his face change. "I need your help, Sarah Booth."

"Harold, you know that Humphrey Tatum has already hired us to help Allison. Besides, you don't have a thing to worry about. Gordon would never seriously consider you a killer."

He frowned. "I'm not so certain. I don't think Tinkie conveyed the full scene to you. Because I didn't convey it to her."

Looking into his dark eyes, I could see he was genuinely worried. Though I might not take his predicament seriously, he did. To belittle his concern was not the action of a friend. "Tell me what happened."

He leaned closer, glancing left and right as if he were about to reveal a state secret. "I was in the bar at The Club. Rachel and I had had a terrible row in the dining room. It was"—he grimaced—"tasteless and regrettable."

"You really care for her, don't you?"

He dropped his gaze, and I could read nothing on his face. When he looked up again, he was composed. "Rachel has such a gift for life. To be with her makes me feel more fully alive than I've ever felt. But it isn't fair for me to hold her back. She wants to travel, to live in Europe, to experience life. I'm happy here in Zinnia, living my dull life with the people I've grown to care about."

I swallowed, thinking of Hamilton. He'd offered me the chance of a lifetime, to live in an exotic city with a man who stopped women in their tracks, a man who loved me. For another woman, it would have been the perfect match. Somehow, though, Mississippi had gotten into my blood, and I couldn't abandon her. My roots had grown too deeply in the rich Delta soil. I understood what Harold was saying. "I just played out this scene, I'm afraid."

"I know that Hamilton offered you Paris. I'm sorry. It's hard to tear your heart in half." He picked up my hand, and I felt the weakest pulse in my thumb. It made me smile.

"We're a lot more alike than you once believed," he said.

"We are." It was an easy admission. "That's how I know you couldn't hurt Quentin. But tell me the rest of the story."

Harold released my hand and looked down at his coffee cup. "As I said, Rachel and I had had an argument. She'd given me back a ring. Not an engagement ring, but a gift

I'd bought her. She left, and I went into the bar and proceeded to polish off my image as an ass."

I grinned. "So you got drunk."

"Drunker." He signaled the waiter for the check. "I don't remember everything I said or did, but Marcus Kline came up to me in the bar and started picking at me about the things Quentin had written in the book."

"I haven't read it."

"She detailed my aunt's unhappy love affair, her suicide." He shrugged. "I swung at him, but Bobby Deneff pulled me off. I was spoiling for a fight."

"That's when Quentin arrived."

"Right. She came in the bar with an attitude. She plopped a hundred down, and when Bernard Jacks couldn't change it, she acted like a little bitch. I told him to put her drink on my tab. That's when she got really nasty."

"How so?"

"She told me that I couldn't bribe her to leave my family out of her second book. She said she was going to dig up every bone I had buried and pick it to death. That's when she stood up and stumbled. Her drink flew all over me. I was furious."

"Charming," I said, hoping to take the edge off. Harold was frowning as he twirled his coffee cup in the saucer.

"She downed the remains of her drink and stalked off, and I followed her outside. I intended to tell her off. In my drunken stupor, I thought it would be better to do it outside rather than in public."

This wasn't good news. After a public argument, Harold followed a lone woman into the night—right before someone murdered her. On a positive side, no one heard what must have been a heated exchange between them.

"So the only person who heard you was Quentin, and she won't be talking," I said, hoping to make light of the situation.

"If only that were true."

"Who heard?"

"Marcus."

"Good grief." Marcus and Harold were bitter enemies. Long ago, Harold had foreclosed on the Kline plantation. The bank can carry a debt for only so long; it was an economic fact even I understood. Rather than accept that the bank had acted in a prescribed way, Marcus found it easier to blame Harold for his personal failure.

"It gets worse. I threatened Quentin." He refused to look up at me. "She said some nasty things, and I responded by telling her if she didn't leave my family out of her books, I'd"—he finally looked up—"kill her."

"How long did it take Marcus to beat a trail to the sheriff's office?"

"He was there as soon as he heard that Quentin's body was found. Gordon came by to talk to me. I admitted the whole thing."

My exasperation with Harold made my voice sharp. "Don't you watch any television? The airwaves are filled with cop shows with the mantra 'don't talk to the police.'"

"I didn't touch Quentin."

"Neither did Allison, and look where she is."

"My point exactly. I need you and Tinkie to help me out."

I sighed. After the things Harold had done for me, I could hardly say no to him, yet I was obligated to work for Allison. When I hit on the solution, I smiled. "You're both innocent, so when Tinkie and I find the real killer, it'll clear you both."

He leaned forward and picked up my hand, his fingers stroking it gently. "You're a clever woman, Sarah Booth."

I shook my head. "Not really. But *you* are a good man, Harold. I can prove that."

He squeezed my hand, and my thumb tingled. Then the waiter brought the check, and we were out in the cold night, with a starry drive back to Zinnia.

Harold left me at the door with a kiss on the cheek. As I watched his taillights disappear down the drive, I felt a sense of foreboding. Gordon Walters knew that Harold wouldn't kill Quentin or anyone else, but I had a feeling this case was going to get much larger than Sunflower County and the reach of local law enforcement. I was worried about Harold.

Sleeping late is an art form at Dahlia House—and one that both Sweetie Pie and Jitty seem to take as a personal affront. The bedside clock showed eight when I heard Sweetie's tail thumping the floor and felt her hot breath on my face. Groaning, I rolled over and tried to burrow beneath my pillows.

"I would have thought you'd get more than a kiss from Harold Erkwell, Sarah Booth."

I opened my eyes to find Jitty standing at the foot of the bed, a shaft of morning sunlight falling directly across her. The peacock blue of her dress was so bright, I held up my hands in the sign of the cross. "You're about to fry my eyeballs. Pull the shades!"

Jitty, of course, didn't move an inch. I got up and closed the shades. I gave the bed one last, lingering glance. "What do you want?"

"Some action." She swished by me as she took a seat on the side of the bed, petticoats rattling.

I wasn't ready for verbal combat with Jitty, but I had no choice. "What about a society that has no morality? I thought you were for rules and order and propriety. How would it be proper for me to sleep with a client?"

"If he became a husband, it would be just fine. Sarah Booth, a whole year has passed, and you're not any closer to the altar than you were in New York City."

"Go away." I went to the bathroom and began my morning ablutions.

"You like Harold." She harangued me through the closed door of the bathroom.

"Which is the best reason I know to stay away from him. Every time I get the idea that I like a man, he ends up in a world of hurt."

"My, my, who are you feeling sorry for, Hamilton or yourself?"

I was saved from answering by the sound of the doorbell. As I zipped my jeans and ran barefoot down the stairs, I considered the advantages of finding a roommate. Jitty didn't appear when anyone else was in the house. A roommate would solve a lot of problems.

"You aren't going to believe what I found out," Tinkie said as she hurried through the front door and headed east rather than west. She was going to our office instead of the kitchen. That in itself intrigued me enough to follow along, my bare feet slapping on the cold wood floor as my brain murmured "coffee, coffee, coffee."

"What?"

She went in the office and plopped down at her desk. She'd learned that from me. In her formal DG days, Tinkie would never have plopped. A true DG descended into a chair.

"The McGee family has refused to claim Quentin's body!"

"Are you sure?" This was scandalous.

"Absolutely. I heard it directly from the horse's mouth—"

There was a light in her eyes that told me more was to come. "And—"

"Mrs. Virgie Carrington is coming down to claim the body and handle all of the funeral arrangements."

"*The* Virgie Carrington? Founder and director of the Carrington School for Well-Bred Ladies?"

"None other."

"I didn't realize Quentin had connections with the school." I should have. She was a McGee, and as such, she'd undoubtedly graduated under Virgie's guiding hand.

"She and Allison both are graduates." Tinkie frowned. "I just can't imagine the family not handling the funeral, though."

"Obviously, they're very angry with Quentin."

Tinkie nodded. "I have to wonder if the whole book wasn't written just to get even with Franklin and Caledonia."

I picked up a pen and scribbled a few notes for future reference. "Do you know the McGees?" In a strange twist of fate, Tinkie hadn't gone to the Carrington School. Her family had certainly had the bucks to pay the tuition, but Tinkie's father had intervened, saying he wanted Tinkie to establish roots in the place she would live, Sunflower County. He was a smart man.

"We're not really friends of the McGees. Daddy and mother have socialized with them in Memphis and Jackson." She tapped the end of her pen against her chin. "They're sort of clannish."

She knew something. Tinkie had the best network of gossip in the Southeast. "So what's the story?"

"If what I'm hearing is true, Quentin had a reason to be angry with her family."

I settled onto the edge of my desk, my desire for information even stronger than my need for caffeine. "What have you heard?"

"Umbria, the older daughter, has always been the favorite. To the point that when Quentin was born, her mother put her in the arms of a nanny and almost never touched her. She was too busy dressing Umbria and fixing her hair. Umbria was the hope of the family." Tinkie leaned forward to lower her voice. "There's talk that Caledonia groomed Umbria to marry Prince William."

"Are you serious?" My own childhood had been so different. Thank God my parents hadn't tried to squeeze me into some preconceived mold.

"Dead serious. Umbria spent her sixteenth on the continent, attending parties and functions in the hope of catching the young prince's eye."

"I gather it didn't work. Isn't Umbria married now?"

"Her husband is a real estate developer with his eye on the McGee land. From what I understand, Franklin and Caledonia are bitterly disappointed in her. And it wasn't until Umbria made her matrimonial choice that Caledonia even acknowledged she had another daughter. That's when they started applying the heat to Quentin."

"Who totally rebelled." No plot twist there.

"Not only rebelled, but began to exact revenge. The venom in her book is a clear indication of how much she was hurt by them."

Tinkie had become quite the psychologist. "What a shame," I said and meant it.

"Yes." She stood up and yawned. "Why don't we go to Millie's Café and get some breakfast. I'm starving."

"I thought you'd never ask." I looked around. "Where's Chablis?" Tinkie always brought the dust mop.

"She's having her nails done and her teeth whitened. Shall we take Sweetie Pie down to stay with her at the Cut and Curl?"

"Sure. But no beauty treatments." Tinkie had once dyed my red tick hound a shade called Ravishing Redbone. It was not, and it had taken months for her to shed out.

"Whatever you say. I don't know why you have this block against cosmetic treatments," she said as she preceded me out of the house. "The idea that someone figured out how to use a deadly poison to kill wrinkles is a sign that God wants us to look better."

"If you're so eager to see a doctor with a needle, why

don't you get that lump biopsied?" I asked as I opened the back door of the Cadillac for Sweetie.

"Because it isn't necessary. End of topic."

Oh, but it was. Though I would remain silent, for the moment, I hadn't given up on making Tinkie take care of her health. I had the best partner in the world, and I didn't intend to let anything happen to her.

4

Millie set the platter of eggs, bacon, grits, and biscuits down in front of me and then sat down herself. The breakfast rush at the café was over, and she had a moment to talk with us. She was a pretty woman somewhere in her forties who wore her life experiences—happy and sad—on her face without shame or make-up. She was also an avid reader of the tabloid papers who had an impressive memory.

"Back several years ago, I found a picture in the *Globe* of Umbria at one of the royal parties at Buckingham Palace. She was hanging all over some dark-haired man who definitely was *not* Prince William." Millie pushed the maple syrup over to Tinkie for her stack of pancakes. "Mrs. McGee had high expectations for her girls, but apparently, neither of them wanted to cooperate."

"Did Umbria go to the Carrington School?" I asked.

"She did. Graduated with highest honors, too." She frowned. "There was some trouble with Quentin, though. What I heard from Chapel Brentworth's nanny was that Quentin 'didn't fit the school.' There was no explanation, but I guess now I know what it was."

"The whole purpose of the Carrington School is to instruct young women in the art of marrying with purpose," Tinkie said. "Quentin and Allison couldn't marry. It isn't legal."

"So two money magnets were suddenly useless," I agreed. "What a tragedy for both families."

My sarcasm was ignored as Tinkie ate her breakfast and Millie got up to serve another round of coffee to her customers. I watched her work, her quick smile at the ready. No wonder Millie's was the most popular Zinnia place to dine for all classes of Sunflower Countians.

When Millie returned to our table, she had another interesting tidbit. "Several of the graduates of the Carrington School were in here earlier this morning."

"Earlier?" I asked in mock horror.

"Who were they?" Tinkie asked more sensibly.

"I didn't get their names, but they were wearing the uniform."

"I didn't realize the school had a uniform dress code."

"It doesn't, but there is a code for girls of that ilk. *The* uniform," Tinkie said, "is a black or navy dress or suit, hose, sensible pumps, and pearls."

"That's it," Millie said. She patted my shoulder. "You can recognize one of the Carrington girls from half a mile away."

"That'll make it easier." I picked up the check over Tinkie's protest, placed an order for two sausage biscuits to go, and went to cash out.

Since we were already in town, I suggested we take the biscuits to Cece, our friend at the local newspaper. Cece had helped us more than once on dangerous cases, and since she was the society editor, I knew she'd have lots of scoop on what was happening with Quentin McGee's murder.

Her office was in the back of the newspaper, behind a wall of file cabinets. She was at her desk, typing furiously on her computer. I tapped on her open door, dangling the bag of biscuits.

"So you two come with a peace offering," she said, waving us inside. "Close the door, please."

As always, I admired Cece's style. She wore a hunter green sweater dress that hugged her slim hips and emphasized her bosom. There wasn't a scrap of fat on her frame, and her make-up, showcasing the latest muted colors of fall, was flawless. I shook my head. "You look marvelous, darling."

"I'll bet you say that to all your transsexual friends." She took a bite of a biscuit with her perfect white teeth.

It was true. Cece had once been Cecil, but a trip to Sweden had made her dreams come true. Now she was a sought-after journalist who'd just turned down a dream job in New Orleans to stay in Zinnia. I had to wonder about this sudden rootedness displayed by Cece, Harold, and myself. Had we lost our marbles?

"What's the scoop on Quentin?" Tinkie asked, moving a stack of books to find a chair.

"Virgie Carrington is at the funeral home now. She got in late last night," Cece said. "I'm trying to get an interview with her, but Gertrude Stromm is guarding her like a one-eyed dog on a gut wagon."

Cece's colorful descriptions were one of her best traits. I could see Gertrude, red hair standing on end, snarling at anyone who dared approach her prize.

"Why won't the McGees step forward and make the arrangements for Quentin?" I still found it a little too harsh to believe. "She's their daughter."

"There's the issue of the trust," Cece said.

"What trust?" Tinkie and I asked in unison.

"Quentin was due to inherit the bulk of the McGee estate."

"Quentin?" Tinkie and I sounded like surround sound.

"A small matter in the way the McGee monies were originally set up," Cece said, her perfect teeth looking wolfish. "According to the trust, the estate could only be inherited by a single female on the occasion of her twenty-fifth birthday."

While we processed that information, Cece continued. "Quentin was due to turn twenty-five yesterday."

The implication wasn't lost on us. Tinkie looked at me before she spoke. "So someone who didn't want Quentin to inherit could have killed her only hours before her birthday."

"Too true," Cece said. "And it gets better. Doc Sawyer ruled that she'd been killed *after* midnight."

"So she did inherit." I felt like I was volleying in a Wimbledon match.

"The McGee family has asked that the body be removed to Memphis for a second autopsy," Cece said.

"I thought they'd yielded the body to Virgie Carrington."

"It would seem they've reneged, or at least they're trying to."

"What does Gordon say?"

"What he says off the record is that he can't wait for Coleman to get back to town."

"Coleman is coming back to town?" I couldn't help that I sounded breathless and sixteen.

Realizing her mistake, Cece shook her head. "I'm sorry, Sarah Booth. I didn't know you'd take it literally. No, he isn't. Or at least no one knows if he is or isn't. Gordon hasn't heard from him in over a week. No one has."

I looked at the floor before the tears spilled down my face and made me look even more foolish than I felt. For one second, I'd believed Coleman was coming home. Until then, I hadn't realized how much he still meant to me. Now I was suffering bitter disappointment, and it was just as unpleasant as I remembered.

"Do you know when the services are set for?" Tinkie asked Cece. They were both trying to give me time to recover. They might not approve of my passion for a married man, but they hated the fact that I was hurting.

"That's a little up in the air. If the McGees regain control of the body and send it to Memphis, there may not be a service at all. Or it could be a week or more."

"And if Virgie Carrington gets her?" I asked.

"Funeral etiquette requires a certain amount of time for a wake. Say two days. And the funeral on the third day. So if that's the case, there should be visitation tonight."

"Do you think they'll hold the services here in Zinnia?"

"What's the point of moving her somewhere else?" Cece noted. "Quentin is, effectively, a woman without a country. The women of the Carrington School are gathering here in Zinnia as we speak. I think this will be where the funeral is held if Virgie gets her way. Probably burial in the local cemetery."

It was something to ponder as Tinkie and I headed back to the jail for another word with Allison.

Deputy Dewayne Dattilo was in charge of the sheriff's office when we got there. He was greener than Gordon, and I was tempted to pump him for details about Coleman, but Tinkie kept a watchful eye on me.

He led us back to Allison, who looked more tired than she had the day before.

"Humphrey was just here," she said. "They're fighting over Quentin's body. She would hate this!" Tears hung on her bottom lashes, but they didn't spill.

"What did Quentin tell you about her trust?" I asked. There was no point beating around the bush.

"She was due to inherit the bulk of the McGee estate." A faint smile crossed her face. "I guess Quentin and I really messed up the game plan for everyone."

"How do you figure that?"

"Her folks had her lined up to marry Talbert LaRue, a lawyer in Baton Rouge. They'd planned to make the announcement last year, with the wedding to be held just after her twenty-fifth birthday. Sometime this week, I guess it would have been." She wiped a tear away. "But Quentin and I fell in love, and that screwed my family's plans."

"Which were?"

"To have Humphrey woo Quentin and marry her—after she'd inherited—thereby securing the future of Tatum's Corner."

"The best laid plans of mice and mamas," Tinkie said softly.

"Can you do something for me?" she asked.

"We can try." I'd learned to be hesitant in granting wishes.

"Have some kind of court order issued so that no one gets Quentin's body. I'd like to make the arrangements myself. I know what she'd want, and it wouldn't be this nightmare." She gripped the bars. "Is Virgie Carrington in town?"

"I've heard she's here."

Allison swallowed dryly. "We were a big disappointment to her. I can't believe she's actually here."

"Once a Carrington girl, always—" Tinkie started.

"A Carrington girl," Allison finished. "Right. That was the motto. But the truth of the matter is that neither Quentin nor I was really a Carrington girl. We didn't live up to the image. We weren't the only ones, but we were the ones who became celebrities, and that was our greatest sin."

I had another matter to take up with Allison. "We found the threatening note sent to Quentin. It was printed out on a laser printer. Do you have any idea where the envelope might be?"

"Quentin had a journal. Maybe in there. She got other notes, too. Some may be in the house in Oxford."

"We'll check it out." I touched her hand on the bar. "Do you have any idea who might have sent the notes? Who knew the content of the book?"

"Quentin wasn't bashful about letting folks know she was getting ready to bloody them in print. She told at least two dozen people."

This was going to increase our legwork, but I was never one to complain about too many suspects. "Can you make us a list?"

"Talk to the owner of Booking It. A lot of the customers who were there yesterday were furious. Quentin's sister was the angriest of all. I still believe she was the one who bought all the books and burned them."

"Umbria," I said, looking at Tinkie. It was almost time for a visit to the McGee family. "Did anyone see Umbria burn the books?"

Allison shook her head. "I don't think so."

"But you said it was her."

"Maybe I'm guilty of the same thing everyone else is. I jumped to the conclusion based on what Quentin told me."

"Which was?" Tinkie asked.

"That Umbria hated her and had vowed to spend her entire inheritance buying the books and burning them."

"Pretty strong circumstantial evidence," Tinkie said.

"Thanks, Allison. We'll be in touch."

"Will they let me go to Quentin's funeral?"

If Coleman had been in charge, the answer would have been yes. He'd allowed Lee McBride to attend her scoundrel husband's funeral, and I felt certain he wouldn't view Allison as a great flight risk. Hell, where would she go? There was no one to help her. The jail docket had showed she hadn't had a single visitor except her brother. "Maybe. We'll have to see," I said.

Tinkie and I said our good-byes and were almost out of the jail when Allison stopped me.

"Humphrey was asking about you," she said. "He's interested."

Tinkie grabbed my arm and whispered in my ear, "He recognizes another deviant."

I pulled free of her. "He's my client," I said a little stiffly. "I don't date clients."

"That's a new rule," Tinkie said drolly, and as we left the jail, I could hear Allison's laugh. I couldn't help but wonder how long it would be before she might laugh again.

Booking It was a quaint shop on a side street not far from The Gardens B&B. Pots of yellow and orange mums accented the gray steps that led to the front porch of the old house that had been converted into a bookshop. Pumpkins were lined up in the front window, along with a display of cookbooks featuring Thanksgiving recipes.

The store owner, Jasmine Paul, was a slender blonde with an amazing knowledge of books and a keen ability to see the bottom line. She wasn't a native of Zinnia, but she'd managed to become an indispensable part of the town, matching book and reader with a skill that bordered on psychic talent.

"Sarah Booth," she said when I walked in. "How did you enjoy that Dean James book?"

"It was perfect," I said. The book's clever plot and unique humor had gotten me through the first few days of Coleman's disappearance and Hamilton's return to Paris.

"What can I do for you today?" She included Tinkie in her question.

"We need a copy of *King Cotton Bleeds*," Tinkie said.

"You're in luck. The publisher just overnighted fifty copies, and they arrived about ten minutes ago." She bent behind the counter and pulled out a box, which she opened with a sharp knife.

The book she handed Tinkie was heavy, with a photograph of a cotton field, computer enhanced so that the plants dripped blood. Effective and grim.

"I heard you ran out of books for the signing Saturday," I said.

"Umbria McGee bought every copy I had." She frowned. "I had mixed feelings about selling them to her. Had I known she was going to burn them, I wouldn't have."

"Did she actually burn them?"

Jasmine nodded. "It had to be her. She came in and paid by credit card for all seven cases of books. That was about an hour before the official signing. She said she wanted to surprise her sister." She rolled her eyes. "Now that's an understatement."

"So she left with the books?" Tinkie asked.

"She had her own dolly. I thought she was going to take them out and then return at the book signing, like a surprise."

"But she never returned."

"She never left. She carted them down to the end of the driveway and dumped them in a pile. She poured gasoline over them and set the fire."

"Did you see her do this?" It was a crucial detail. Assumption could be a fatal mistake.

"I didn't see her pour the gasoline or throw the match, but there's a pile of ashes at the back of the driveway. I saw the flames, but by the time I ran back there, whoever set the fire was gone." She touched one of the books. "Whether you agree or disagree with a book, it shouldn't be burned."

"When Quentin arrived for the book signing, what did she say?" Tinkie leafed through the pages of the book she held, feigning simple curiosity. "She must have been furious."

"She chewed me out, and then she went outside to the ashes."

"Was she aware Umbria had bought all the books?"

"She was. She said something to the effect that within twelve hours, Umbria wouldn't have three thousand dollars to spend on destroying her dreams."

Tinkie and I stared at each other. It was a damning tidbit, as far as Umbria's motive went. "Did she say anything else?"

Jasmine straightened a neat stack of children's books on her counter. "She said I should have known better than to sell all the books to one person." She looked up. "She was right about that. I should have known better."

"Do you have a list of the people who showed up for the signing?"

"A few people ordered the book. They should be back today to get their copy." She pulled a notebook from behind the counter.

I wrote down the names of Lorilee Brewer, Marilyn Jenkins, and Jolene Loper. The names weren't familiar to me, but Tinkie was far better versed in Delta society than I. Once we were out of the shop, we could talk more freely.

We thanked Jasmine and heard the tinkle of the bell behind us as we closed the door. A gust of wind sent a flurry of brown pecan leaves skittering across the porch, reminding me of my childhood and the joys of fall at Dahlia House when my mother was alive to make candied apples, pumpkin pies, and steaming pots of soup.

When we were in the Caddy, Tinkie turned to me. "What's wrong, Sarah Booth? You look as if the life was sucked out of you."

"I was just thinking of the past. Don't you find fall a sad time of year?"

She thought about it as she drove. "Sad because the year is ending?"

"It's a time of change." I touched the window, feeling the chill. "Change has never been easy for me."

"Nor me. But I do love the cold weather and the fires and sitting beside Oscar under a blanket." She slowed the Caddy as we turned down the drive to my home. Her gaze swept the long driveway, past the leafless sycamores to Dahlia House. "Fall isn't so bad if you have someone to share it with." She touched my arm. "You're just lonely, Sarah Booth."

She was right about that; I was lonely. Perhaps that was all that was wrong with me, and I was just too self-absorbed to see it.

"Thanks for the ride, Tink." I leaned over and pecked her cheek. "I count on you a lot, you know." Sweetie Pie and Chablis came running from the back of the house, where I'd had a doggie door installed. Obviously, the groomer at Cut and Curl had delivered them for us. The dogs, so different and yet such good friends, bounded toward us. Chablis barely touched the grass as she ran. With one giant stride, she leapt into the front seat of the car.

Tinkie dazzled me with her smile. "Isn't that odd? A year ago, I thought you might actually have stolen Chablis just to get some money."

Her words struck deep into my heart. I had stolen her dog for the ransom. Had I not done so, Dahlia House would be a shopping mall. "Tinkie, I—"

"Oscar just laughed at me when I told him that. He said you couldn't have thought of something so clever."

I wanted to kiss Oscar and then slap him silly. "I'm surprised with Oscar's opinion of me, he allows you to work in the PI agency."

"Oh, he doesn't *allow* it," she said, and her smile was even more radiant. "One thing I've learned from you, Sarah Booth, is how to stand up for what I believe in. I count on you a lot, too."

She gave a cheery wave and headed down the drive.

5

Not every county in Mississippi has a doctor to perform autopsies. State law has few requirements for a coroner. But with Coleman's help in the last election, Doc Sawyer had won appointment to the post. For the most part, Doc had retired from the medical profession, but he often took emergency calls at the hospital and maintained an office in a back corner of the emergency suite.

"Help yourself," he said, pointing at the coffeepot.

I got a Styrofoam cup. The coffee was slightly thinner than molasses and twice as black. "Yum."

"I'm sixty-four and have the heart of a forty-year-old," Doc said. "It's all due to that coffee. It's a wonder drug."

With such an endorsement, I couldn't decline a cup. I took a sip and felt my jaw lock.

"Good, huh?"

I nodded, trying to swallow.

"You're here about Quentin McGee."

"Yes." I put the cup down on the table and inched away from it.

"What can I tell you?" Doc leaned back in his chair, the

late afternoon light from a window catching in his wild thatch of white hair.

For a split second he looked like an angel with a halo. I realized then that the coffee had some type of hallucinogenic properties. "Time of death is critical." I forced my thoughts back on the business at hand.

"I've put Quentin's death at two in the morning. I understand her family isn't happy with that."

"Is it possible she was killed before midnight?"

He frowned. "I've heard a lot of money rests on my answer."

"I gather it does. It also speaks to motive."

He sipped his own cup of coffee and rubbed his chin. "Quentin's body was found before dawn, as you well know. She hadn't been dead more than three hours. I won't go into all the medical details, but I'm positive of it. The McGees can have the autopsy repeated, but unless they pay off the examiner, he's going to find exactly what I found."

"How did she die? Officially."

"Suffocation." He got up and walked to the window. "Death is never a pretty thing to see, but it's especially hard when a young person is murdered. Someone held her face down in the mud." He faced me. "That's hard to think about."

"Would it have to be someone strong?"

"Not necessarily. Quentin had been roped, like a steer at a rodeo. The rope caught her initially around the waist. There was severe bruising, such as what would happen if the person on the other end of the rope were in a vehicle. She was pulled off her feet, and once she was injured and on the ground, the rope was shifted around her feet. She was dragged behind a vehicle into the bog. By that point, I doubt she had a lot of fight left in her."

I sat forward. "That's awful."

"Someone had it in for her." He sat back at his desk. "I think Gordon's a good man, but I wish Coleman were back on the job."

"Me, too. Have you heard from him?" Whatever Doc thought about my question, he would keep it to himself. He'd treated my scraped knees and coughs when I was a child. He'd given me tonics and vitamins when my parents were killed. Though he'd done his best, he'd had no medicine for a broken heart.

"I have."

"How's he doing?" I forced myself to add, "And Connie? How is she? Is the baby okay?"

He didn't look at me. "Those are questions only Coleman should answer, Sarah Booth. It isn't my place."

"You're right." I stood up, suddenly ashamed at my inability to keep my errant heart in check. "If you talk to him again, tell him I said hello."

"Sarah Booth, whoever killed Quentin meant for her to suffer. There's an element of malice here that I haven't seen in many murders. Be careful."

"I will," I promised. "I think it's a lot more dangerous to drink your coffee."

He shook his head. "You're just like your mama."

Dusk had fallen by the time I got to my car and headed back to Dahlia House. Lights began to flicker on in the houses I passed. In a few, I could see the blue glare of a television, and a sudden longing for family traced through my heart. I was lonely. Tinkie had hit the nail on the head. After a year of being back in Zinnia, I still went home to an empty house.

My last case, with Doreen Mallory, had changed me. Doreen was a woman who believed in miracles. The day-to-day kind and the big ones. She also believed that everything in life happened for a reason. At first I'd fought against such a belief, but now my mind was exploring the possibility. The question I had to answer was why I chose to be alone.

As I pulled up in front of Dahlia House, I heard Reveler whinny a welcome. Sweetie Pie came charging around the house to whip my legs with her eager tail. So I wasn't exactly alone. I just didn't have a man and children—the family that seemed so desirable, and so elusive.

"Pull yourself out of that slump and feed your horse," Jitty commanded from the porch.

How foolish of me to think I was alone. "Yes, ma'am." I detoured from the porch and went to the barn to give Reveler his grain.

His soft muzzle blew kisses on my neck and cheeks as I brushed his coat while he ate. The sound of his chewing was comforting. When he was done, I went back to the house to confront Jitty.

The back door was locked, so I had to walk around to the porch. If Jitty was going to inhabit the house, it would be nice if she could be a little helpful, like opening a door or making coffee in the morning. But no, noncorporeal beings didn't have to lift a finger in the residences they haunted. It was some kind of ghostly union rule.

I was still gnawing on my grievances when I tripped on something. Sitting right by the front door was a big box, gift wrapped.

"Special delivery," Jitty said.

Somehow she'd managed to fit her huge dress into one of the rocking chairs. As she tipped back and forth, I could see her pantaloons.

"It's a good thing you waited for fall to play French Revolutionary. If you'd done this in August, you'd have died of heat exhaustion in all those clothes."

"I don't sweat," she said.

"Ah, another benefit of being dead."

"I can eat anything I want and never gain weight, and my hair never frizzes."

Now she was getting insulting. I picked up the box, which bore no sign of any delivery system. Pulling the red ribbon that tied it, I sat down on the steps and opened the box. Layer after layer of tissue paper concealed the contents.

"What's in there?" Jitty asked. She'd stopped rocking.

"Hold your horses. I'm getting there." I peeled back at least twenty layers of flimsy red paper before my fingers struck something furry. I gave a little squeal as I pulled out a tiny froth of a silk garment.

"The French do have the best design sensibilities when it comes to bedroom *couture*," Jitty said as I sorted out the straps of a risqué red teddy trimmed in fluff.

"Who sent this?" I felt a flush touch my cheeks.

"Harold, I hope," Jitty said. "There's always a strong current beneath those still waters. That boy has some idea of sleep attire, but I doubt sleep is on his mind."

I sorted through the tissue papers only to find stiletto slippers with four-inch heels, also trimmed in red fur.

"Ooh la la," Jitty said, beside herself. "You've inspired me to learn French."

I turned the box over and shook it. The person who sent the gift surely left a card of some type. I couldn't believe it was Harold. He'd truly fallen for Rachel Gaudel, and he knew that my heart was a war zone between conflicting interests. No, this was the work of someone who hadn't heard of my reputation for death in the field of romance.

At last I found a small note card. I took the box and contents into the house, where I could turn on a light to read. I didn't have to invite Jitty to follow. Wild horses couldn't have kept her away.

"Hurry up, Sarah Booth. It isn't every day you get a harlot outfit left on the porch."

Ignoring her, I went to the kitchen, where Sweetie Pie met me. She sniffed the gift box disdainfully and stalked out of the room.

"That hound has an attitude problem," Jitty said.

I sat at the table and opened the envelope. Jitty hovered over my shoulder as I read: *Let's play Scarlett and Rhett! Tomorrow night at eight. You have the plantation house, and I have the champagne. Humphrey*

Humphrey Tatum. At his kinky best. I put everything back in the box and closed it, then retied the red ribbon.

"You aren't sending it back?" Jitty was horrified.

"Of course, I am. Humphrey is my client. I can't accept gifts from him. Especially not boudoir attire."

"Why not?"

I couldn't tell if Jitty was trying to devil me or if she was sincere. "It's unethical."

She arched her eyebrows, which conveyed a world of my past ethical mistakes.

"I'm not interested in Humphrey," I finally admitted.

"Sarah Booth, I have only one thing to say."

"What?"

"Ticktock."

"Maybe I'm not meant to have a baby. Maybe I'm meant to run a private investigators agency." My tone was getting hotter and hotter as I spoke. "Why is that unacceptable? Why can't that be enough for you and Tinkie and every-one else? Why—"

"Because it isn't enough for you," Jitty said, and she wasn't deviling me. "I know you. You want a husband and a fam-ily."

I picked up the box and shook it at her. "This isn't a marriage proposal, Jitty. It's an invitation for sex. There's a big difference, you know."

"In this day and age, Sarah Booth, one often leads to the other."

"I don't want to marry Humphrey."

"Because he isn't Coleman?"

"Because I don't love him."

She walked around the table, the rustle of her petticoats a gentle shush in the room. "You won't love anyone until you get Coleman out of your heart. And Hamilton, too. You're so conflicted over Coleman, you haven't even begun to figure out what you feel for Hamilton."

"Exactly my point. And I don't need to muck up my muddled emotions more by jumping into the sack with Humphrey-the-Humper."

Jitty's laughter was low and rich. "A little bit of two-backed tango might shake loose your heart."

My own laughter matched hers. "Not in my experience. Besides, Humphrey is a client. That has to mean something."

"If you say so," she finally relented. "Now I'm off to the court to see what kind of action I can stir up."

I thought I felt her hand trace across my cheek as she passed me.

"I don't have to point out," she said, "that casual sex without consequence is just one more advantage of being a ghost."

"Put that way, I can't wait to be dead," I said to her vanishing back.

I was sitting on the front porch, sipping coffee, the next morning when Tinkie pulled up. Her blond hair glistened in the pale morning sunlight as she got out of the Caddy. To my amusement, she was wearing a navy suit with a pale pink blouse and a stunning string of pearls. Even her exquisite little feet were encased in conservative navy pumps.

"Where'd you get the costume?" I asked.

"We have an appointment in an hour with Virgie Carrington. I came over to help you pull yourself together."

I held up a hand a la Diana Ross. "Stop in the name of sanity. I'm not putting on some kind of ridiculous uniform."

"Of course you are."

"No way, Jose. I'm not a Carrington girl, and I'm not pretending to be."

Tinkie put her hands on her hips. "Sarah Booth, sometimes you're just plain mulish. Virgie Carrington has spent her entire life training young women to fit into a certain mold. We need her help. We want her to talk to us. The simplest way to do that is to reflect the type of woman she creates."

Tinkie was right, but I felt my Irish dander rise. "I shouldn't have to conform to her dress code for an interview."

"You don't *have* to," she pointed out. "But it will certainly grease the skids if you do. We meet her as equals that way."

"I don't have a blue suit."

She reached into the back seat of the Caddy and pulled out a hanger covered by a Charlene's bag. "Charlene opened the store early for me." She thrust the bag at me. "I picked this out for you because I knew you'd try that excuse."

"I don't have any shoes," I countered.

"You get dressed. I'll find some suitable shoes." She marched past me into the house. I was defeated. I had the choice of surrendering with honor or whining. Only because I figured Jitty was eavesdropping did I choose the former. Carrying the dress bag, I marched behind Tinkie to my doom.

An hour later, we were sitting in the formal den at The Gardens B&B. I was wearing a Donna Karan designer suit and holding a cup of tea—Earl Grey—which looked like thin milk. I had no intention of drinking it, especially since Gertrude Stromm had made it. Hemlock was the word that came to my mind. Tinkie had no such apprehensions. She sipped her tea and chatted with Virgie Carrington about the desperate need in society for more Sunday brunches.

"What would you view as the perfect menu for a brunch?" Virgie suddenly asked me.

Her blue grey eyes were shrewd and a perfect match for the silk dress she wore. Her pearls had the sheen of age, as if they were family heirlooms. I knew her question was a test. "I don't think the menu matters as long as the Bloody Marys and mimosas flow freely," I answered, ignoring the daggers Tinkie shot at me.

To my surprise, Virgie laughed. The iron maiden had a sense of humor. "I remember your mother, Sarah Booth. She was unconventional, but always with kindness. I see you're a page from the same book."

It was a compliment I couldn't ignore. "Thank you, Miss Carrington. I didn't realize you knew my mother."

"Everyone knew her. And everyone adored her."

"Not everyone," I said.

"Everyone I knew," Virgie insisted. "I don't find it peculiar that you've become a private investigator, Sarah Booth, but Tinkie is another matter." She turned to my partner. "I can't believe Oscar has agreed to this."

Tinkie's smile never slipped. "Well, Virgie, Oscar didn't really have a choice. I bought my freedom a long time ago."

The blade was presented with such deftness; at first, I didn't recognize the sharpness. Virgie surprised me again by laughing. "In a way, I'm glad your parents chose not to send you to my school, Tinkie. You would have been a real problem."

I saw that the conversation was going south fast. "Miss Carrington, as we mentioned, we've been hired to help prove Allison's innocence. We're hoping you can help us."

"How?"

"Quentin's book has upset a number of people, many of them your former students."

"The book is vile. Quentin has ignored every commandment that I teach, but the one most offensive is the violation of family. She must have broken Franklin's and Caledonia's hearts."

"Not to mention Umbria's," Tinkie said smoothly. She'd regained her equilibrium.

"Poor Umbria." Virgie poured more tea for Tinkie and herself. I guarded my cool cup. "She's had a rough life, thanks to Quentin."

"Tell us about Quentin," I urged.

Virgie leaned back in her chair. Her posture was perfect. "Quentin was perhaps the smartest girl I'd ever had at the school. She could learn anything. Algebra, literature, languages. She was fluent in Spanish, French, Italian, and German. She had the ability to read something once and to own it. She had such potential."

"Did she always want to write?"

Her laughter this time was without humor. "Writing was the tool of revenge for Quentin. She didn't intend to make her mark in the literary world. She intended to settle some scores."

"But why?"

"Can't you guess? Once she let it be known that she wasn't interested in men, the other girls were merciless."

"Was she outed?" Tinkie asked.

Virgie shook her head. "That's one thing I never understood. Quentin told the girls herself. It was as if she defied them. She announced one day that she was a lesbian and that she thought they were all stupid cows—her words—headed for the butcher block of marriage. She told them she was going to inherit a considerable fortune, and she'd never be saddled with a man to please. In essence, she rubbed their noses in it. In return, the girls ganged up on her and tormented her. And Allison."

The picture she painted was unpleasant. "Do you think any of the other girls were capable of hurting Quentin?" I asked.

Virgie put her teacup on the coffee table. "Have you read her book?"

"Only a few chapters."

"Read on. Though my girls are well trained, they're human. Quentin attacked numerous families with malice. Those who live by the sword, die by the sword, Tinkie dear. It's a Biblical prediction that's true today."

"And Allison?" I asked.

"Allison couldn't harm a fly," Virgie said. "Whatever I can do to help her, I will."

"She wanted some say in planning Quentin's funeral," Tinkie said.

"I'll stop by the jail today and speak with her." Virgie rose. "Now, ladies, I have an appointment with the funeral director. I have much to do today."

We rose and shook hands. As we walked out of the B&B and into the November sunshine, I could only think about getting out of the clothes Tinkie had forced on me.

6

Tinkie sat at my kitchen table as I made chicken salad sandwiches on wheat bread and poured two glasses of iced tea. To avoid another brown meal, I added a sprig of parsley to her plate.

"Virgie gave us some good leads." She bent to pick up a square of paper from beneath the table. "What's this?"

I hesitated. "A card from Humphrey Tatum."

She opened and scanned it, her eyes widening as she read. "Are you going to play Scarlett to his Rhett?" she asked. "I'll bet the two of you could make Atlanta burn for the second time."

"Absolutely not." I pulled the gift box out from the cabinet and tossed it onto the table. "Subtlety isn't Humphrey's strong suit."

Tinkie dove into the package like a kid at Christmas. Her squeal was one of wicked pleasure. "Sarah Booth, he realizes that red is your color." She held up the teddy and matching slippers. "You could bring a man to his knees in this outfit."

I took it from her hands and put it back in the box. "It's going right back to him."

"We could have delivered it ourselves this morning," she said, with a sly grin. "He's staying at The Gardens. Were you afraid you might be tempted?"

"It seems everyone is staying at Gertrude's place. She must be making a fortune off Quentin's murder."

"It's not like Zinnia has a Paradise Resort," Tinkie said, tapping the gift box with her Classic Red fingernails. "Why don't you at least go to dinner with Humphrey?"

"I think he's made it plain that he isn't interested in food or conversation."

"A little liaison with Humphrey might help your heart heal. Sometimes, a bit of uncomplicated fun is the ticket." There was sincere concern in her voice.

"Did you take a look at the outfit? I wouldn't call that uncomplicated. I'd never figure out the straps, hooks, and laces. I'd need a maid to help me get into it."

Tinkie bit into her sandwich. "Very funny, Sarah Booth. So what do you have planned for the rest of the day?"

"A horseback ride and then set up some appointments with the women who were at Booking It."

"I've made my own list of suspects." She reached into the pocket of black slacks that hugged her petite figure, brought out a piece of paper, and handed it to me.

Her neat handwriting scrolled down the page. "There are eighty-four names." She'd conveniently numbered them.

"All taken from Quentin's book, and all with plenty of motive to want her dead."

I put the list on the table. It was overwhelming in a way. Most of the names were high society, too. Not the most co-operative element in a murder investigation. Often people with money and social power felt they were insulated from the law.

"I've put a red check by the names I think we should in-vestigate first," Tinkie said.

"A little organizational nut you picked up from Oscar?"

My teasing was good-natured. Tinkie's mind was often more practical and organized than mine. I sat down with my iced tea and read through the list.

The entire McGee family was listed with red checks. Aunts, uncles, cousins. "All of them?"

"They'll all be greatly impacted by the inheritance of the trust," Tinkie pointed out. "Not to mention that they were dissed in print."

"Lorilee Brewer?" I pointed to another red-checked name.

"She was at the book signing Saturday. That's opportunity, and the motive is in the book."

"The name is vaguely familiar. Something unpleasant?"

"She was behind us at Ole Miss, but word from the sorority sisters is that she was a legendary bitch!" Tinkie swallowed the last bite of her sandwich. "Lorilee had good reason to want Quentin dead. Quentin went straight for the jugular when she printed that Lorilee was sexually desperate."

"Sexually desperate?"

Tinkie rolled her eyes. "I don't have all the details, but you can read as well as I can. Look her up in the book, Sarah Booth. See what Quentin wrote."

"Tinkie, I find it difficult to believe someone would kill over what's printed in a book."

"Lorilee was at the book signing Saturday afternoon and she stayed overnight at The Gardens and she has a big four-wheel-drive pickup. I think that makes her a superior suspect."

I thought about the crime scene. By the time I'd arrived, several vehicles had gone in and out, so I couldn't say for certain about tire treads, but Gordon might know more.

"Lorilee could have stolen Allison's shoes from her

room at The Gardens. She could have done the whole thing."

Tinkie was right. "Is she still in town?"

"She's staying for the funeral."

"How did you find that out?" I was curious. Tinkie had her ways, and I was always impressed with them.

"I called Gertrude Stromm." She smiled sweetly. "From Oscar's office at the bank. She was eager to cooperate with me."

"You're very bad, Tinkie."

"I know. I learned it from you."

Glancing down the list, I saw another name I'd heard before. "Marilyn Jenkins?"

Tinkie nodded. "If you'd ever take the time to read the book, you'd find that almost every prominent Delta family has been *honored* by inclusion. Marilyn, too."

I had a vague memory of tragedy striking Marilyn Jenkins in the last few years, but I couldn't put my mental finger on it. "Didn't something awful happen to her back in the nineties?"

"Her mother was killed in that freak rock slide in that exclusive neighborhood in Birmingham, Alabama. She was showing a house or something like that when half a mountain tumbled down on top of her and crushed her flat, but that wasn't how Marilyn got into the book."

Tinkie wanted me to beg, and I obliged. "What got her in the book?"

"Quentin dug up the fact that Marilyn had entered into secret negotiations to sell her Rankin County property for a toxic waste landfill. She's ruined in her neighborhood! The gossip is that the neighbors have formed a tomato squad, and whenever they see Marilyn, they pelt her with rotten tomatoes."

"Good lord, Tinkie. From what you're saying, half the

state's in the damn book." I had a sudden thought. "Am I in it?"

Her look was knowing. "You aren't in the index, Sarah Booth, but if Quentin had spoken with me, I would have given her a few of your more interesting biographical details. I think your romance with Hamilton Garrett V would have made fascinating reading."

The memory of those few days with Hamilton made me blush, but I wasn't worried. Tinkie would never do a single thing to hurt me. "My point is that almost everyone we know could be a suspect."

"I haven't had a chance to read the whole book yet, but whatever else you say about Quentin, she was a damn good detective. She dug up the dirt on everyone."

"She hurt a lot of people."

Tinkie stood up. "Enough procrastinating. We need to get to work." She took the list and tore it in half. "Sound fair?"

"More than." The McGee family was at the top of my half of the list.

"I'm going to stop by and talk to Cece before I tackle my names," Tinkie said. "Want me to return that little nightie to Humphrey?"

"Be my guest." I was amused. Tinkie was more interested in Humphrey's sex games than I was. "It might be a little big on you, Tink, but—"

"Oscar would never approve," she said drolly. "He doesn't share his money or his wife."

"A good motto to live by." I pulled a map of Mississippi out of the kitchen drawer. "Let's check in with each other around eight."

"Fine by me." She whistled up Chablis and left with the dog under one arm and the gift box under the other.

Before Jitty could cinch herself into another gorgeous French outfit, I darted out of the house. Reveler seemed eager for a ride, and we set off at a brisk trot, paralleling the road in front of Dahlia House. It had occurred to me more than once how lucky I was that cotton farmers didn't feel the need to fence. I had vast expanses of land to ride without the worry of wire and gates.

A car slowed behind me, and I signaled Reveler to walk as Harold eased closer. The Porsche was a beautiful machine, but he was right. It didn't really suit him. He was too dapper for a racing convertible.

"I was looking for you," he said.

I checked my watch. The bank was open; therefore, Harold should have been at his desk. "What's wrong?"

"Gordon stopped by the bank first thing this morning."

I eased Reveler to a stop. "For what purpose?"

"To ask a few more questions about my argument with Quentin. It would seem there was another witness to my death threat to Quentin at The Club."

"I'll stop by and talk to Gordon today," I said. "He has to question you, Harold, but it doesn't mean he suspects you."

"I want to help clear Allison's name."

Now that was a surprising twist. "Okay. But why?"

"I was thinking about it this morning, after Gordon left. It's a terrible feeling to be accused of something. For Allison, it has to be a million times worse. This was someone she loved, someone she planned to marry. I don't believe she did it, and I want to help."

"Without violating any of your banker ethics, could you find out the financial status of the Tatum family?"

"They don't bank with us, so I can make a few discreet calls."

"That would be a big help."

"Anything else?"

I shook my head.

"Sarah Booth, you should know that Humphrey Tatum

was at Playin' the Bones last night, telling folks that he was smitten by you."

Gossip is the lifeblood of a small town. "He can say whatever he wants, but it doesn't make it true."

"He's a little peculiar, but he's smart." He hesitated. "I've heard he can be very seductive."

"Once he finds out I don't have any money, he'll move his interest elsewhere."

He studied me for a moment, and I wondered what he was thinking. "Just keep your guard up."

He eased the Porsche past me and waited until he was far ahead to press hard on the gas. The little car shot forward in a blur of power.

After a shower and a change of clothes, I picked up my purse and keys and headed to the courthouse. There were a few things I wanted to check with Gordon.

There is little cold weather in Sunflower County, and none in November. Brisk days can happen, but not often. Thanksgiving, which was just around the bend, often brought weather warm enough for shorts. Ninety-five percent humidity and temperatures above seventy made it difficult to be festive. I dreamed of snow as I drove past the fallow cotton fields.

The statue of Johnny Reb on the courthouse lawn looked a little sad. A committee had formed to demand that the statue be removed, saying it was offensive. I couldn't look at the worn bronzed face of the "everysoldier" and see anything offensive. I saw sadness and loss and bitter disappointment. The statue didn't glorify the war that had torn my country apart, but it did honor the sacrifice of many families. My idea was to add other statues, not to destroy what had always been a part of my childhood.

I walked into the sheriff's office and looked around. It

was empty. Coleman had fired Rinda Stonecypher, and no one had been hired to replace her.

"Gordon?" I called as I walked into the office and slipped behind the counter where the jail docket lay. "Gordon?"

It seemed no one was home. The door to Coleman's office was open. Gordon hadn't moved in, which I thought was a wise decision on his part. It was one thing for him to act like sheriff in Coleman's absence, but it was another to try and take his office.

From the doorway, I could see a sheaf of paperwork still on the desk and a small, framed photograph. I walked to the desk, feeling very much like the intruder I was. I picked up the frame and turned it around. It was a picture of cotton fields and, far at the back of the horizon, a horse and rider skimming over the fields. No one else could possibly have recognized me. I put the picture down.

"Can I help you?"

I looked up, guilty as a felon, at Gordon standing in the doorway.

"Any word from Coleman?" I asked. I didn't know how much Gordon knew about my feelings for his boss, but he was astute. He certainly knew there was something between us.

"He called about an hour ago."

"He did?" I sounded too eager.

"He's coming back. Thursday. For the board of supervisors meeting."

"Is he coming back to work?"

"You'll have to ask him." Gordon stepped out of the doorway and went to his desk out front.

I followed him like a puppy. "Did he say how Connie was feeling?"

Gordon bent his head for some paperwork. "He didn't say. I don't mean to be rude, but those are things you should take up with him, not me."

I felt a flush touch my cheeks. Gordon was absolutely right. I'd gone all over town asking questions about Coleman and his personal business. Coleman knew my phone number. If he had something to tell me, he would have called. "Thanks, Gordon. I only need one more thing. Did you match the prints at the murder scene with Allison's shoes?"

He nodded. "A perfect match. Those shoes were in that mud hole. Now if you can convince me Allison wasn't in the shoes, we'll be getting somewhere."

I thought about what he was offering. "Do you think Allison killed Quentin?"

"The evidence tells me she did. The tissue sample taken from beneath Quentin's fingernails belongs to Allison."

"But Allison said they had an argument and Quentin scratched her face."

Gordon tidied his desk. "People don't always tell the truth, Sarah Booth. You know that. But I will say that watching her and seeing how hard she's taking it . . ." He shrugged. "But guilty people are often remorseful."

"Do you have any other suspects?" I asked, not wanting to be too obvious and bring up Harold's name.

Gordon smiled. "Coleman told me to cooperate with you, but he didn't say to give away the farm."

"Thanks. I'll check back with you later." Gordon wasn't going to give me anything else, and if I was going to Leflore County, I needed to get on the road.

Heading vaguely northeast, I notched the roadster up to eighty on the empty, flat highway and let my mind wander over what I knew of the case.

The way Quentin was killed indicated rage and a desire to punish. She'd pissed off a number of people, but 99 percent of angry people don't commit murder. I was looking for that 1 percent, that one person in all the suspects who could step over the line and take a human life.

I'd only been a private investigator for a year, but I'd worked on some interesting cases, and I felt I'd learned a lot about human nature. The seed of Cain was in all of us, but most people never acted on a hot desire to murder. Whoever had killed Quentin had plotted it out. She'd been lured into an empty cotton field in the middle of the night. The killer was someone she knew, or someone who could convince her to ride into the darkness with him or her. Quentin's vehicle was parked at the bed-and-breakfast.

I picked up the cell phone Tinkie insisted that I carry and dialed her number. "If you get a chance, could you stop by the jail and ask Allison a question?"

"Sure."

"Quentin must have ridden into the cotton field with her killer. Who was she talking to the last time Allison saw her? And we need to have the tires on Quentin and Allison's vehicle analyzed for composites of mud. We may be able to prove that Allison never went into the cotton field."

"Good thinking, Sarah Booth. By the way, I returned the little gift to Humphrey."

I could hear the amusement in her voice. "And?"

"He said he had another idea for something that might be more up your alley."

"I hope you convinced him to cease and desist."

"No, I told him I thought black leather was more your style."

I couldn't be certain she was teasing. Tinkie enjoyed tormenting me as much as I did her. "I'll get even."

"Oh, no doubt. I mentioned that he might want to take a camera. Just think, Sarah Booth, our client list would double if you'd pose for a few snapshots in a little leather outfit. Thigh-high boots, something with chains on the front."

She was having way too much fun. "I'm in front of the

McGee estate." I gave a low whistle as I took in the manicured twenty acres with the curving drive, white fences,
and Thoroughbreds grazing in a field. "Very nice."

"Old money is always the best," Tinkie said. "Before you
hang up, the wake is set from six to nine. A lot of our suspects are still in town. I'm hoping a few of them will show
up at the funeral home."

"We'll meet there, then." I hung up and drove toward
the white-columned mansion, which would have done any
Southern belle proud.

7

The McGees weren't expecting me, and the maid let me know it at the front door of the Monticello-style mansion.

"Miss Caledonia didn't say she was expecting anyone." She glared at me as I read her nameplate. Wow. Imagine having so many servants they had to wear name tags.

"I realize that, Tonya, but I'd like to talk with her and her husband, anyway."

"Do you have a card?"

It took me several minutes, but I dug out a slightly used looking business card and put it on the silver tray she extended.

"Wait here." The look she gave said "don't touch anything."

The entrance hall was beautifully appointed with marble floors, taupe-colored plaster walls, huge mirrors, and a vase of fresh lilies. Stargazers. Not so long ago a man had sent me such a bouquet. Standing in the foyer of the McGee home, I wouldn't allow myself to think of Hamilton Garrett and the future I'd thrown away.

"Miss Delaney, follow me."

Tonya had reappeared, and I straightened my posture as I followed the gray uniform–clad maid through a formal dining room to a music conservatory dominated by a grand piano.

Franklin and Caledonia McGee sat on a brocade sofa. She held a book, her thumb marking her place, and a newspaper was scattered at his feet.

"What brings a private investigator to our home?" Franklin stood as he spoke. He walked behind his wife, his stance protective.

"I'm working for Allison Tatum."

"I think you should leave." Franklin's voice thickened with emotion. "That young woman killed our daughter. We have no business with you."

"I think Allison is innocent." I spoke quietly but with the force of my convictions. "Surely you want to find the real murderer."

"And if Allison is the real murderer?" Caledonia's tone almost frosted my eyebrows. "Get out of our house before I slap your face."

"Darling, remember your blood pressure." Franklin put a hand on her shoulder. He looked at me. "As you can plainly see, you're upsetting my wife. It would be best for you to leave. Now. We deserve, no, demand the right to grieve in private."

The lord and lady of the manor act had worn a little thin with me. "You're so upset over Quentin's death, you didn't even claim her body for burial."

Franklin flinched, but his wife only grew angrier. "Get out of this house," she said, her voice harsh.

"Miss Delaney, we haven't spoken to Quentin in over a year. She made it very plain to us that she'd severed her ties to this family. I think it would be fair to say that she hated us." Franklin held his wife on the sofa with a discreet grip.

"Why was she so angry with you?" I asked.

"Quentin was born angry," Caledonia said. "She came out of the womb with a chip on her shoulder. And don't think you can blame it on us. Umbria is our daughter, and no one could ask for a more loving and devoted child. Quentin was a changeling. The fairies must have swapped her at birth."

I saw Franklin's grip increase as he sought to stop his wife's tirade. "We gave Quentin every opportunity that money could buy," Franklin said. "Just as we did Umbria. Quentin took the money and all it could buy, and then she wanted to act like it was tainted." His smile was tired. "She could have gone to public school. She didn't have to ride on the equestrian team at Ole Miss. No one forced her to accept vacations in Europe, week long spa treatments, and a dietician to plan her menus. In my mind, she was the worst kind of hypocrite."

Caledonia had gotten as stiff as a board as her husband spoke.

He released his wife's shoulder and came to stand in front of me. "Perhaps Shakespeare said it best in *King Lear*. 'How sharper than a serpent's tooth.'"

An ungrateful child could break a parent's heart, but I wasn't certain either Franklin or Caledonia was suffering from heart problems. It was possible they were only worried about their own necks. "Who would want to kill Quentin?"

"Almost everyone we know," Caledonia said. "Can you possibly understand what she did to us? To our friends. All of their private shame, dug up and put in print. We're social outcasts now because of the action she took."

What I wanted to say had something to do with the loss of a daughter versus the loss of social position, but I kept my comments to myself. I had no right to judge the McGees because they hadn't loved their daughter the way I'd been loved.

"Quentin was a great disappointment to us," Franklin said. His mouth quivered. "I'm glad she's dead."

Even if the words were spoken in anger, Franklin McGee was a fool. His wife knew it, too. I could read it in her cold eyes.

"We're both terribly upset," Caledonia said. She stood up and walked to stand beside her husband, her hand on his arm. "It's just like Quentin to start a mess like her book and then to duck out on the consequences of her actions. She was an irresponsible child."

I was having a hard time believing what I was hearing. "Quentin was murdered." I said. "She didn't 'duck out.'"

Caledonia waved a hand as she spoke. "You know what I meant."

"Where were you the night Quentin was killed?"

"Are you implying—" Caledonia started.

"I'm not implying anything." I was way out of patience. "I simply want an answer. Where were you?"

"It's none of your business, but we were at the Greenwood Public Library. A fund-raiser. For new books." He barked a laugh. "Isn't that bitterly ironic?"

"What time was it over?"

They exchanged a glance. "Sometime after ten," Caledonia said.

I calculated the distance from Greenwood to Zinnia. They could have made the drive, killed Quentin, and gone home. "After you left the fund-raiser, where did you go?"

"Home." Caledonia answered quickly. "We had a nightcap, and then we went to bed."

"Can the servants verify this?"

Caledonia laughed. "Do you think we keep them chained in the kitchen until we go to bed? They leave each day after dinner. No one was here."

She was an insulting woman. "Then you have no alibi." I didn't smile. "And where was your daughter Umbria?"

They both started, refusing to look at each other. It was

the most telling action they could have taken. "She was home with her husband, I'm sure," Franklin said.

"She was in Zinnia for the book signing," I pointed out. She bought a number of books."

"I'm sure she was home by dinnertime," Franklin said. "Her husband enjoys his family time. I do believe Lizzie, the cook, said Umbria stopped by here for some spices Saturday evening."

"Could I speak with Lizzie?" I asked.

Rather than walk to the kitchen, Caledonia rang a small bell that rested beside the sofa. Tonya silently appeared and was dispatched to retrieve Lizzie. We waited in strained silence until Tonya returned.

"Lizzie has gone to the grocery store," she said, darting a look in my direction. "She left not ten minutes ago. She should be back within the hour."

"I'll stop by another time," I said, aware of the relief on the McGees' faces. "Could you direct me to Rutherford Clark's real estate office?" When they spoke of Umbria, it was as if she were single. I could see by their expressions that Franklin and Caledonia wished she were single.

Caledonia leaned forward. "Umbria made a wonderful match, a Delta boy with an impeccable bloodline. We can't wait for our first grandchild."

How nice for them that one child lived up to expectation. I'd gotten all the information I was going to get. Now it was time to pay a call on Rutherford Clark, and I hoped to catch him before he was warned that I was coming.

I found his real estate office in the heart of Greenwood's historic district, right beside the Dancing Rabbit Bookstore. To my surprise, the door was locked. When I rattled the knob, a beautiful young woman with long legs, a short skirt, and a large bosom opened it from the inside.

"Is Mr. Clark available?" I asked.

She frowned, causing a harsh line to divide her eyebrows.

"Rutherford isn't here. He's"—the frown deepened—"Who are you, and what do you want with Rutherford?"

"I'm a private investigator, and I want to talk to him." As I'd hoped, my words caused her more worry.

"He's away on business."

"When will he return?"

"In a week or so."

I almost laughed. "Where is he?"

"Russia," she said, without a hint of a smile. "It was the opportunity of a lifetime." She sounded as if she'd memorized words that had no meaning.

"When did he leave?" I asked.

"Sunday."

From inside the office, I could hear what sounded like television coverage of some type of sporting event. The young woman glanced over her shoulder, clearly nervous. "Could I step inside?"

She shook her head. "We're closed."

Before I could respond, she shut the door, and I heard it lock. Peering in the window, I watched as she walked to the back of the office, clicking off the lights as she went.

Since I was so close, I stopped at the bookstore to check on the availability of Quentin's book. The store owner told me that she'd sold over two hundred copies. It was impossible to keep the book in stock. Umbria McGee Clark had bought almost all of the copies.

I left the bookstore and took a drive around the town. Greenwood is where the Yazoo and Tallahatchie Rivers meet, and for many years it was a big cotton town. The cotton would be brought in from farms all around, ginned and baled, sold by the pound, and shipped downriver or sent by rail. Since the bottom had fallen out of the cotton market, the town had not prospered. There were empty storefronts, neglected streets, and some beautiful older homes needing a coat of paint. I drove to the local library and checked to make sure there had even been a fund-raiser.

Peggy Greene, the librarian, was excited to tell me that the fund-raiser had been a great success. The McGees had donated five thousand dollars. They'd been the guests of honor at the event. She moved around the children's section of the library, restacking books as we talked.

"Franklin and Caledonia have always supported the library," she said. She was a trim woman with intelligent brown eyes. "Why are you asking about them?" She rolled her cart full of books farther down the aisle.

"It's just routine."

"My eye," she said. "You know, we were afraid that after Quentin's book came out, the McGees might not support the library. They aren't really readers, you know."

"Do you have any copies of *King Cotton Bleeds* here?"

She shook her head. "We don't intend to stock it."

"Because it's controversial?"

"No, because it would be stolen." She stared into my eyes and dared me to question her logic. "We've had at least a hundred people call to ask for it, and none of those callers are regular library users. They're just the type of people who steal books. Isn't that ironic? We have a wealth of wonderful books, great literature, which folks won't consider reading. But something scandalous, something that impugns their neighbors, they can't wait to see it."

The McGees held the reins of power at the library. I wondered how much money they'd donated in the last year. "What time was your fund-raiser over?"

"A little before ten. Several people stayed to talk afterward."

"And the McGees?"

She thought for a moment. "They went home, I believe. Yes, Franklin said he'd been up early. He'd gone to Memphis to take care of something."

Because I have a suspicious mind, it naturally jumped to the postmark of the last threatening note Quentin had received. But the timing was off. Franklin couldn't have mailed the note the same day Quentin received it. I needed to study the date of the postmark more closely, though.

"Ms. Greene, did you know Quentin?"

"As a child, she came to the library frequently. Loved to read. Adventure stories and mysteries. Couldn't get enough of them. Over the summer she was eight, she read the entire Hardy Boys series." A faint smile touched her mouth as she talked.

"You were fond of Quentin?"

"She always seemed a little out of place."

I had to tread cautiously here. "I never knew her, but I'm trying to get an idea what kind of person she was. Can you help me?"

She considered for a moment as she put two books back in their proper places. "Quentin was a kind child. She was tenderhearted. I remember one summer day she found a kitten behind the library, just about starved to death. She pleaded with her mother to take it home, but Caledonia wouldn't let her. She said cats where filthy creatures, and she wouldn't have one on her place. Quentin sobbed like she was going to die." Peggy looked down at the books on her cart and blinked her eyes. "It still upsets me. Caledonia forced Quentin to put the kitten down. It was frightened and ran out in front of a car, and was almost killed in front of Quentin's eyes."

"Quentin must have been very angry with her parents to write that book."

Peggy shook her head. "She changed as she became a teenager. She did everything she could to defy her parents. Umbria, of course, only made it that much worse. She was the perfect child. Caledonia was always throwing Umbria up in Quentin's face. It was horrible."

"Do you remember anything else?"

"When Quentin was younger, she excelled at sports. Caledonia wanted her to take ballet. Quentin refused and played Softball. I don't think the McGees ever went to a single one of her games, but they drove all over the Southeast to watch Umbria dance."

It sounded as if Franklin and Caledonia had done everything in their power to drive Quentin out of the family. They had succeeded, but Quentin's revenge had come in a way they could never have anticipated.

"When was the last time you saw Quentin?" I asked.

"She stopped by a few weeks ago to tell me the release date of the book." Her hand faltered as she slotted a book back into place. "She was so different."

"How so?"

"She was hard. She knew her book was going to hurt a lot of people, and she was glad about it." Peggy turned to me. "She did say that with her advance money, she and Allison were going to fund an animal shelter for stray cats. I think the incident with the kitten really scarred Quentin. Of all the things Caledonia did to her, that hurt the worst."

My own mother had been the queen of stray animals. Not only did she pick up strays on the side of the road, she was notorious for snatching hunting dogs that ran illegally across our property. Perhaps that was where my passion for hounds had developed. "I can't imagine upsetting a child that way," I said.

"Quentin was so tender. It was what drew me to her. She was so compassionate and kind. When I saw her last, it seemed all of that had died in her."

"Did you know Allison, too?"

"I met her that day. She was so in love with Quentin. I remember thinking that at last Quentin had found someone who could truly love her, truly appreciate her spirit.

They told me they were getting married and invited me to the wedding."

"She must have thought highly of you."

"I took that stray kitten home with me. Miss Vesta lived to be seventeen."

"No wonder Quentin called you her friend." I put my pad and pen in my purse and pulled out a business card. "If you think of anything, or hear anything, please call me."

"Librarians aren't generally included in the local gossip clubs." Her eyes crinkled at the corners.

"Just in case."

"I hope you can help Allison," she said. "She doesn't strike me as the kind of girl who could kill anyone. In fact, I got the distinct impression she wasn't thrilled with all the pain Quentin caused with her book."

I nodded. "Thanks."

Peggy turned back to her work, and I left for the drive back to Zinnia. Dusk had fallen, and as I drove out of town, I passed a pecan orchard, the delicate branches of the trees like gray fans against a pinkened sky. The Delta was one of the most beautiful places on earth. I wondered at the strange pull of land, home, and memories that had brought me back to a place I'd been busting to leave. It made me wonder why Quentin hadn't simply left Mississippi. Left the South. She could have gone to a big city and lived her life with Allison and never raised an eyebrow. Instead, she'd come home to rub her book in the faces of her family and their social peers. It spoke of a hurt bone-deep and a desire for revenge that overrode a desire for happiness. Somehow, I couldn't help but believe that the answer to Quentin's murder would be found in her own dark ambitions.

Just as I hit the city limits of Zinnia, my cell phone rang. Tinkie was calling.

"We need to be up at the funeral home at seven o'clock for the wake," she said.

I wasn't about to argue with her. "Do I have to wear the uniform?"

She considered. "Slacks will do just fine. Black or navy. Nothing too bright in the blouse department."

I sighed. "I'll do my best."

"Sarah Booth, you make it sound like putting on some decent clothes is worse than cutting off a limb."

I considered the horrors of each. "Almost."

"I'll pick you up at six forty-five."

"Got it." I'd already sped through town. I'd be home in another few minutes, with plenty of time to feed Reveler and my hound and get ready for the next leg of the investigation.

8

Tinkie wasn't a woman to keep waiting for a social event as potentially delicious as a wake, so I went straight to the barn and fed Reveler. As I ran the brush over Reveler's golden hide, I heard the mournful sound of baying and barking. Sweetie Pie was after the armadillo that had taken up residence under the front porch. Once Reveler had gobbled his grain, I retraced my steps and went to retrieve Miss Pie. For a few minutes I watched the antics of my hound as she cornered the armor-plated rodent. They raced around the yard, with the armadillo freezing and then dashing off in another direction, with Sweetie hot on its trail. Sweetie didn't have the instinct to kill that a terrier might, but I wished she'd run the varmint out of the yard. It was doing a major job of destroying what was left of my mother's flower beds.

Once Sweetie grew tired of barking at the armadillo, she followed me up the front steps and to the door. Just as I was reaching out my hand for the knob, I saw the handcuffs. My heart did a double take. Coleman! He was the only man I knew who might leave handcuffs at my door as a coded message. But it was strange that he hadn't simply left a note to let me know he was back in town.

I unhooked the cuffs from the doorknob and took them inside. Sweetie paced to the kitchen, obviously hungry. I had part of a roast in the fridge, so I put the cuffs on the table, pulled out the roast, and began to cut it up for my hound.

"That dog is spoiled rotten."

I didn't bother to look. Jitty was back from her ball or wherever she'd been. I cubed the meat with my sharpest knife. Sweetie liked bite-sized chunks. She was the most ladylike resident of Dahlia House.

"Where'd the handcuffs come from?" Jitty asked.

I finally turned to address her. She was dazzling in umber brocade. Whoever managed her wardrobe deserved an Academy Award nomination for best costume design. "You're the resident haint. You're here all day long, lurking and spying. I was out working. You should know who stopped by."

"You're *thinkin'* it's that married lawman." She didn't smile.

"I'm *hoping* it's that married lawman," I corrected her.

"You're just a hussy."

Jitty's name-calling hurt my feelings. "Maybe I am," I said hotly. "I'm tired of pretending I don't care about Coleman. I do. I care a lot."

"It's not about carin'. It's about a code of conduct. It's about livin' in a way that stands for something."

That was too much. "Oh, Miss High-and-Mighty, you're living in an era when children starved in the streets while the court dined on delicacies. If there was one word to describe the period you've chosen, it would be excess. A code of conduct! I think you'd better get your historical facts straight before you call me names."

Jitty shifted closer to me. "I'm not tryin' to hurt you.

I'm tryin' to protect your heart. Fallin' for a married man only leads to suffering. For everybody involved."

"I'm already suffering," I snapped. "Stay out of it." I picked up the handcuffs. "I have to get ready for a wake!" I stormed past her and went to my bedroom. In a few moments I had my bath running.

I picked up the cuffs again and looked at them. Coleman wasn't the type to leave enigmatic messages. So why hadn't he just written a note?

On the off chance he'd called, I lifted the phone beside the bed and heard the beep-beep-beep that let me know someone had left voice mail. Tinkie had convinced me that my old answering machine was no longer adequate, but I'd resisted caller ID, which took the anticipation out of messages. I put in my code and waited, my heart pounding in a way that was exciting and uncomfortable.

There was no message, only a hang-up call.

Punching in new numbers, I waited for Tinkie to answer. "I don't feel like going to the wake," I told her. "Can you handle it?"

After a lengthy silence, she spoke. "What's going on?"

I couldn't tell her I'd had a fight with Jitty. The men in white coats would be at my door in a matter of hours if Tinkie thought I regularly bickered with a ghost. Out-and-out lying wasn't an option, either. Tinkie was my partner and deserved the truth.

"Someone left handcuffs on the front doorknob."

"Sarah Booth, are you thinking it might be Coleman?"

She knew my heart. Silence was my answer.

"Girl, you're setting yourself up for real heartbreak. You have to let Coleman go."

Tinkie was parroting what Jitty had said. "So I keep telling myself."

"I've been debating about whether to tell you this or not."

"What?" This was going to be painful. Tinkie never withheld unless it was in an attempt to avoid hurting me.

"Oscar got a call today from Coleman. He's putting his house up for sale."

"He's selling his home?" Repeating a question was an old Daddy's Girl ploy designed to give one an opportunity to think.

"He told Oscar that Connie will never come back to Sunflower County. They've decided to sell." Emphasis on the "they've."

"Why did he call Oscar?" Surely there was a mistake. Coleman and Oscar had never been confidants.

"Oscar's arranging the financing on the sale."

"But Coleman's supposed to be back in town this week. Gordon said he planned on—"

"Did it ever occur to you that he might be coming back to Zinnia to sign the papers on selling his house and to tie up loose ends for a permanent move? Sarah Booth, you have to stop living in a fantasy."

Tinkie wasn't a cruel person, but her words cut me like sharp blades. "That isn't true."

"It's time for you to let go of the past. All of it. You don't have room in your life for anything new, because you're stuffed full of the past."

"I don't want anything new." There it was. The truth at last. I clung to the past like a favorite sweatshirt.

"Don't take this the wrong way, but I'm worried about you."

That was great. Tinkie had a lump in her breast, and she was worried about me because I had a faulty heart and a hole in my head. "I'm okay. I just want a chance to talk to Coleman. If he's in town tonight, he might decide to stop by here. I want to be home in case he does."

"You're going to get you heart broken," she warned.

"It's my heart to abuse," I said softly. "Tinkie, I have to see this to the end. You can understand that, can't you?"

She sighed. "I'll take care of the wake. The funeral's been set for Wednesday morning. A memorial service and then burial of the urn."

"The urn?"

"Mrs. Carrington has requested that Quentin be cremated."

"What does the McGee family have to say about that?"

"Not a word," Tinkie said. "They gave up the right to complain when they failed to claim the body. I understand Virgie and Allison had a chat this afternoon, and both agreed that cremation was what Quentin would have wanted."

"Are you sure you're okay to handle the wake?"

"I can cover the wake, but we both need to attend the funeral tomorrow at ten."

Her tone told me I was making a bad choice. "I'll be here if you need me." I hung up and hurried to the tub full of hot water for a long soak and a few healing daydreams.

I spent forty minutes sinking beneath the warm water and imagining various scenarios where Coleman had a reasonable explanation for why he'd chosen his insane-pregnant-lying-manipulating wife over me. I understood what it meant to stand by a vow, but there came a point when a commitment was null and void. A marriage was a contract. A partnership. When one partner began to lie and cheat and abuse the other, it was time to sever the contract.

My parents had occasionally argued. Twice they'd gotten so angry, they'd mentioned divorce. Both times it had involved conduct one felt violated the spirit of the vows. The first time was over the attentions of another man toward my mother, and the second involved a piece of land that my father wanted to sell. Those arguments had been resolved before night had fallen on the house. That was the pattern I'd learned for marriage. If it was going to be different than that, I didn't want it. I didn't want Coleman to settle for less.

The bathwater had grown cold, so I got out and dried off. I'd just walked into my bedroom when I heard the doorbell chiming. My heart began a sickening staccato beat as I scrounged around my closet for my "company" dressing gown. Normally, I wore an old terry-cloth robe that had belonged to my father, but if Coleman was at the door, I wanted to look more elegant.

In the back of the closet, I found a short silk kimono in a shade of green that intensified the color of my eyes. I slipped it over my head as I started down the stairs. It settled around my thighs just as I opened the door.

"Hello, Sarah Booth," Humphrey Tatum said, his canines showing as he took in my bare legs and braless state.

Disappointment has a bitter taste. I knew instantly that Coleman had never stepped foot on my front porch. The handcuffs were from the deviant standing in front of me.

Humphrey leaned against the door frame. "I wondered if the handcuffs would do it for you. Obviously, you like the idea of playing strip search."

Blushing wasn't something I did often, but this was a major power surge. I felt the heat rise from my neck up into my cheeks. I'd been played and played well. "Humphrey, have you lost your mind?" Not the most brilliant question I might have asked, but I was trying to find my composure and hide my tattered heart.

"I haven't lost anything. Yet. I think I may have underestimated you, Sarah Booth. Are you playing naughty games with someone else?" He maneuvered so that he was halfway in the door.

"What is it with you, Humphrey?" I decided to stand on dignity.

"Now that's a question," he said, his mouth twisting in amusement. "You meet me at the door half naked in a silk dressing gown and nothing else, and you wonder why I keep trying to hop in bed with you. Could it be that you're sending mixed signals, Sarah Booth?"

Damn it, he had me there. "I was ex—" I stopped myself. Humphrey didn't need to know anything about my private life, especially not my feelings for Coleman. "I'm sorry, Humphrey, I . . ." What did I have to be sorry for?

"Are you in the habit of speaking in incomplete sentences?" He glanced over my shoulder. "Perhaps you intended to invite me in for a drink?" He coughed delicately. "I'm parched."

I sighed. "Come in. The liquor is on the sideboard. Help yourself. I'm going to grab some jeans." I didn't give him a chance to question me. I ran back up the stairs to my bedroom. I pulled a clean pair of jeans from the closet and a sweatshirt from my drawer. I was dressed, complete with sneakers, in less than five minutes. I didn't bother with make-up.

He was sipping a Scotch on the rocks when I found him in the parlor, looking at some of the family pictures. He pointed to one, and I leaned closer to see my mother holding me on her lap. On my round, bald head, I was wearing a headband with two little horns. A forked tail hung from my red diaper. Mother wore a damsel costume. I had no memory of the event, but Aunt Loulane had repeatedly told the story of how every year my mother dressed up to take me trick-or-treating.

"I've heard a few stories about your mother," Humphrey said, tapping the photo.

"I'm sure." I bristled. "Which ones? The ones where she slapped the mayor or the ones where she was starting a communist commune here?"

He chuckled. "You're a little on the sensitive side. I guess it's difficult to have a mother who was both brilliant and beautiful."

If he was trying to win me, he was on the right track. "What stories did you hear?"

"My father was a great admirer of your mother. He wooed her in college, but your father beat him out."

This was news. I'd known that several local men had fallen in love with Mother after she was married to Daddy. This was different. This was a pre-wedding story, and one I hadn't heard before. "So tell me."

"The Booth family was well known in Delta society," Humphrey said. "When your mother came of age to be considered as a bride, she was known to be the catch of the season. At one point, she had dates booked for lunch and dinner for an entire semester. After a few months of that, she'd had enough. She called the remainder of the men she was supposed to dine with and told them all she was on a diet, and to save time, they should just submit a list of their marital demands."

"You're teasing, aren't you?"

"Absolutely not. I know it for a fact. My father was scheduled for a Friday evening. He realized then that she was more woman than he could manage, and he dropped out of the running."

"Why was Mother so popular? The Booths didn't have a lot of money." My grandparents had been comfortable, but that was a long, long way from being rich.

"Your mother had so much more than money. She had class and intelligence and beauty. She was a woman who could turn around the fortunes of a family."

"How so?" I saw that his glass was nearly empty, so I made him a fresh drink and one for myself.

"You greatly underestimate the power of a woman with brains and ambition." His gaze held mine.

"My mother was smart, but I wouldn't say she was ambitious. She didn't seem to care a lot about money."

"Perhaps not, but she was ambitious. Look at the way she raised you."

I arched my eyebrows.

"Independent, a woman capable of living alone, running her own business, a horsewoman." He smiled. "I would give a lot to see you astride."

Just when I was beginning to enjoy the conversation, Humphrey had to go kinky on me. "Do you ride?" I decided to ignore the innuendo.

"Yes," he said. "I used to show jump. I'd love a brisk ride through the autumn afternoon."

Now that was interesting. "Perhaps I can borrow a horse from my friend Lee."

"It would mean a lot to me. We haven't had horses at Tatum's Corner for a long time. You've probably heard that the Tatum family has fallen on hard times financially."

Since Humphrey had brought it up, I decided to dive in. "Yes, and I've also heard that you were interested in marrying Quentin because she was due to be an heiress."

He leaned back against the horsehair sofa. "That's true. My parents had settled on Quentin as my bride-to-be. I didn't object. She was a beautiful woman."

I couldn't tell what he was feeling. "But Quentin wasn't interested in marrying you."

"My little sister grabbed the brass ring." He shrugged. "What difference did it make? The money would be in the family."

"It truly made no difference?"

"Not to me. Once Quentin and Al hooked up, it took the pressure off me. Quentin was certain to remain unmarried until she gained the inheritance. Once she grew tired of Al, I was prepared to step in and pay court to her."

"You would have married Quentin without loving her?"

"You are naïve." He finished his drink. "Name me one marriage that isn't based more on economic need than romance."

"Tinkie and Oscar." I said it without thinking.

"The question to ask is, would either of them be happy married to a pauper?"

I didn't know. They were perfect for each other because they came from the same background, shared the same values. "In your quest for financial stability, have you considered a profession?"

He laughed out loud. "Very cutting, my dear. Actually, I have an MBA in business. Unfortunately, it doesn't do any good if I don't have a business to manage."

"So why are you leaving questionable gifts for me?" I asked. "I have nothing to offer in the way of financial security."

He rose in a graceful motion. When he stood in front of me, he held his hand out. I accepted it, and he lifted me to my feet. "You have fire, Sarah Booth."

"Not exactly a marketable quality."

"But one that intrigues me."

"I hear a lot of women intrigue you."

He touched my cheek. "Someone has been listening to dirty gossip." He leaned closer so that his breath ruffled the curls beside my ear. "I do like my games, Sarah Booth, and I think you like them, too."

He gently hooked his thumb beneath my jaw and tilted my face so that we looked at each other. "Tell me you don't."

It was a dare, a challenge. "You're . . . interesting," I admitted, stepping away from him.

He chuckled. "You're too honest for your own good."

"Perhaps." I freshened my drink and made him another. "You're a handsome man, Humphrey. There aren't many women alive who don't enjoy the attentions of a handsome man."

"I'm good in bed." He took the drink, his fingers brushing mine.

"You're also too modest."

My sarcasm only made him laugh. "Why did you come back to Zinnia, Sarah Booth? You could have stayed in

New York. You could have married well and had the perfect life."

I was surprised to discover that I wanted to answer him honestly. "This is my home. This is where I belong."

"That kind of attitude will only get you into trouble."

Beneath his glib remark, I saw a flicker of something. "You love Tatum's Corner, don't you?" I saw I'd hit my mark.

"I have fond memories of the town. It's dying, you know. We need jobs and industry. We—" He realized how passionate he sounded. "I didn't realize I brought my soapbox inside with me. I apologize."

"Quentin's money would have come in handy."

He nodded. "Yes, it would. But that's a moot issue."

"Who will inherit?" I asked.

He shrugged his shoulders. "If the death certificate reads that she died after she turned twenty-five, then I presume she has a will."

"You don't know for certain?" I found that hard to believe.

"Okay, she has a will, but no one knows the terms."

"No one?"

He finished his drink. "You're a born schemer, aren't you? The will is to be read Thursday morning, but enough about money. I'm going to further shock polite society by skipping the wake tonight. Why don't we step out for dinner?"

I wasn't a fool. Humphrey was in town because of the will. I wondered what he hoped to gain, and if the help he'd extended to Allison was a bid for managing her money, should she inherit. "If I go to dinner with you, I'm not changing clothes."

"Heaven forbid that you should make an effort on a man's behalf," he said as he crooked his arm for me to take. "I'll take you somewhere dark and low class. It'll be a perfect evening for you."

9

I had to wonder about my baser motives as I let Humphrey Tatum drive me through the brisk November night. My partner was working a wake, and I was going to dinner with a man who touted his kinkiness. Somewhere, my life had gone terribly awry.

Humphrey pulled into the parking lot of Playin' the Bones, a nightclub run by an old client of mine.

"This is high class, not low," I said. Patrons of the blues club might show up in jeans and work boots, but it still reeked of class. The music was hot, and the barbecue, which was smoked out back on an open pit, was tart. It fit my mood perfectly.

"I understand you know the owners," he said, grasping my wrist to prevent me from getting out of the car. "Please, Sarah Booth, give me a chance to be the gentleman."

He walked around, opened my door, and helped me out. "Thank you, Humphrey." I did a royal curtsey. "I just don't know how I could have managed to open that heavy ole door all by myself. A big, strong man like you"—I squeezed his bicep for good effect—"well, you just make me glad I'm a helpless little woman."

His laughter was rich. "When you were in New York, they obviously failed to offer you the role of Betsy Iron Magnolia. What a shame."

I was surprised that he knew about my former client list as well as my failed acting career. Humphrey had done his homework, which told me his romantic maneuvers were calculated.

Inside the club, we found a table against the back wall. He ordered our drinks, naming my preference without asking. Once the drinks arrived, he ordered our dinners. My job, apparently, was to sit still and be quiet.

"I took Quentin out once," he said. "She was insulted by the way I ordered for her."

"It is insulting." I sipped my drink.

"Did I get it wrong?"

"It's not about the menu. I'm not a mute; I can speak for myself."

"But"—he stopped himself—"the world is changing."

He looked so lost that I felt a twinge of sympathy for him. He'd been raised to inhabit a world that no longer existed. For the second time that evening, I thought of Ashley Wilkes and his attempts to hold together his family heritage. He'd loved Scarlett, yet he'd married Melanie. That choice had destroyed both of them.

"What will become of Tatum's Corner if Allison doesn't inherit, or if she's sent to prison?"

"I'll marry well."

"That simple?"

"For me, it is." He finished his drink and signaled the waiter for another one. Percy Sledge was playing on the juke box, and I couldn't help but contrast the lyrics of his classic song "When a Man Loves a Woman" with the reality that Humphrey faced.

"How old are you, Humphrey?"

"Thirty-nine." He tipped the waitress a ten. He might be on the edge of financial ruin, but he was going down as a man who knew how to live well. "My birthday is December fifth. I'll be forty."

"And Allison is twenty-five?"

"Yes. Her birthday was last April." He swallowed half his drink and signaled for another. Though he showed none of the affects, he was drinking hard. "Allison was still in diapers when I went to Livingston Academy in Richmond, Virginia. She was in fifth grade by the time I returned to Tatum's Corner. We never had a chance to be close."

"Were you ever friends?"

"No." He rattled the ice in his glass. "Allison stayed in her room. She read a lot. She wanted to be a writer."

That was news. "Yet Quentin wrote the book."

"My parents ignored Allison. I was the apple of their eye, and there was no room for her. Whenever she told them about her dreams, they were amused. I remember one Thanksgiving dinner when she wanted to read a poem aloud. They shushed her." He leaned toward me. "They literally shushed her. I don't think she ever said another word about writing. If they'd ever taken the time to encourage her, things would be a lot different."

The waitress brought his drink and our food just as a lone guitarist walked onto the stage and strummed his guitar. The club gradually quieted. The young man adjusted the mike, shifting from foot to foot as he did so.

"Hi, folks. I'm Adam Sinclair. I'm glad to be here at Ida Mae's club. I have some exciting news. I just signed a record contract with Bristol Studios."

He waited for the applause to die down. "I owe this to Rutherford Clark." He pointed to a table at the front of the stage where a balding man sat surrounded by three beautiful young women and thousands of dollars worth of silicon. "Stand up, Rutherford," Adam said.

The balding man beamed a smile around the club as he stood to applause. The young women at his table all but hung on his arms.

The singer spoke again. "Mr. Clark heard my songs, and he made some phone calls. He got me this chance, and this first song is for him." He sat back on the stool that had been provided for him and began to play.

"Sarah Booth, what's wrong?" Humphrey asked.

I was staring at Rutherford Clark, husband of Umbria McGee. The man who was supposed to be in Russia. Instead of attending his sister-in-law's wake, Rutherford was in a blues club with a bevy of buxom women.

"Do you know Rutherford Clark?" I asked.

"We've met before." He made a mock-surprise face. "You're shocked that he's here instead of at the wake."

"Yes," I said. "Quentin was his sister-in-law. I would think he'd be with his wife."

"Have you met Umbria?"

"Not yet, but what's that—"

"Wait until you meet her. As every good warrior knows, never face the dragon head on."

"Is she that bad?"

"Only if you're sober, and Rutherford has found that the McGee money is adequate compensation." He nodded toward the girls. "They don't last long, but there's always a new one to take the empty place. I think Rutherford must go to Memphis to pick them out."

"And Umbria? Does she have her little flings?"

"What's sauce for the goose is sauce for the gander, or so the saying goes."

"You wouldn't happen to have any names of the men she sees, would you?"

"I can supply you with a list if you're really interested." He studied me without a qualm.

"I am interested. Very." My gaze rested on Rutherford. He sipped champagne from the blonde's glass while one brunette fed him pieces of barbecue she tore into bite-sized chunks. I provided that kind of service only for my hound.

"Rutherford better enjoy it while he can," Humphrey said.

"Why is that?"

"Once the family accepts the time of death, and Quentin is posthumously crowned heir apparent to the McGee fortunes, I have a funny feeling his life will change dramatically."

All the more reason for him to want Quentin dead before her birthday, I thought. It was another lead to investigate. We'd finished our barbecue, and I rose from the table. "Will you excuse me?"

"Headed for trouble, I see. I'll pay the tab just in case we need to leave in a hurry."

I walked over to Rutherford's table. He ordered another bottle of bubbly and ignored me. "Mr. Clark," I said.

"Who are you?" He was annoyed by my interruption. "Can't you see someone is singing?"

I introduced myself and leaned down. "How was Russia?"

"You're that private investigator," he accused. "What do you want?" He took another bite of barbecue.

"Where were you on Sunday night?" I asked. "Don't bother with the whole Russian lie. It won't take me any time to check the airports."

"He was with me," the blonde said. She laced her arm through his. "We had a wonderful time. What's it to you?"

"And your name?" I asked, pulling a notebook from the back pocket of my jeans.

"Brittany Spears." She didn't bat an eye.

"Very amusing, but you're a little long in the tooth to pretend to be Brittany."

She stood up, her chest heaving in indignation. "You bitch!" She swung hard, but she was slow. I ducked and the force of her swing tipped her off balance. She fell across the table, sending champagne flying.

"Catfight! Catfight!" The cry echoed throughout the club. Before I could do anything, one of the brunettes jumped on me. She was tugging my hair and trying to bite my ears as I stumbled into the stage. The singer stopped, putting aside his guitar so that he could jump into the middle of it.

I felt the screeching brunette pulled off my back, and Leo, Ida Mae's bouncer, appeared at my elbow.

"Ida Mae told me to get you outside," he whispered just before he bodily lifted me and carried me toward the door. Behind me I could hear the sound of chairs being smashed, fists thunking into flesh, and loud cursing.

As we slipped through the door, we passed two women coming in. They wore the Carrington uniform and carried themselves with the attitude of proper debs. They disappeared inside as Leo set me on my feet.

"You were just about to get your ass whipped, Miss Delaney," Leo said. "Don't you know better?"

"I didn't start it." I was already laying the groundwork for my defense. "That blond bimbo jumped me."

Humphrey sallied out the door, his face wide in a grin. "Sarah Booth, I didn't realize you were a woman of so many talents. That was one helluva bar fight you started."

"I didn't start it," I protested.

"I doubt Rutherford Clark will ever forget you. The last I saw of him, he was calling his lawyer. I think he may sue you. Leo, Ida Mae needs your services inside."

The bouncer went back in, and I sat down on the bumper of a pickup and put my face in my hands. My ears were ringing. My head throbbed. I felt Humphrey's hand on my elbow as he lifted me to my feet. Before I knew it, I was seated in his car and riding through the night toward Dahlia House.

To my surprise, Humphrey left the motor running when he helped me out of the car and walked me to the door. "I'll give you a call tomorrow." He kissed my cheek and walked across the porch. On the top step, he turned. "You may think I'm shallow and a game player, but just understand, Sarah Booth, I like my opponents worthy and prepared to play. I'll see you again when you're at your best."

I watched as he roared down the driveway, beneath the bare white limbs of the sycamores, and turned onto the main road.

"I'd like to see that one in knee breeches and a cod-piece."

Jitty had joined me on the porch. I didn't have a ready answer, because I was conflicted where Humphrey was concerned. Just when I thought he was too shallow to hold rainwater, he surprised me. "What do you make of Humphrey?" I asked.

"He's a gentleman out of time."

She was right, dang her. "What are his motivations in hiring me to help his sister?"

She opened a fan and whipped it rapidly in front of her face even though I was freezing. "If Allison inherits, he needs to be in her good favor. If she doesn't, he can appear to be the loyal brother. It's a good place to be, whichever way it plays out."

Jitty was the ultimate pragmatist. "You find Humphrey insincere?"

"No." She slapped her fan closed in her palm. She'd added a beauty mark to the corner of her mouth. "The fate of his home rests in his hands." She pointed the fan at me. "Much like Dahlia House rests on you." Her lips lifted just a fraction. "I remember when you stole Chablis."

She could have hit me in the head with an axe and not delivered such an effective blow. In my life I'd done things I wasn't proud of, but stealing Tinkie's dog was the worst. I sat on the steps, ignoring the icy bite of the wood on my butt. "I did a terrible thing."

She sat beside me, her skirts rustling in the night like the whisper of dying leaves. "You saved your home."

"I stole my friend's dog."

"Life isn't simple, Sarah Booth."

"I should tell Tinkie what I did."

She shook her head. "Never. You owe it to her to keep that information to yourself. That's part of the bargain of friendship. Tinkie looks up to you. That's your penance." She stood up. "Sorry to rush off, but I've got a date."

"Jitty—" But it was too late. She was gone. Evaporating after a zinger was her specialty.

I sat alone on the steps, thinking about the past. I might want to clear my conscience by telling Tinkie the truth, but Jitty was right. I owed it to Tinkie to keep my mouth shut. There was nothing for it but to get to bed and face the prospects of Quentin McGee's funeral service the next morning.

Tinkie was waiting in the parking lot of Rideout Funeral Home, wearing a perfect navy "uniform" and a frown. "I tried to call you three times last night, and you didn't answer." She didn't tap her toe at me, but she wanted to.

"I was having dinner with Humphrey."

Her entire demeanor changed. "That's great, Sarah Booth. And to think I was afraid you were holed up in bed, pining for Coleman." She looked me over from head to toe. "You look perfect. So where did you and Humphrey go?"

I told her about my dinner date and my run-in with Rutherford and his chicks.

"A bar fight!" She was about to give her Daddy's Girl squeal when I grasped her arm.

"I didn't start it."

"Sure." She rolled her eyes. "While I'm working the case, you're going out to dinner with Harold and then Humphrey, and you're starting bar fights. Let's see. I got to stand beside a spray of roses while wearing sensible shoes. Someone is getting the best end of this case."

"Tinkie!" I was shamed. "I apologize. I—"

Her laugh was mischievous. "I'm only pulling your leg, Sarah Booth. I learned a lot at the wake. Umbria was there all night, lurking in the back of the room. There was no family receiving line." She adjusted her veil. "There wasn't even a picture of Quentin. It was like a bad cocktail party where all the guests hate each other. I hear Gordon is allowing Allison to attend the service."

Tinkie steered me up the steps. The service was going to be in the chapel of the funeral home. A man in a dark suit with a boutonniere opened the door, and the scent of carnations floated out on air conditioning. Tinkie steadied my elbow as we walked in together and found a seat at the back of the chapel.

"Virgie's picking up the cost of the funeral. The McGees refused to pay for the cremation or the burial," Tinkie whispered.

"She told you that?"

"No, I overheard her talking with the funeral director. The body was finally released last night. He had to take it to Memphis for the cremation, and Virgie was writing him a check."

Tinkie had become very good at eavesdropping. I nudged her shoulder. "What else?"

Tinkie didn't get a chance to answer. A gaggle of gray-suited women came down the center aisle. Their heads were covered, and their faces hidden by veils. To a woman, they were wonderfully groomed, physically fit, and elegantly coiffed. Even if my mother had sent me to the Carrington School for Well-Bred Ladies, I would never have been able to live up to the standard of dress. As I sat on the bench, I had a sudden urge to snatch off my panty hose and throw them.

"Look." Tinkie nodded toward the front of the chapel.

Allison, escorted by Gordon, entered the chapel from a

side door. To my surprise, she wore a carnelian red suit with matching lipstick. She took her place on the first pew, the one reserved for family.

"Umbria is going to love this," Tinkie said. "All last night she was spewing vitriol about how Allison corrupted Quentin and virtually forced her to write the book."

There was a commotion behind us, and everyone swiveled to watch Umbria McGee stalk through the church, headed straight for Allison.

"Get out of here," Umbria said, pointing at Allison. "You killed my sister. You have no right to be here! Get out!" She made a lunge for Allison, her fingers curled into claws.

Deputy Dewayne Dattilo materialized. He made an effort to detain Umbria by stepping in front of her, but when she resisted, he simply picked her up and carried her, squawking like a hen, out of the chapel.

As the doors closed behind them, I could still hear Umbria's angry remarks, but I couldn't tell if they were directed at Dewayne or Allison.

The chapel doors opened again, and all heads swung around. At this point, Elvis could have walked in and no one would have been surprised. The striking figure of Humphrey Tatum strode down the center aisle to a few low murmurs of feminine approval. He stopped beside the pew where Tinkie and I sat.

"Sarah Booth," he said, reaching for my hand and kissing it. "Thank you for supporting my sister." He released my hand and walked to the front pew to sit beside Allison.

"My, my, my," Tinkie whispered. "Don't look now, Sarah Booth, but two-thirds of the women in this room would like to cut off your head. The other third would like to find out what you did to charm Humphrey." She leaned a little closer. "What, exactly, did you do?"

"Check out the altar," I whispered, pointing to the front of the chapel.

10

Virgie Carrington took center stage in front of a spray of red roses and calla lilies. It was the only stand of flowers in the small chapel, jammed with dozens of women in the prerequisite Carrington suit, hat, and veil. A few men, including Harold, were also in attendance. Tinkie and I moved up about midway in the chapel. The one thing I noticed was that not a single person shed a tear. The Carrington class of 1999 was in attendance, but no one was mourning the passing of Quentin McGee.

We took our seats just as Virgie Carrington stepped forward. A buzz emanated from the vicinity of two women I'd seen the night before at Playin' the Bones. I poked Tinkie in the ribs. "Who are they?"

She tilted her lips up and beckoned me to lean close. "That's Lorilee Brewer and Marilyn Jenkins. Honestly, you'd think they could can the whispering for the length of a funeral."

I couldn't understand any of what was being said, but it had the angry tone of hornets, and the two women were intent on what they were saying.

From the front of the chapel came Virgie's sharp voice.

"This is a funeral service, not an opportunity for gossip."
Silence as heavy as a shroud fell over the chapel. "Quentin
McGee was the most talented student I ever taught." Her
gaze seemed to rest on each of the women in the chapel,
measuring them and finding them wanting.

"With one exception," she continued. Her gaze focused
on the front row. "Allison Tatum."

Several people gasped. Propriety warred with curiosity
until, at last, I swiveled around to look. Everyone in the
audience was surprised by Virgie's statement. Marilyn and
Lorilee were whispering again. Only Allison failed to show
any emotion. She sat rigidly beside her brother, looking
neither left nor right.

Virgie's tone had grown gentle. "Allison truly has the
talent to write. She has the heart and imagination to create a novel, yet it was Quentin who published a book. That
is an irony bitter beyond belief. The only thing I have to
add is that Allison is no killer. Certainly not of the person
she loved above even her talent."

No one moved as Virgie talked. The chapel was so still
that when the air conditioner kicked on, the sound was
disruptive.

Virgie looked over the crowd. "At first, I would have
said that Quentin and Allison made an unlikely pair. But
as I came to know them, I saw the love they shared."

A whisper moved around the chapel. The only indication that Virgie heard was the tightening of her mouth. "It
will surprise some of my Carrington girls to realize that I
had agreed for Allison and Quentin to be married at the
school. Neither of their families would allow the cere-
mony to be held at their homes. In fact, the families requested that the wedding be moved from their towns. So I
offered the school. I saw the love these two women shared,
and I wanted to help them celebrate it. The wedding date
had been set for December twenty-first, only a few short
weeks away. Now, instead of celebrating a union, we're

here to grieve a passing. The joyful plans that Allison and Quentin made are ashes."

She stepped out from behind the podium. "Allison is left alone, accused of murdering the companion she intended to spend the rest of her life with."

Virgie walked slowly across the front of the chapel. She seemed to study her next words. "Quentin was a woman who made enemies more easily than friends. I've known her since she was a young girl. When she was ten or so, she'd occasionally come to the school to visit her sister, Umbria. Her parents were hoping that some of Umbria's social skills and ambitions would rub off on Quentin." She shook her head. "Never were two sisters more opposite."

Virgie's hand went up to touch the triple strand of pearls at her neck. "Quentin was a neatnik." Her fingers clutched the pearls. "It has always been one of my tenets that an ordered house reflects an ordered mind, but Quentin was more than ordered. She was compulsively neat. Once when she came to spend the weekend with Umbria at the school, Umbria went through her suitcase and didn't put things back in order. I thought Quentin was going to have a conniption on the spot." The memory made Virgie smile. "Quentin was a stellar student. She had a photographic memory. She loved sports, especially riding horses. She was kind and generous to those who treated her with kindness and generosity. She was a champion of the underdog to the point that she often aligned herself against authority. Any authority. And more than once I found her taking the leftover food from the Carrington kitchens to the homeless on the streets of Memphis. These are things few people know about her. She never needed public approval, or acclaim, for her deeds."

In the front row, I saw Allison's head bow. She sobbed once, and to my surprise, Humphrey put his arm around her.

Virgie paused, but only for a beat. "I have such vivid

memories of Quentin. I see her in the classroom, helping a student. I see her on the hockey field, running with such joy. In fact, when I think of Quentin, I always remember her passion for whatever she turned her hand to. Quentin had the potential to be my masterpiece."

She walked slowly in front of the podium. "Life is never a straightaway. I try to prepare all of my girls for the bad things in life, as well as giving them the necessary polish to become excellent wives. I was never able to put a buff on Quentin." She shook her head. "Quentin defied me. She rejected the values I taught. But—" She held up her hand. "Quentin had her own values, and I, for one, am here to honor them."

Tinkie shifted her knee so that it touched mine. "I never thought Virgie Carrington would bend like this," she said.

"Was she that fond of Quentin?" I asked softly.

"I never thought so. Maybe Allison," Tinkie whispered.

Virgie riveted us with a gaze of disapproval. "I can see not everyone in the audience has learned proper behavior at a funeral. Miss Delaney, Mrs. Richmond, do you have something to add?"

"No, ma'am." Tinkie seemed to slink down in her seat.

I merely shook my head.

"Then I'll continue. Quentin McGee has written a book hurtful to her family and her class. I don't approve of it."

Virgie walked to the podium and removed a copy of *King Cotton Bleeds*. She held it up. "Quentin hurt many people with this book, but she was hurting, too. All she wanted was love. That's what we've come here today to give her. A final farewell, from her classmates and friends. And at least one member of her family."

Virgie walked to the front row and sat down beside Allison.

Two rows in front of us, a plump woman rose. She turned and looked around the chapel. "I have something to say. Allison, you know this is true. Quentin cheated me. She promised to put me in her book and didn't."

Virgie started to rise to her feet, but Allison stopped her with a hand.

"It's true. Quentin promised me that she'd put me and my family in her book. I have the highest IQ in the Southeast. Along with all of the terrible secrets she found out, she was supposed to include some of the good things, too. But she didn't. She didn't put in a single good thing."

"Who is that?" I whispered to Tinkie.

"Genevieve Reynolds." Tinkie put her hand on my knee to silence me.

Genevieve took a deep breath. "I just want you all to know that I'm writing my own book. One that will reflect some of the positive accomplishments of the people we know. So there."

She sat down to a round of applause.

The funeral director, Roger Dendinger, stepped forward. "There will not be a graveside service. Miss Carrington will transport Quentin's ashes to her family cemetery in Clarksdale."

Before he'd finished speaking, Gordon Walters walked through a back door and escorted Allison out. She never had a chance to speak to anyone.

The attendees rose and began to file slowly out of the chapel and into the bright November day. I pulled at the back of my skirt until I felt Tinkie's hand slap at me.

"Sarah Booth, you act like you're trying to pull your panties out of your—" She broke off.

"It's these damn panty hose. I couldn't put them on straight, and now they're all twisted around the tops of my thighs." I was finding it difficult to take a normal step. My stride was restricted to no more than six inches.

"Can I help you with something?"

I looked up to see Humphrey watching me with amusement. Tinkie was trying to hide her smile.

"Sarah Booth has some binding garments," she said, with a sparkle in her eyes. "I think she needs some assistance getting out of her panty hose."

"It would be my pleasure to offer assistance." Humphrey bowed slightly and held out his arm. "There's a small alcove just over here. Perhaps I could escort you and remove those offending garments."

"This isn't the freaking eighteen hundreds," I snapped. "They aren't garments. They're cheap panty hose, and I can take them off by myself." They'd had their sport with me. "How's Allison holding up? I didn't get a chance to talk to her."

"She was swept away like some kind of dangerous criminal." The humor was gone from Humphrey's eyes. "She's seriously depressed. I'm worried she might try to hurt herself."

"Gordon will watch out for her," Tinkie reassured him. "To be honest, Allison is safer in jail than anywhere else."

"Are you recommending that I don't bond her out?" Humphrey asked. I couldn't read a thing in his expression.

Tinkie exchanged a look with me. "I think, for right now, Allison is better off where she is." Tinkie frowned. "We've found several potential suspects, and if the book is at the bottom of all of this, Allison could be in danger, too."

Humphrey maneuvered so that he had one of us on each arm as we walked along the sidewalk toward our cars. I had to admit that he was the most fluidly social man I'd ever met. If a gracious gesture was called for, he was Johnny-on-the-spot.

"Sarah Booth, may I have a word with you?"

I recognized Harold's voice and turned to face him. He didn't look well, and my concern must have registered on my face.

"I'm fine," he said. "Has Humphrey told you that the reading of Quentin's will is set for ten o'clock tomorrow?"

"Yes." I didn't want Tinkie to think Humphrey was holding out on us.

"Does anyone have a clue what Quentin may have done in her will?" Tinkie asked. She tapped her tiny little foot impatiently on the sidewalk as she turned to Humphrey. "Surely you have an idea. I mean no one in Zinnia can prepare a will without most of the town knowing the terms."

"Quentin was very secretive. Ladies, let's talk about this over lunch," he said as smooth as butter.

"Sarah Booth doesn't have time for lunch," Harold said as he put his arm around me and moved me away. "I need her."

"Are we talking emotionally or sexually, dahling?"

None of us had noticed that Cece had walked up. She had a notepad and pen in her hand. "I need a comment for tomorrow's paper," she told Humphrey.

"My sister is innocent." Humphrey said it with conviction. "She's as much a victim as Quentin. Once Sarah Booth and Tinkie find the real killer, Allison will be vindicated."

"And free to inherit?" Cece asked, with arched eyebrows.

"The will hasn't been read yet." For the first time, a note of testiness was in Humphrey's voice. "Quentin never divulged the contents of her will to Allison. If Allison inherits, it'll be a surprise to her."

"Oh, really? They were partners, were they not?"

"If Quentin and Allison had been allowed to actually marry, they would undeniably be partners. But as it stands now, Allison is merely a close friend. She inherits only what is named in the will. If anything is named."

Cece closed her notebook. "Do you have any idea what's in the will, Mr. Tatum?"

The irritation was gone from Humphrey's face. "No,

and I will tell you this for print. I don't care what's in the will. In some ways, if Al inherits, it'll look worse for her. So it's a catch-22. The best thing that could happen would be to turn the clock back and prevent Quentin from going to that cotton field."

Cece nodded. "Do your parents feel the same way?"

Humphrey shrugged. "I have no idea how my parents feel. I haven't spoken to them since I came here and hired the Delaney Detective Agency. Ladies, are we going to lunch?"

"I need to speak with Harold," I said, detaching myself from Humphrey's arm. "Tinkie?"

"I'd be delighted. I'll fill Humphrey in on what we've done so far."

"I have a deadline." Cece turned to me. "Sarah Booth, give me a call later, when you have time."

The group split, everyone going in different directions. I stood in the warm sunshine and faced Harold. "What is it?"

"Gordon stopped by to see me today. He found my fingerprints in Quentin's room."

"But that's impossible. You—"

"I was there."

I tried to pull myself together. "What were you doing in Quentin's room?"

"I stopped by with some papers from the bank for her to sign."

"Was Allison there?"

"No. It was on Friday, before she was killed Saturday night."

Harold hadn't been exactly square with me, and I felt the slow fuse of anger begin to burn. "You had to take them to her?"

"Rachel was staying there. I stopped by for lunch and brought the papers with me."

I sighed. "We'll get it straight. Don't worry." I gave his arm a squeeze.

"There's something else."

I dreaded to hear what he might have failed to tell me. "About Quentin's murder?"

"About Coleman."

My throat constricted. "Tell me."

"I'm not sure I'm doing the right thing, but Coleman will be here tomorrow. He's meeting with the board of supervisors at ten."

My heart was pounding in my chest. "Why?"

"I'm not certain." Harold gave me an odd expression. "I don't mean to pry, Sarah Booth, but why hasn't Coleman called to tell you this?"

I shook my head. "I don't know. I haven't heard a word from him since he left with Connie."

Harold took my arm. "Both of you are trying to do the right thing here. If he hasn't called, it's because he has nothing to offer you."

A year ago I would have questioned Harold's motives. Now, though, he spoke as my friend. "I know."

"Let it go, Sarah Booth."

"I'll talk with Gordon about the fingerprints. I need to see Allison, anyway."

He released my arm. "Would you like some lunch?"

I shook my head. "I'm not hungry." It was true. I'd lost my appetite. "I'll be in touch." I walked to my car, hoping no one else would attempt to waylay me. I needed a little time to recover.

11

Jitty must have sensed my mood, because when I got back to Dahlia House, she was nowhere in sight. I tore off the aggravating panty hose, slipped into some jeans and my boots, and went out to saddle Reveler. There are times when the kingdom of animals is the only place to find comfort. With Sweetie at my side, I rode into the cotton fields.

Once upon a time, the vast expanse of the cultivated fields had been forest. Man had worked tremendous change on the face of the Delta. Not all of it good. Once, the forests had been filled with wildlife. Teddy Roosevelt had hunted bear here. In some of the old groceries that dot the crossroads, there are photographs of hunters standing proudly beside the carcasses of bears, panthers, wild hogs, deer. Whatever they could kill. The carnage is celebrated in the smiles on the hunters' faces. The excess of the kill—a slaughter of wild creatures—is considered something to be proud of.

Once the value of the land for crop cultivation was understood, the wealthy planters moved in and put their slaves to pushing back the forests. Fields that stretched for two and three miles were cleared, the rich soil tilled for the sowing of cotton.

The edges of the fields had been left wooded, and I rode beside the remaining trees, listening to the fussing of the squirrels as I passed. Cotton was still king in the Mississippi Delta, and its rule had been bought with blood. It was this heritage that Quentin had trashed in her book. She had used words to cut deep into the land, revealing things that Delta families had wished to keep hidden. And it had cost her her life. Blood to blood.

I thought about the photograph of the hunters, the casual brutality of their smiles as they gripped the horns of a deer to twist its head, glazed eyes staring into the camera. Quentin had stirred that bloodlust.

Struck by sudden inspiration, I turned Reveler toward home. I needed to find some annuals of the Carrington School and compare the photographs of the girls to the names in the book Quentin had written. More importantly, I needed to find her notes for the proposed second book. It seemed to me that it was the second book that surely prompted her murder. The idea of killing for revenge was entertaining, but more likely was the prospect of killing to prevent the revelation of some other dark secret.

I allowed Reveler his head, and we galloped through the fields in the bright sun. Sweetie, ears flopping, raced with us. For a brief few moments, I forgot about Quentin and murder and Coleman and love, and I gave myself to the pleasure of the ride.

We arrived at Dahlia House breathless. After cooling him out, I untacked Reveler and set him loose in the green winter rye pasture and headed into the house. To my surprise, the back door was locked. Sweetie slipped through the doggie door, but I was forced to walk around to the front. Who would have locked the door, and why? It wasn't Jitty. She didn't lift a finger to do a single manual chore, not even turning a lock. Perhaps I'd palmed the door-knob by accident when I left.

I trudged around to the front and stopped. A car was pulling down the driveway. A car I didn't know. I looked down at my jeans, spattered with mud from my ride. My hair was unbrushed, my face daubed with dirt. I wasn't prepared to entertain guests, but I didn't have a choice. The champagne-colored town car barreled toward me at breakneck speed. The dark-tinted windows concealed the occupants. I stood at the edge of the lawn as the car slid to a stop in the loose oyster shells only five feet from me.

The driver's window lowered automatically. A veil-covered face was revealed. It took me a moment to recognize Marilyn Jenkins.

"Do you have a moment, Miss Delaney?" Marilyn asked. "Lorilee and I want to talk to you."

"About what?" It was my understanding that graduates of the Carrington School for Well-Bred Ladies didn't just show up at someone's door.

"About Quentin's murder. We may have some information."

Sighing, I signaled them out of the car. I walked to the porch and waited. Together, we walked into Dahlia House. I herded them toward the office.

"Sarah Booth, how quaint that you'd set up your office in your home." Marilyn's amber-tinted fingernail traced the glass door with mine and Tinkie's name stenciled on it.

"Yes, quaint is exactly the word I would have used." I showed them to chairs in front of my desk. Psychologists were correct; the desk gave me an advantage. I sat behind it and smiled. "I would have thought you two would have gone to talk to Tinkie."

"We did," Lorilee said. "She wasn't home. The maid was rather rude to us. She said that all official detective business was done out here at Dahlia House." She looked around the room. "I could give you some tips on decorating. I redid my brother's real estate office, and it turned out stunningly, if I do say so myself. The social status of his clientele rose instantly."

"Thanks, but our client status is just fine." The Lorilee I remembered from Ole Miss was completely gone. The shy young woman of my memories had been replaced by a tigress. She'd even traded in her brown hair for tawny curls.

"I suppose. Folks who need a private investigator are criminals, after all," she drawled.

"What can I do for you?" If I hurried to find out what they wanted, maybe they would leave.

"We know who killed Quentin." Marilyn tilted her head.

"Oh, really? Have you told Deputy Walters?"

"We thought we'd let you do that," Marilyn said. "We don't want to get involved."

"You know who the murderer is, but you don't want to get involved? Okay, so who did it?" I didn't have a lick of faith in their accusation, but I was curious.

"Jolene Loper." Lorilee sat forward, her brown eyes intense. "That's who we figure did it."

"Do you have any proof?" I didn't know who Jolene Loper might be, and I didn't want to give them the satisfaction of asking. I hoped to draw it out of them.

"Proof!" They spoke in unified outrage.

"That would be the necessary ingredient before you ruin someone's reputation."

"Jolene's capable of anything. We've known her for years." Marilyn jutted her chin out in defiance.

"Tell me what you have," I said.

"Did you see Jolene at the funeral?" Marilyn asked.

How could I tell the difference among the conservatively dressed Stepford wives? "No."

"She was wearing the burgundy suit." Lorliee could

barely suppress the shudder. "She sat at the back of the room."

I did remember a woman dressed in a burgundy suit. I'd only caught a glimpse of her, a cardinal amongst the wrens, and I hadn't figured her for a Carrington graduate. While red was my favorite color, it wasn't on the approved list at Virgie Carrington's school. "I saw her." So what? was left unsaid.

"Tacky, tacky, tacky." Marilyn's lip curled. "A football color. At a funeral."

Had Tinkie not brought me a navy suit, I might have shown up in jeans. "I doubt tackiness is such a grave character flaw that it leads instantly to murder. If you don't have something more concrete"—I rose—"I have business to finish."

They looked at each other and smiled. "We have more."

"Then spill it." I sat slowly.

"Jolene had an older sister," Marilyn said. "Belinda. She was several years ahead of us at school, but the stories lingered on and on."

Lorilee rolled her eyes. "The Loper girls simply weren't Carrington material. I realize Mrs. Carrington was trying to help them, but it was a true disservice. In many ways, they were as out of place as Quentin and Allison were."

"They wore red lipstick and bleached their hair blond," Marilyn said.

"Not just blond, that white blond that looks so fake." Lorilee flipped her own multitoned tawny locks off her shoulder. "I mean cosmetics are meant to improve, not create a freak show."

I didn't have to say a word. The two women were capable of bouncing the conversation between themselves without any help from me.

"Belinda died last year." Marilyn shrugged. "It was a bizarre accident."

Now that was interesting. "What happened?"

"She had a beauty salon in West Memphis. She inhaled some dry peroxide and had an allergic reaction. Or at least that's the story I heard." Marilyn had the decency to look sorry.

"Well, it just goes to show that you can only expose yourself to so much of a toxic substance. She put enough of it on her head that I guess she used up her quota." Lorilee rubbed her perfect nail polish with her pointer finger. "I realize it's poor form to speak ill of the dead, but that beauty shop Belinda ran was a scandal."

Her eyes were bright with malice as she leaned forward. I instinctively withdrew.

"That salon catered to nothing but whores."

"Even hookers need to look good," I said, trying to lighten Lorilee's intensity.

"Well, if that's true, then they only looked good for their clients. It wasn't their heads Belinda was working on." She smiled. "I guess you could call it Cooter Couture." She put a hand over her mouth to signify that such a phrase was embarrassing, even to her.

"How did you find out about this?" As soon as the words left my mouth, I realized how dumb they were.

"Page 447. Quentin goes into great detail about how Belinda used the horror of September eleventh to her personal benefit. She gave all those whores a red, white, and blue dye job on their private parts and made it seem like screwing them was a patriotic deed." She folded her arms across her chest and leaned back in her chair.

The Loper girls were younger than me by nearly a decade, but I had heard that Belinda Loper ran a top-end salon in West Memphis. I just hadn't realized what "top-end" signified. But Lorilee's animosity seemed a little beyond Belinda's betrayal of the Carrington tradition. If I had to bet, it would be that Lorilee's male interest had paid a few trips to the red, white, and blue. Marilyn Jenkins, on the other hand, looked uncomfortable at the turn the conversation had taken.

The red telephone on my desk gave a brisk ring, and I picked it up with some relief. No one could be worse than Lorilee Brewer.

"Sarah Booth, I've been to see the Tatums, and we need to talk."

Tinkie was driving a hundred miles an hour with the window of the Caddy down. I could hear the wind rushing. "Stop by Dahlia House."

"I'll be there in half an hour."

Marilyn Jenkins rose. "If Lorilee is finished spewing venom, I think we should leave." She didn't wait to see if Lorilee followed. She got up and left.

My admiration for Marilyn was cut short when Lorilee put her hands on my desk and leaned to within ten inches of my face. "Marilyn is just upset. Her mother was a common slut, and Marilyn was terrified Quentin was going to print that in her second book. I guess the parallel to Belinda Loper was too much for her to take."

"Thanks for the hand grenade of a motive," I said, smiling brightly. "How long have you and Marilyn been friends?"

"Since first grade." She stood up and straightened her suit. "I can't wait to get to my room and out of this horrid outfit. I'll be in town for a few more days, should you need to talk with me again. I'm staying at The Gardens."

"Sure." It was the only syllable I could muster. I remained behind my desk as she left.

I'd barely gotten out a sigh of relief when Jitty drifted through the south wall of the room. "I hope you had your vaccinations," she said. "That woman is rabid."

"If she'll eviscerate a friend like that, imagine what she would do to someone who pissed her off."

"She'd be perfect at court," Jitty said.

Something in her tone caught my ear. I looked at her, really looked at her. Even beneath the ridiculous white face paint, she was pasty looking. "What's wrong? The glamour of the court wearing thin?"

"Don't be impertinent." She walked to the windows and looked out.

Jitty was many things, but she was seldom melancholy. That was my specialty. "What's wrong?"

"What is happiness?"

Though she remained looking out the window at the sweep of Dahlia House's brown front lawn, I knew she wasn't teasing me. She was serious. Her back was rigid, and she stared as if her question would cavort across the lawn.

"It's a feeling, a sense of . . . contentment."

"Are you sure?"

Once she questioned me, I wasn't. "Do you think it's something more, like a spike of pleasure or a bubble of intensity?"

She shook her head. "I think it's knowing where you belong."

I took in her finery, the dress that must have taken ten seamstresses six months to create, the jewels that adorned her bosom, ears, and fingers. "You belong at court."

At last she turned to face me. "Today. That's where I belong today. But what about tomorrow or next week?"

"You belong here. At Dahlia House. With me."

Her smile was luminous, possibly because the light from the window was shining through her. "And where do you belong, Sarah Booth?"

That was a harder question. "This is my home," I said.

"But it doesn't bring you happiness."

"It holds the past, which gives me a sense of identity. That's part of happiness. You have to know who you are to know where you belong."

"One day you might belong somewhere else."

This conversation was making me uncomfortable. "The Buddhists believe that living in the moment is the ultimate happiness. And right now, this moment, I belong here at Dahlia House."

She reached out a hand, and I felt a cool breeze graze my cheek. "You're clever."

"Jitty, we have a case to work on. We have food. Sweetie Pie and Reveler are in good health. We have—"

"You have a suitor." Her smile was impish. "And I have to go because company's coming."

"Jitty, damn it! Wait!" But it was too late. She was gone in a shimmer of light. I shook a fist at the empty air. She was always getting in the last word and then vanishing. It was one of her worst ghostly traits.

My irritation was short-lived. A knock at the side door of the office forced me to straighten up.

"Sarah Booth, I found this up at the road. It was leaned against your mailbox." Tinkie walked in with a round tube tied with a black velvet ribbon. "Did you order maps or something?"

The package did resemble a mailing tube for posters or paintings or maps. But there was no mailing label, no stamp. Someone had hand delivered it. I opened one end of the tube. A slender black leather riding crop slid into my hand. Tied to the handle was a note.

If you want a really exciting ride, give me a call. Humphrey

Tinkie read over my shoulder. She gave a squeal of delight. "I don't think you'd need spurs for Humphrey. Are you going to call him?"

"Do you see a hole in my head?" I couldn't believe she was asking.

"Sarah Booth, he's a handsome man. You're all the time saying you don't want a serious involvement. This sounds like you could have your cake and eat it, too. Humphrey must be good in bed. I'll bet he's very original." Her eyebrows rose suggestively. "That's the most creative invitation I've ever seen."

I put the riding crop down on my desk. "He's a client."

"Are you talking to yourself or to me?"

I plopped into my chair. "Enough about Humphrey. What happened at the Tatum's?"

12

"Before I reveal anything, I need food."

Tinkie's jaw had that set to it that let me know facts would not be forthcoming until she had food.

"Let's go to Millie's. The cupboard is bare here."

She dangled her keys. "We'll call on your cell phone and order. That way the food will be ready when we get there."

Tinkie was serious. She was starving. I followed her to the Caddy, and we roared down the driveway. By the time we got to the blacktop, I had her order phoned in.

We were seated at a table in the corner of the café in less than fifteen minutes. Millie brought iced tea and a basket of corn-bread muffins to tide us over until the real food came. As Tinkie slathered butter on the hot corn bread, she glanced around to be sure no one was listening.

"Jay and Jennifer Tatum are furious with Allison and with Humphrey."

"Why?" Allison was innocent, and Humphrey was trying to help his sister. I could understand worried, or confused, or maybe even hurt. But furious?

"Allison skewed their plans, and now Humphrey has fallen out of order." Tinkie bit into the corn bread, an expression of complete contentment settling over her face. "This is delicious. Aren't you hungry?"

I hadn't been—until I watched her eat. I picked up a muffin and buttered it. "What did they say?"

"At first they didn't want to talk to me at all. When I showed them the receipt for Humphrey's check, they were so shocked, they let me in. They were upset that Humphrey spent ten grand on his sister's defense."

"Did they express an opinion about Allison's guilt or innocence?"

Tinkie's face grew hard. "Allison is a bitter disappointment. They don't care if she goes to jail. As far as they're concerned, she's dead. That's a direct quote."

I ate the last bite of my muffin, trying to understand how parents could treat a child so coldly. My own parents would have died for me. If I'd been locked in a jail, my mother would have figured a way to break me out. She would have pulled the jail down brick by brick, if she had to. "And Humphrey? Is he dead to them, too?"

"They don't have the luxury of writing him off. He's the last hope. And he bears the name. They dote on him."

Such a position couldn't be easy for Humphrey, either. Perhaps it was why he'd developed into such a Lothario. "Are they just angry about the book, or do you think they're willing to write off their own daughter?"

"Hmm, how would you view telling me that they're going to stop payment on the check Humphrey wrote us?"

I shook my head. "Too late. It's cleared already. And where were they the night of the murder?"

"Believe me, I asked. I wouldn't put it past them to kill Quentin, but they have an airtight alibi. They were in Washington. Jay had gone up to see if he could get some federal funding for Tatum's Corner. The town has dried up and is blowing away. He'd hoped for some grants and was in meetings all Friday with Senator Trent Lott."

"I'd rather see ticket stubs from the airlines than take their word for all of this."

"I did get Oscar to call Lott's office, and the senator's secretary confirmed that the Tatums were on Lott's appointment book for Friday evening."

"Did the secretary actually see them?"

"Not personally. She was sick on Friday. But she did say that the senator kept a strict account of all his appointments."

"That still leaves all day Saturday."

"I stopped by the sheriff's office. Gordon is checking with the airlines in Memphis to see when the Tatums returned from D.C. If what they told me is true, which was a return flight that arrived in Memphis at ten p.m., that should give them a clear alibi for the time of the murder."

Tinkie was thorough. And hungry. Millie swept over to us with her arms loaded with platters of food. Pork chops, turnips, fried okra, squash, and sweet potato casserole. There was enough for eight people.

"I'll be back in a minute," Millie said. "There's something you should see."

"By the way, I talked to Cece, and she gave me the lowdown on your two visitors." Tinkie's lips curved up.

"Marilyn Jenkins and Lorilee Brewer? What gives with those two?"

"It's an interesting story, but it's going to have to wait for dessert." Tinkie's focus was on food and tormenting me.

"Tell or I'll steal your fork."

"Okay. It's too juicy to keep to myself." She leaned forward slightly. "Quentin hammered Marilyn on the land deal for the toxic waste disposal, but there was another story she didn't put in the book."

"Quit doling out details and tell me."

"Marilyn's mother died in a freak rock slide."

"We covered this already." I picked up another muffin. Damn, Tinkie was driving me to eat.

"She died naked."

"Naked?" Now Lorilee's comment about Marilyn's mother being a woman of loose morals made more sense. "Why would she be naked at a house she was showing?"

"The story I heard was that she was supposed to meet a contractor for a nooner. The rendezvous point was this picturesque stone wall in the backyard. Flat surface, secluded, the exotic sounds of nature all around."

I held up my hand. "I get the picture. Was Mrs. Jenkins married at the time?"

"Right. Anyway, no one is certain of the details, but something happened farther up the steep hill that caused several tons of rocks to shift and tumble down right on top of that wall where Mrs. Jenkins was—"

I held up my hand to stop her. "I get the picture." And I did, rather vividly. "Rather biblical, isn't it? She was committing adultery. The penalty for that in some countries is stoning." I shuddered.

Tinkie slowed her fork long enough to shoot me a wicked look. "I guess Quentin was so caught up in the toxic waste story that she let the landslide slip. I'll bet it was scheduled for the second book."

"And the contractor? Did he survive?"

"He must have been on top and seen the rock slide coming, because he escaped. There was no sign of him, but an agitated man called in the accident anonymously."

I nodded. "Lorilee was eager to *imply* all of this, but she was too cowardly to come right out and tell me."

Tinkie's grin was a million watts. "Remember that old saying 'People in glass houses . . . '?"

"One of Aunt Loulane's favorites."

"Lorilee should keep her rocks to herself. Quentin had the goods on her. Page 217." Tinkie picked up her tea.

"You'd know all of this if you took the time to read the dang book."

I suddenly had an inkling of the power of Quentin's book. I disliked Lorilee, and I wanted the story. "Tell!"

Tinkie daintily wiped her lips with her napkin. "According to Quentin's book, Lorilee's husband caught her in a delicate moment with the weed-eater boy!"

"He caught her in the act?" Talk about getting caught with her pants down.

"It's in the book, and there's not been a lawsuit filed, so I gather it must be true. Charlie Brewer followed a trail of grass cuttings and clothes to the pool cabana and caught them on one of last season's lawn chairs."

I could only shake my head. "The weed-eater boy? Would it have been more socially acceptable if he was the pool boy?"

"Make fun if you want, but it gets worse. According to the passage in the book, Lorilee was so taken with the boy's vigorous 'mulching' that she started a college fund for him. He was fifteen at the time of the affair."

"Damn. That's illegal, isn't it? Talk about a motive for murder. And Lorilee was so busy trying to point the finger of guilt at others."

Tinkie nodded. "Quentin as much as said that Lorilee was a desperate thirty-four-year-old who had to *pay* a child for sex. Desperate doesn't begin to do it justice."

Such a portrayal certainly made Lorilee Brewer look desperate, old, and over-the-hill. But it raised an even more interesting question. "Did Quentin have it in for Lorilee for some reason? They weren't in the same class. Lorilee's at least ten years older."

"I can't answer that. But Lorilee also had plenty of motive to want to hurt Quentin. Lorilee had managed to keep all of this hush-hush until the book came out. Now I hear her husband is talking divorce. Lorilee will be out in the cold without alimony or any job skills."

"The weed-eater boy? And she was paying him? Lorilee isn't so ugly she'd have to pay to get laid."

"Not on the outside, at any rate." Tinkie pushed her plate away. Beneath her stylish brown corduroy slacks, her tummy had taken on the slightest hint of a bulge.

"I've got to read that book." I'd have to dedicate an evening to go through it.

"Sarah Booth, your aversion to the written word is appalling."

"I don't have an aversion to reading. I love mysteries, but I don't like nonfiction. This isn't really nonfiction, though. It's more like an evening at The Club where everyone talks about each other's dirty secrets."

She shook her head. "Let's just say that Lorilee has as much motive as anyone else for killing Quentin."

Millie finished her work and came to the table with something in her hand. Before I could ask, she spread the pages of a national tabloid, the *Galaxy Gazette,* on the table in front of us. "Look at this." Her finger stabbed at a huge tabloid headline: DELTA DARLINGS DISH DEATH.

"Zinnia has made the big time, but the alliteration sucks," I said. "I'm sure Cece will be amused."

"Read the article," Millie insisted.

"Sarah Booth is typographically challenged," Tinkie said as she scanned the story. "Why, this paints Allison as the killer. The only person who even tries to show sympathy is Virgie. At least, they interviewed her."

"What does she say?" I couldn't read because Tinkie's and Millie's heads were in the way.

"She urges people not to judge Allison until all the facts are in. 'It isn't ladylike to judge,' she says."

"I think our next stop should be a visit to Virgie." I pulled my billfold out of my purse. "It might be good to get her take on the suspects we have so far, since they're all her girls."

Tinkie picked up the last corn-bread muffin. "If we're

going to have to see Gertrude Stromm, I'm taking provisions. If she gets half a chance, she'll lock us in the basement."

"That house doesn't have a basement," I pointed out. It was built off the ground, with a crawl space.

"For all you know, Gertrude's out there right now digging a basement." Tinkie popped the muffin into her purse and led the way to the cash register.

Gertrude was busy serving tea in the conservatory when we arrived, and Tinkie, with the help of a forty-dollar tip, managed to get one of the maids to tell us Virgie's room number. Glancing over our shoulders to make sure Gertrude hadn't spotted us, we hurried down the hallway to Room 12.

"Do you remember sneaking through Mrs. Hathaway's yard?" I asked Tinkie.

"Of course. We were always terrified her Doberman would bite us." She slowed enough to look at me. "We're having exactly the same feeling now, aren't we? And it's only Gertrude."

"I'd rather face that Doberman than Gertrude Stromm," I said. We rounded the corner, and Tinkie knocked on the door of Virgie's room.

She answered it quickly, almost as if she'd been standing right beside the door. Her pearl gray suit was rumpled, and she looked worn and tired.

"What can I do for you?" she asked, forcing a smile to her face.

"How about a cup of coffee?" Tinkie, always the perceptive one, made the offer. "Sarah Booth and I would like to chat with you, but you look done in, Mrs. Carrington."

"I am tired." She straightened her shoulders. "This whole thing has been hard on me. I'm fond of Allison, and I hate to see what she's being put through."

"There's a lovely table out in the garden," Tinkie said.

"Sarah Booth, why don't you escort Virgie there, and I'll stop by the kitchen and order us all some coffee."

"Sure." I offered Virgie my arm and was surprised when she actually leaned a bit of weight on it. Watching her command performance at the funeral, I'd forgotten she was in her sixties. Now, she looked every bit her age.

"The wedding was going to be beautiful." She stared straight ahead as we walked along the polished pine floor. "I didn't approve of it. I mean my entire life has been focused on preparing my girls for marriage to a suitable man; I couldn't approve. But when I saw Quentin and Allison together, I couldn't deny what they felt for each other. I let my heart rule my head."

"That's not always a bad thing to do." I felt at a loss. Of all the people I imagined I might comfort, Virgie Carrington wasn't one of them.

"If my girls start letting their hearts rule, the structure of our society will erode. Why, look at you, Sarah Booth. You're a perfect example of that."

She'd almost won my sympathy—until that comment. "Right. I'm such a danger to the fabric of society."

Her grip on my arm tightened. "Deny it if you wish, but had you married properly, Dahlia House would be in excellent repair. You'd be planning day care for your children and the menu for your Thanksgiving dinner, not running around chasing murderers."

"That might be true, Mrs. Carrington, but what you haven't taken into account is my wishes. I don't wish to be married to someone for the sake of security and children."

She stopped and looked at me, her pale eyes amazed. "My dear, those are the only two reasons to *get* married. Why else would you even consider it?"

"For love?" I couldn't help myself. I made it a question at the end instead of the declarative I intended.

"Love? What poppycock!"

"It's become a popular concept in the last half of the twentieth century." I couldn't help myself. She'd insulted me and was now treating me as if I had a mental disorder.

"Have you bothered to check the statistics on these so-called love matches?"

I didn't say anything.

"Do that, Sarah Booth, before you go making such bold statements. That's one of your problems, you know. You step out front before you realize what's happening. If you aren't careful, you're going to wind up in trouble."

"I didn't mean to offend you." I might not have a diploma from the Carrington School for Well-Bred Ladies, but my mother had taught me respect for those older than I.

"The divorce rate today is close to seventy-five percent. Of the people who stay married, many of them have more at stake than simply romance. Properties, lifestyles, investments, the concept of building a life together instead of randomly falling into bed—that's the glue of a good marriage."

Thank God we were at the back steps. I helped her to the table in the shade of a magnificent oak. The garden was a riot of yellow, orange, amber, and garnet mums. "I'll check on Tinkie." I started to turn away.

"Sit down, Sarah Booth. I won't fuss anymore." She sighed. "I'm an old lady, and I find that I grow quarrelsome. I'm sorry."

I took a seat across from her. Her face was pale, except for her cheeks, which were flushed. She'd gotten upset, and it was my duty to calm her. "How many girls have graduated from your school?"

"When we first opened, the school was small. Our original class was ten girls. It was the height of the youth rebellion. Marijuana was being grown on the fringes of the cotton fields. Young girls were throwing away their brassieres, their morals, and their bodies. Society was under siege. I was a young woman of twenty-seven, and I saw what was happening. I knew I had to fight against it."

I glanced toward the house, praying Tinkie would appear. This was a conversation I didn't want to have with Virgie. We were polar opposites, and another clash of values would only upset her further. "Quentin and Allison graduated when?"

"Seven years ago." Her face clouded over. "Who could have foreseen all of this?"

"No one. Not even you." That was true. There was nothing to be gained by Virgie kicking herself over something she couldn't possibly have stopped.

"Quentin had an element of spite in her nature. I remember one time when she was visiting Umbria—she was just a child then—she took a dislike to the young man Umbria was seeing and put Red Devil lye in his shoes."

"That sounds a little extreme."

"Quentin lived on the edge. The book is mean-spirited. What she did to her own family, I don't understand it. What did she hope to gain? The book has a limited audience. No one cares about any of it except for those in the immediate area. It's caused a sensation now, but in six months no one will remember it."

"The book must be true, though. Otherwise, someone would have sued."

"There is factual truth and emotional truth, Sarah Booth. The sooner you learn that, the easier your life will become."

I knew what she meant, but as a private investigator, I dealt with the facts. The emotional shadings were another matter.

At last I saw Tinkie carrying a tray of cups, condiments, and a pot of coffee. There was also a bottle of expensive brandy. *Good thinking, Tinkie.* I needed a shot, if no one else did.

She set the tray down and poured for all of us, adding a dollop of brandy to each cup of coffee. "You look like you could use a little pick-me-up," she told Virgie.

To my surprise, Virgie accepted the brandy-laced coffee without complaint. She drank it down, and Tinkie prepared another.

"What's the story on Lorilee Brewer?" I asked.

"She was a Frazier before she married." Virgie sipped her coffee. "She had a vicious streak a mile wide. Most of the other girls despised her, and to be honest, I never thought she'd land a man. But Charlie Brewer married her. I dare say, he'll be divorcing her after everything Quentin revealed in the book. No man wants to be shamed like that. In many ways, men are so very fragile. It's a woman's duty to protect them from this type of shame."

"Lorilee said some vicious things about Marilyn," Tinkie said. "I can't imagine why they hang around together."

"Since Quentin revealed Marilyn's plans to sell her property for the landfill, Marilyn doesn't have a friend left in the world. All of her neighbors felt betrayed. I guess Lorilee is the best she can do." Virgie sighed. "It's so hard to watch my girls go wrong."

"Do you think either of those women could have killed Quentin?" I asked.

"When Marilyn was one of my students, she was sweet. A little withdrawn. She's changed. But if I had to pick one or the other, I'd say Lorilee. Then again, Marilyn lost a lot because of what Quentin and Allison revealed." She shook her head. "The truth is, either one could do it."

"Who else?" Tinkie asked.

Virgie put her empty cup on the table. "I'd certainly put Umbria at the top of the list. And that low-life husband of hers, Rutherford Clark. Why Franklin and Caledonia allowed that marriage, I'll never understand. Now that's something worth looking into." She slowly rose to her feet.

"I'm sorry, but I need to go and lie down. I hope you'll excuse me. And Tinkie, thank you for the refreshments."

When I made an effort to help her, she waved me back into my seat. "I'm not helpless yet," she said, "but I am tired. Good day, ladies."

13

We left The Gardens and slowed for school traffic. Tinkie was pensive behind the wheel of the Caddy. "Do you really think the murderer could be a woman?" she asked. "Quentin's murder was so brutal."

"You're the one who made the list of names from the book. Almost everyone on the list is female."

"I've been giving it some thought. Quentin's murder seems to be something a man would concoct. I mean, most women wouldn't think of suffocating someone in a mud hole."

That was true. But there was the note. "Dragging the family's name through the mud . . ." I pondered the genderlessness of it. "Could be a woman or a man."

"We should go and look for those other notes."

Tinkie was right. I checked my watch. We still had two or three hours of daylight. "Let's go to Oxford."

Never one to miss a chance to show off her driving skills, Tinkie whipped a U-turn in the middle of Main Street. The school traffic deputy blew her whistle and started running toward us, white gloves waving frantically in the air.

"Go!" I urged Tinkie. The traffic cop was faster than she looked. "Go!"

Tinkie hit the gas, and the Caddy jumped forward. I looked back to see the cop shaking her fist at us.

Tinkie was laughing as we left Zinnia behind and headed up the highway to Oxford, Mississippi, and the rental house where Allison and Quentin had lived.

The topography of the Delta changed as we moved eastward across the state. The flat land gave way to hills and rises. Development was everywhere. When I'd gone to college, the drive to the university had been isolated. Now there were homes and businesses everywhere. I saw the death notice for the thousand-acre farms writ large on the canvas of the earth. Land would soon be more valuable for subdivisions than for growing things. Factory farms, where cattle and hogs were penned in squalid feedlots, were already replacing the sprawling grassland ranches.

"You're mighty quiet." Tinkie kept her gaze on the highway in front of her.

"I've been stuck in the past because what I see in the future terrifies me."

"Coleman?"

"No." I smiled. "Not Coleman but another lost love."

"Hamilton?"

"The land."

"Oscar and I were talking just last week. Politicians associate progress with growth, when it's exactly the opposite. If we could freeze the development in Sunflower County, in ten years we'd have something really special—a town that isn't jammed to the seams with people."

"Oscar said this?" My understanding of bankers was that they encouraged development, because it meant more people borrowing more money.

"Sarah Booth, you consistently underestimate Oscar and yourself."

I was saved from a reply because we hit the outskirts of Oxford, Mississippi. It is a picturesque town that had developed around the University of Mississippi, or Ole Miss, as it is fondly known. Oxford was also the home of William Faulkner. Tinkie had accused me of not liking to read, but it wasn't true. In my youth I adored Faulkner and Miss Welty. In the past year I'd added books by Larry Brown and Brad Watson to Dahlia House's library shelves.

We passed the square, which housed, brilliantly enough, Square Books. Oxford had grown around a central courthouse square. William Faulkner had hung his hat here, and a lively group of writers of all genres now lived in the area. Many of the authors hung out at the bookstore and taught, when they could, at Ole Miss to supplement their incomes. The mystique of Faulkner could still be found in the shade of majestic oaks and along a rural dirt road.

The house that Allison and Quentin had shared was on the north side of town, a cottage really, tucked among second growth pines and oaks. The yard was a jungle. A storm that had come through in September had knocked trees down, and they remained partially draped across the driveway, which wound through the winter-bare trees and vines. In the summer, the place would be hidden by thick leaves.

"This is a little on the creepy side," Tinkie said as she maneuvered the car around a fallen pine. "It's been two months since the storm, yet debris is everywhere."

"Quentin had been on a book tour." I had to suppress a tiny shudder myself. The place was creepy. It was a strange blend of the witch's cottage in *Hansel and Gretel* and a Tolkienesque hobbit's hole. We pulled to a stop beneath the lattice-covered portico.

"We didn't bring a key," Tinkie said.

I could read her desire to leave on her face. But we'd driven hours to look for the threatening notes. "I'll go in a window." I got out and walked to the side door. To my surprise, the knob turned easily, and the door pushed open. "It isn't locked."

Tinkie reluctantly got out of the car and followed me up the steps and into the kitchen. I stopped. The room was painted barn red, with white fixtures and white trim on the windows. Lacy curtains fluttered in a breeze that blew through a crack. An old white farm table with four oak chairs stood at the center of the room. Copper pots gleamed on the walls, along with pen-and-ink drawings, done by Quentin, I noted.

"This is very nice," Tinkie said.

She was so close, I could feel her breath on my shoulder blades.

"I would never have suspected they were such traditionalists." She stepped forward and touched a vase full of dead flowers on the table. They'd been spider mums. "They were happy here, weren't they?"

I nodded. "Let's find those notes." We were trespassing on a past that was dead. The sensation made me uncomfortable, and I realized that this was what Tinkie had not wanted to feel. The life Quentin and Allison had shared was over. This was the last vestige of it. We had tainted it with our presence.

"I'll take the study." Tinkie scooted past me, leaving the bedroom for me.

"Thanks," I called after her as I moved down the hallway to the bedroom. The bed was made, covered with heirloom quilts. On the lavender walls magnificent Wyatt Waters artwork hung beside black-and-white photographs. I went through the bedside table drawers and then the bureau and highboy drawers. There were no notes, but I did find what appeared to be several digital camera diskettes. I slipped them into my pocket and went to find Tinkie.

She sat in the middle of the office floor, with pieces of paper all around her.

"These are serious," she said, her face pale in the fading

light. "Someone really meant to harm Quentin, and finally did." She handed the note to me.

You are a disgrace to your family. Stop this foolishness or pay the consequences. There was no date, and I couldn't tell if the note was about Quentin's book or her relationship with Allison. I took another note Tinkie handed up to me. *Your conduct will be the death of you.* The note was still ambiguous. The third one, though, was more telling. *The pen is mightier than the sword. Beware the consequences of what you write because you will pay in blood.*

"There aren't any dates," I pointed out.

"If they were mailed, she didn't keep the envelopes. They could have been left here for her."

If that were the case, then the murderer most likely lived in the vicinity and would know their routine of coming and going. "Where did you find them?"

"In her address book. There were just the three of them, all together."

"Under which letter?" I thought the alphabet might be a clue.

"Just shoved at the back, with some bills." She handed the letters up to me. I noted that the unpaid power bill was for October, along with a platinum MasterCard bill. It was possible that one of the notes was received in October, at the same time the bills arrived. Which indicated to me that the threatening notes were mailed, not hand delivered. Then again, Quentin may have stuffed the threatening notes in with other mail she didn't take seriously, like her bills.

Tinkie was scanning the purchases on the credit card bill when she looked up. "There's a charge on here for three thousand dollars to a lawyer, Linda Feinstein."

"Where's her office?"

"Clarksdale." Tinkie tapped the bill against her palm. "We should pay her a visit."

"Tomorrow," I said. "Let's make certain we have all the notes."

We spent the next hour going through Quentin's desk, but we didn't find any other threatening notes. We did find one strange handwritten letter, which was unsigned. Instead of trying to intimidate Quentin, the note demanded that the author receive just due for her contributions to the book. The script appeared to be feminine.

"We need to check and see if Quentin had some kind of researcher working for her." I bundled that note with the others.

We unplugged the computer and loaded it in the car. If Quentin was murdered because of what she intended to write next, we might find some good leads on her hard drive.

Night had fallen as we slowly drove along the highway toward home. Tinkie slowed a bit so she could look at me. "We'll leave the computer at the bank. Oscar has an employee who can do anything with computers. He'll make us copies of everything on it."

I nodded. "Who would know enough about what Quentin intended to write to threaten her?"

"She had a big mouth. She could have told anyone."

Tinkie spoke the truth. "That woman who spoke up at the funeral. What was her name?"

"Genevieve Reynolds!" She turned to me. "She *wanted* to be in the book. Could she be the one wanting recognition for her contributions?"

"We need to check it out."

"She lives in Rosedale. We could go there now."

"Now?" It would be seven at the earliest before we got back to Zinnia. If we went to Rosedale, it could be as late as midnight. "What about Oscar?"

"If he hasn't learned to use the microwave by now, he's due for a crash course."

"You go, Tinkie." I settled back into the comfortable leather seat for a ride to Rosedale.

The Reynolds home was set back off the highway, on what appeared to be a manicured lawn, complete with several spruce trees and fairy lights along the driveway. Someone in the Reynolds family enjoyed gardening, but somehow I didn't think it was the woman I'd seen at the funeral home. She was too pale, too intense.

Genevieve Reynolds was not excited to see us, and it showed on her face. She pushed her brown hair behind her ears and took off her glasses to study us.

"Tinkie Bellcase. Sarah Booth Delaney." Her lips thinned. "What do you want?"

"To chat." Tinkie breezed by her and into the foyer.

I had no choice but to follow suit. "We have some questions for you."

"If you don't have the authority of a badge, I don't have to talk to you at all." Genevieve swiveled her finger from me to the front door. "Out."

"Perhaps you should listen to us first." Tinkie cocked her head. "We have the note you sent to Quentin. Some people could interpret that as a motive for murder."

It was a bold move to make, but as I watched Genevieve's face, I realized Tinkie had played her hand admirably.

"Posh!" Genevieve's hand flew all around her. "No one could possibly think I killed Quentin McGee. That's the most ridiculous thing I've ever heard." She put both hands on her hips.

"I'm sure Allison feels the same way." Tinkie's mark hit home. Genevieve stopped in her tracks. She turned to us. "What do you two really want?"

"Information," I said.

She rolled her eyes. "Come into the library. But keep your voices down. My father is resting, and I don't want him disturbed. Ever since my mother died, he's had such a difficult time. His only consolation is the lawn. He works all day and paces the house all night."

We followed her into a huge room with a cathedral ceiling. Shelves of leather-bound books reached twenty feet high. The smell was wonderful; it reminded me of the tack room in the barn. A small fire burned in a fireplace, and a chair, covered with a maroon chenille throw, was drawn up there. Genevieve had obviously been reading. From the folds of the blanket, an old black head lifted.

"Grrr-rrr-rrrr!" The poodle looked ancient and half-hearted in its attempts to intimidate us.

"Beowulf, hush!" Genevieve hurried to the chair and scooped the poodle into her arms. "He's a fierce one, isn't he? He can't see and he can't chew, but if anyone tried to hurt me, he'd do his best to get them."

For the first time I felt a glimmer of compassion for Genevieve. She adored the old poodle. "What kind of work did you do for Quentin?"

She held the poodle in her arms as she paced the library. "Some fact-checking, that kind of stuff. Quentin knew a lot of dirt on people, but she didn't have the documentation. She was too impatient to bother with actually getting the proof. If it hadn't been for me, she would have been sued for every penny she ever hoped to inherit."

The dog began to growl. Tinkie walked up to Genevieve and took the dog. "You're exciting Beowulf." She cooed softly to the old poodle, who immediately relaxed in her arms. The growls were replaced with the short, snuffling sounds of a dog falling into contented sleep.

"I'm glad my mother is dead." Genevieve turned her face away to hide the tears that filled her eyes. "She would be so ashamed of how this all turned out. She was so proud of me, so glad that I was finally going to get the recognition that I deserved."

"Recognition?" Somewhere along the way, Genevieve's train had derailed. I didn't have a clue what she was talking about.

"Quentin promised me that if I helped her, she'd devote an entire chapter to me. I became the youngest person ever inducted into Mensa. I write brainteasers for the *New York Times* that are so difficult, I have to send the answers. I'm a bonafide genius, and Quentin was supposed to put that in the book." She dropped her head. "My mother hoped that some intelligent man would read it and see my value as a mate. I just wanted some recognition, instead of being the butt of everyone's jokes."

"Whatever made you think Quentin would include anything nice about anyone?" Tinkie's tone was sharp.

"She said she would." Genevieve's head came up, and there was fire in her gray eyes. "She promised. I told my mother about it, and Mom thought it was great." Her voice broke. "Right before she died, she told me to order a dozen copies of Quentin's book so we could mail them to all the family for Christmas." Her sobbing was in earnest.

Beowulf began to squirm in Tinkie's arms. She put him on the floor, and he ran to his mistress and began to paw at her knees.

"Poor baby. He misses Momma, too." Genevieve picked the old dog up and sobbed into his fur.

I looked at Tinkie and mouthed, "What happened to her mother?"

Tinkie shrugged. "Genevieve, how did you lose your mother?"

"It's all Quentin's fault!"

"How?" I was losing patience.

"See those big reference books?" She pointed to a pile of huge books sitting on the floor beside the fireplace. "They belong up there." Her finger moved to point out the very top shelf, which was strangely bare. I glanced around until I located the library ladder, which was a necessity to get that high.

"Yes," I said.

"I had those old books out. They're bloodlines of all the best Delta families, a sort of register. I was looking up a particular request for Quentin. I got the books down and used them, but I didn't put them back up."

Her face had grown pale, and the little poodle was trying to burrow up under her chin in an effort to give his mistress comfort.

"And?" Tinkie and I said in unison.

"Mother decided to tidy up the library. She was having some of her friends over for tea. She picked up those heavy books and climbed that ladder." Genevieve turned to look at the ladder as she spoke. Her face was deathly pale. "Something happened. All of the books on that shelf came tumbling down on top of her." She took a deep breath. "She was dead when the ladies found her."

Genevieve might have the highest IQ in the Southeast, but in my opinion, she didn't have walking-around sense. "You got the books down, didn't you?"

She whirled on me. "Yes, but it isn't my fault. I was going to put them up. I told Mother that."

I held up a hand. "I didn't mean to imply otherwise."

Genevieve sniffled. "Okay. But everyone is always on me about being too smart. Mrs. Carrington told me one time that I'd never catch a man, because men don't like to have their noses rubbed in a woman's superior intelligence." She looked at me. "Something you don't have to worry about, Sarah Booth."

I was about to take offense when Tinkie intervened. "Was there anything you were working on for the second book?"

Genevieve considered it. "Quentin had it in her head

that the Eastmans were the product of a relationship between Jebediah Eastman and one of his slaves."

The Eastmans were an old, prominent Southern family raised in the tradition of segregation. They'd fought long and hard against integration. Such a revelation would be a bitter irony indeed. "Is it true?"

Genevieve thought about her answer. "I had information—I found a marriage certificate that isn't recorded in the formal Eastman family tree—that appears to confirm this. Quentin was dying to get her hands on it." She put her hand up to her mouth. "I didn't mean that literally. But she was due to come by here and talk to me before Halloween. Mother's death . . ."

"When did Mrs. Reynolds die?"

"October the twenty-second. I haven't been able to work. I can't concentrate. You can't begin to imagine. Dad is just destroyed. We both sit across the table from each other and stare."

"It's okay," Tinkie said soothingly.

"I got that awful note and everything—"

"What note?"

My tone stopped her in her tracks. "The note telling me that I would suffer for being so smart."

"Where is it?" I demanded.

"In the trash, where it belongs! What's wrong with you?"

Tinkie put a gentle hand on Genevieve's arm. "Do you remember exactly what the note said?" She nodded at me as she encouraged Genevieve.

"Not exactly. It was a stupid, threatening note. Why should I recall it verbatim?"

"Think, Genevieve." Tinkie patted her arm. "Trust us, it's important."

"Okay." She closed her eyes and frowned. "It went like this. *Back off or you'll die under the weight of your own intelli-*

gence.'" She opened her eyes. "That was it. I'm sure. Only the note didn't use a contraction."

Across the top of Genevieve's head, my gaze met Tinkie's. We shared the same thought. Before we could say anything, we heard footsteps in the hall, and the library door opened. A man in his late fifties stopped in the doorway. He clearly wore the traces of grief on his face.

Genevieve rose to her feet. "I'll be back in a few minutes." She left.

Tinkie and I didn't waste any time. We pushed the library ladder over to the area where Mrs. Reynolds had been trying to reshelve the books. I scurried up the ladder, holding tight. I'd never liked heights. When I got to the top shelf, I reached out and tugged. The wood tilted down with the slightest pressure—enough so that the weight of the books would have caused them to fall right on top of the person shelving them.

"Was it deliberate?" Tinkie asked as she held the ladder.

"I'll have to take the shelf down to be sure."

"Do it!"

I gave a good tug, and the wooden shelf came out in my hand. I turned it to examine the sides. I couldn't be certain, but it appeared that the wooden dowels that would have held it in place had been sawed clean through on one side.

Easing down the ladder, I handed the shelf to Tinkie. "We should take that to Gordon," I said.

"This is going to be a neat trick—getting out of the house with their library shelf."

I hurried to the window and dropped the shelf out on the ground. "In case Genevieve objects," I said. And just in time. The door opened and Genevieve returned.

"We have to be going," I said as I sidled out the door.

"We'll be in touch," Tinkie said as she slipped out with me. Once we cleared the front door, I waited several minutes before I hurried to the side of the house and re-trieved the shelf.

"Don't you think they're going to eventually notice a shelf is missing from their library?" Tinkie asked.

"In this case, it's better to beg forgiveness than ask per-mission." I put the shelf in Tinkie's backseat and signaled for her to take off.

14

The courthouse was empty, except for the sheriff's office. Gordon Walters glared at us as I handed him the shelf and the three notes we'd found at Quentin's cottage.

"Sarah Booth, what if there were fingerprints? Now you've pawed all over the dang things."

He was tired and worried, but it had been a long day for me and Tinkie, too. "You wouldn't have the evidence at all if it weren't for us. You could at least act grateful."

Gordon ignored me and turned to Tinkie. "Oscar is fit to be tied. He's called up here four times, and he said you'd turned your cell phone off."

Tinkie bristled. "Oscar doesn't own me. I can come and go as I choose, and I'm not attached to him by a telecommunications leash."

"If he acted the same way, you'd be singing a different tune." Gordon slipped on a pair of heavy blue latex evidence gloves and examined the notes for the second time. Once he was done with them, he turned his attention to the shelf. "I'll get all this dusted for prints. Sarah Booth, I'm sure yours are on file."

"They are," I conceded. "Will you call us?"

He considered. "Yes. I owe you that much. But I think we're running down a rabbit trail with all of this. Even if Quentin was receiving threatening notes, why would someone kill Mrs. Betty Reynolds over in Rosedale?"

"I don't think he meant to kill Mrs. Reynolds. I think the trap was set for Genevieve."

"Because—" He arched his eyebrows.

"Because she was working on that book. She was the digger. She found the dirt and then got the documentation so that Quentin could print it."

"That's stretching it a tad, ladies. You're basing everything on the premise that Quentin was killed because of the book. My take on the murder is that it was a crime of passion. Allison Tatum and Quentin McGee had a lovers' spat. In a fit of fury, Allison killed her."

Gordon's skepticism was about to drive me over the edge. "Are the dowels cut or not?"

He examined the shelf again. "I can't say for certain."

"But an expert will be able to tell if they broke or were cut?"

He nodded.

"And you promise to call us as soon as you hear?"

He nodded again.

"Thanks," we said together as we walked out of the sheriff's office and into the empty hallway of the courthouse. Our footsteps echoed as we headed toward the doors and stepped out into the clear November night. A million stars winked down at us.

"I don't want to encourage your feelings, Sarah Booth, but I wish Coleman would come back." Tinkie sat on the top step.

I sat beside her. "I miss him. A lot."

"I know you do."

The step was cold and it was late. Oscar was already worried. I wondered why Tinkie was lingering.

"Oscar has told me if I don't go to the doctor and get my lump biopsied, he's going to divorce me."

She'd put me between a rock and a hard place. On one hand, I completely agreed with Oscar. Tinkie needed to get medical attention for the lump that she'd found in her breast almost four weeks earlier. Seeking a biopsy seemed the responsible, adult thing to do. But on the other hand, Tinkie had a right to determine her own fate. It was her body, and she should have the final say. She shouldn't be blackmailed into doing anything.

"You know Oscar won't really divorce you." I tentatively put an arm around her. When she didn't pull back, I gave her a squeeze. "Oscar couldn't make it without you."

"That's why he's going to divorce me. He said he won't hang around to watch me die a slow and awful death when I could avoid it. He said I have until the end of the week, or he's going to file the papers."

I didn't know what to say. But it's the job of a friend to try. "Tinkie, what would it hurt to have the biopsy?"

She turned to me, tears hanging off her bottom lashes. "I believe I'm fine. If I question that belief, maybe I won't be."

"If you're fine, you're fine. The test will only confirm that."

She sighed. "It's an issue of faith, Sarah Booth. It's between me and God. I don't need a doctor to tell me, and I won't have a needle jammed into my breast to prove what I already know. I've had more than enough of doctors."

I sat quietly beneath the stars for a little while. "Is there something else going on here, Tink?"

"Like what?" Her tone was angry.

"Are you trying to make Oscar squirm?"

"Why would I do such a thing?"

Again, there was anger in her tone. "I don't know, so you'll have to tell me." There was a reason she wouldn't go to the doctor, and why she wasn't eager to get home. She and Oscar had the marriage I envied. Oscar doted on her, and she adored him. Something was very wrong and had been when we went to New Orleans.

"Spill it. What's going on?"

When she looked at me, I was completely unprepared for the anguish in her face. "I want a child."

"Tinkie!" I put my hands on her shoulders.

"I went to the doctor last week. There's some scarring in my fallopian tubes. He confirmed what the fortune-teller in New Orleans told me."

"Wait a minute," I said, recalling the conversation she'd had with the reader in the tearoom. "She said she saw a child, a girl. She was swinging. I remember this clearly."

"And she said the girl was happy, that she forgave me."

"Forgave you?" I didn't remember this part.

Tinkie wiped the tears from her face and looked at me. "When Oscar and I first married, I got pregnant. He didn't want a child then. He said we should wait, that we should plan for a child, for a future. He convinced me that I should abort our baby." Her throat began to work, and she stopped talking.

"I'm so sorry." I felt the inadequacy of anything I might say. Tinkie sat in the cold, wrapped in guilt and regret, and there was nothing I could do to help my friend.

"I've begun to dream about her, Sarah Booth. She's nine now. The perfect age, don't you think? I've gotten her horseback riding lessons from Lee and dance lessons from Madame."

Tinkie was scaring me. "Nine is a good age. But she's a dream. A fantasy."

"Maybe everything else is a fantasy. Did you ever consider that?"

"Oscar loves you, Tinkie. That's solid and real. He had no reason to believe you wouldn't have another baby. It was a decision the two of you made together."

She shook her head. "It was his decision. Not mine. I wanted her. I wanted Madeline."

I closed my eyes. She'd named a dream child, and she was choosing a fantasy over her own husband. I had to think. "What I'd like is for you to go to another doctor. Get a second opinion." I squeezed her shoulders. "I remember when you used to love to go to the doctor, if he was handsome. I'm sure we can use the Internet to find a terrific-looking fertility specialist."

"I'm going to let Oscar divorce me."

I was at my wit's end. I didn't know what to say. "I'm going to be really honest with you. I think you should go to a surgeon and get that lump checked, if it's even still there. Then, you need to go to a fertility doctor. They're doing miraculous things, Tinkie, but you have to be healthy to have a shot at having a child."

She stood up. "I have to get home."

It was where she needed to go, but I wasn't certain her heart was in the right place about going. "Oscar does love you."

She started down the steps and looked up at me. "Almost as much as he loves himself. Come on and I'll drop you at Dahlia House."

I stood on the porch and watched Tinkie pull away. We'd been together all day. In fact, we'd been together a tremendous amount ever since she'd seen that fortune-teller in New Orleans. Yet I'd never picked up on her distress. I was real observant.

Sighing, I turned to enter my home. A large box tied with a rainbow-hued ribbon was propped against the front door. Humphrey had struck again. I picked up the box and took it to my office, where I could check my phone messages, and hopefully, avoid Jitty. She was always throwing Tinkie and Oscar in my face as the perfect couple. She should have warned me that Tinkie was as haunted as I.

My voice mailbox was empty, and there was no sign of the haint, so I opened the gift box, trying hard not to wonder why Coleman hadn't even let me know he was coming to town.

Inside the layers of tissue were a white blouse with drop-down breast pockets and a blue pinafore that was barely long enough to cover possible, as Aunt Loulane had called her hinder region. At the bottom of the box was a pair of white-sequined thongs. And a note. *If you'll play Dorothy, I'll send you over the rainbow.* Even though I was appalled, I couldn't help but laugh. Humphrey was nothing if not persistent.

I felt a cool breeze and turned to find Jitty drifting my way. To my surprise, she was wearing what looked to be my gray sweats and my black "Bad to the Bone" T-shirt. "Night off from court?" I asked.

"I couldn't find my maid to lace my corset." She pointed to the box. "Give the man an A for attempt."

"How about a D for deviant." I put the lid back on the box. I would have to return it tomorrow. But I didn't want to talk about Humphrey and his gifts. I had something serious to discuss with Jitty. "Why didn't you tell me Tinkie is haunted?"

When there was no immediate answer, I turned to confront Jitty. Her brow was furrowed and her gaze distant. Some other scene played out in her mind.

"It's a different thing." She sank down in Tinkie's chair. "A long time ago, when your great-great-grandmother was alive and we were young, she almost made a choice to live in a dream."

The stories of Alice Delaney were legend in the family, and I could have quoted this one by heart, but I loved to hear Jitty tell it. "What happened?"

"The war was on, and both our men were gone. We didn't know they wouldn't come back to us. I guess it's a good thing we didn't, or we would've just quit." She looked at me. "Miss Alice lost a baby. The hardships were too much. She just couldn't carry all the way through, and it likta killed her."

Though I knew the story, I hadn't grasped the similarities. "What did she do?"

"For a while the fever took her." She looked out the window to the drive. "The crops had died in the heat. We were hungry, and nothin' to eat. Miss Alice would hold her arms like an infant was there. She'd tell me to hold the baby. She left me for a time and lived in a place where she had her baby."

"What did you do?"

"Little John was two. He was so afraid. His mama would look at him and see right through him. So one day I took him and stood him right in front of her. I told her that her baby was right there, needin' her. I told him to touch her face and tell her to come back to him. And she did. I made Miss Alice see that the reality of her son was greater than the dream of a lost child."

"I don't know if I can do that." I shook my head. "I'm in my office, having a conversation with a ghost. Who am I to say she can't have dreams about her child?"

"You have me because you need me. I'm here for you."

To dispute Jitty would have only hurt her feelings. "And Tinkie? Maybe she needs her daughter."

"She's haunted by guilt. She dreams about a child who doesn't exist, who never existed. She's being seduced by a fantasy, and there's a real danger there."

Jitty was scaring me, but it wasn't deliberate. "What's the danger?"

"That her fantasy will grow more appealing than her reality. That's the danger of all fantasies, but most especially those spun from the threads of guilt."

"What should I do?"

"Remind her of the good in her life. Make her see what's real is always the best choice. Stand right in front of her, and make her see how much you need her."

"And what about Oscar?"

"The past is done, Sarah Booth. It's as much a dream as the future. There's only the here and now. Once she sees that, she'll be okay." She started to waver. "That's something you need to understand, too. Could be the two of you will teach each other."

"Don't go." I didn't want to be alone.

"Feed the hound and the horse. You'll be just fine."

She was gone. I stood up and walked outside to feed Reveler and to whistle up my hound. Sweetie Pie and I were going to take a ride to the Dairy Queen. I was in desperate need of a chocolate shake and some time behind the wheel. I also wanted to stop by the local pharmacy and drop off the photo diskettes I'd found at Quentin's house. In all of my concern for Tinkie, I'd almost forgotten about the case.

While the one-hour processing of the diskettes took place, I got an ice cream for Sweetie and a double chocolate shake for me and drove around with my hound to look at the Christmas lights.

This had always been one of my childhood highlights. I'd sit in the front seat, between Mama and Daddy, and let the multihued lights blend and whirl in a fantasy of color and bliss. Now, the trend of the more sophisticated white lights had taken over. "Icicles" hung from eaves all over town. It was beautiful, but I missed the red, green, blue, and yellow lights of my childhood. In fact, I missed all of my childhood. And mostly, I missed my family.

I sucked down the last drop of my shake and wadded up Sweetie's clean napkin—she never let a drop of ice cream escape her—and headed to pick up the photos.

The clerk yawned as she bagged everything and handed it over to me. "How's the case coming, Miss Delaney?"

I was surprised that the teenager would recognize me, much less know I was on a case. "It's coming," I replied, with a knowing nod.

She nodded and compressed her lips. "Will these photos help?"

I hadn't seen them yet, but it really didn't matter. "I'm sure they will." I took them and headed into the night.

Sweetie was more interested in the wind in her ears than looking at photos, so we went back to Dahlia House, where I could go into my office with good lighting and privacy to see what I'd netted.

At first I was disappointed. The photos were of Allison and Quentin at a restaurant, then a dress shop, then a florist, all around the Delta. I recognized some of the establishments where they were shopping—ritzy, expensive places. The two women were together in each shot, laughing and looking at each other with obvious love. This was a documentary of their wedding planning trip. When it occurred to me that someone else had taken the photographs, I wondered who. It could have been an employee at each different business, or it could have been someone who was with them, planning the wedding. The photos had elicited another question for me, but they would also be something for Allison to hang on to, once she was cleared.

I put them in my desk drawer and locked it, thinking how fleeting happiness could be. And sometimes what an illusion. Tinkie had me worried. The road to romance was mighty rocky. My heart squeezed as I thought of Coleman. I had to let him go. I had to.

My friends, and Barbara Mandrell, were right. There was no future in loving a married man. Did I love him? I wasn't sure. Love was an emotion that swelled and withdrew. The truth was, I didn't want to plumb the depths of my feelings for Coleman. What good would it do?

Though I expected Jitty to appear and make a comment on my morose attitude, she didn't. Jitty had little tolerance for self-pity and even less for self-inflicted pain. I didn't have to see her to know what she'd be saying, and it was the best advice I could follow.

I headed upstairs for a long bath and the bed, with Sweetie Pie at my side. I'd just made it beneath the quilts when the telephone rang. My first inclination was to ignore it. I was tired, lonely, depressed, and wired from sugar. No one would be calling at eleven o'clock at night unless it was bad news. As unprofessional as it was for a private investigator, I didn't want to hear it.

On the fifth ring, I couldn't stand it and picked up the phone just before the answering machine got it.

"Sarah Booth?" It was Cece's breathless voice.

"What's going on?"

"You'd better get to The Club, quick."

I didn't have ESP, but I knew something serious was wrong with Tinkie. "What's happened?"

"Tinkie is drunk as a lord and on a tear. She slapped Oscar, and he left her there. The manager of The Club tried to contain her, and she slugged him. He's called the police to have her arrested."

I sighed. "I'll go get her."

"I'll meet you there. What's going on with her?"

"It's a story she'll have to tell you," I said as I fumbled for my clothes and began to dress.

15

I was a little too late. When I pulled up at The Club, blue lights were whirling against the front of the exclusive establishment, and Tinkie was sitting in the back of a patrol car. When she looked at me through the window, her eyes wouldn't focus. I'd never seen her drunk before, and it wasn't a pretty sight.

Bernard, the barkeep and an old friend, was talking with Deputy Dewayne Dattilo when I walked up to them.

"She's just upset. Miss Tinkie isn't a problem, and I'm sure Oscar will pay for the damages. Just take her home." Bernard tapped the window and gave Tinkie a thumbs-up.

"She assaulted two women, who say they're going to press charges," Dewayne said. "I called Mr. Richmond, and he hung up on me before I could tell him what was happening. I don't want to take her in, but I don't know what else to do." His face showed no desire to be in the middle of the mess he was in. "When her father hears about this, there's going to be hell to pay for everyone involved. Mr. Bellcase *owns* the bank!"

Tinkie's father was not going to be happy to wake up to a phone call telling him Tinkie was incarcerated for public drunkenness and fighting. "She doesn't have to go to jail. I'll take her home with me. I'll call her father."

He looked at me with relief. "That would be great."

"Once tempers cool, I'm sure Oscar or Mr. Bellcase will pay for any damages." No matter how mad Oscar might be with Tinkie, he would come to his senses and realize his wife should not be in jail. "If you'll tell me who wants to press charges against Tinkie, I'll have a talk with them."

"Me, too," Cece said as she walked up. "I would think most people would prefer to keep this off the society page." She smiled her hungry canine smile. "Give me their names, and I'll explain it to them in a way that makes them understand."

"Suits me," Dewayne said. "Lot less paperwork if all of this fades quietly away."

"We'll handle it," I assured him.

He opened the back door of the patrol car and stepped away. And just in time. Tinkie hurled herself out of the car, grabbing at him.

I stepped in front of her. "Tinkie, don't make me call your daddy."

For most women, but especially a Daddy's Girl, the threat of calling Daddy is the biggest switch of all. Tinkie halted in her tracks. She wobbled unsteadily, and I didn't offer a hand. She had to make up her own mind without anyone touching her or trying to coddle her.

"Mind your own business," she slurred, but there was no fire behind her words.

"I'll take you to Dahlia House, and you can sleep it off." I held her weaving gaze. "Or I can call your daddy to come and take you home with him."

She did the best about-face she could manage while tottering and lurched to the roadster and got in the passenger seat. She promptly opened the door and threw up all over the ground.

"At least she had the presence of mind to open the door," Cece said, one hand on her hip. "Now, Dewayne, who are the women pressing charges?"

He rolled his eyes. "Marilyn Jenkins and Lorilee Brewer. It seems Tinkie threw a drink on them." He shook his head wearily. "I wish Coleman was back at work."

I opened my mouth to echo his sentiments, but Cece cut me short.

"Don't worry, Dewayne, everything is under control." Cece gave me a hug and a kiss on the cheek. "Remember, get her to drink a Bloody Mary with a raw egg in it. That'll make her feel a whole lot better."

"Or give her salmonella." I had no desire to see the offering of a raw egg returned to me.

"Well, at this point salmonella would feel better than the hangover she's going to have in the morning." Cece turned and sashayed over to her car. "I'm off to visit Marilyn and Lorilee. I intend to catch them before they wash their make-up off and reveal scales. Wish them luck!"

I walked into The Club and found Bernard sweeping up a mountain of broken glass. I didn't want to imagine the scene that had occurred there so recently.

"Bernard, are you okay?"

He nodded. "Just feelin' bad for Miss Tinkie."

"What happened?"

"It all started when Miss Tinkie and Oscar got in a terrible fight." He stopped sweeping and held the broom. "It was my fault."

That was impossible. "Why do you say that?"

"Miss Tinkie came in and started drinking vodka martinis. After the fourth one, I tried to cut her off, but she started making a scene. So I called her husband to come get her. I should've minded my own business."

"It isn't your fault, Bernard. Tinkie was primed for a fight with Oscar."

"She sure got one. They had it out, and then he left, and those other two women came up and said something smart to Miss Tinkie. She poured her drink on one and grabbed a drink off the bar and tossed it on the other one. Then all hell broke loose."

"If it's any consolation, those women deserved whatever they got."

He still looked down. "I know. They were no-count women. They been in here before, complainin' about everything. After the drink incident, I had to grab one of them and hold her. But that won't make it any easier on Miss Tinkie."

I gave him a hug. "She'll be fine. Please give Mollie my love." His wife was the best seamstress in the state and had created my unforgettable gown for the Black and Orange Ball last Halloween.

"Will do. You take care, and take care of Miss Tinkie."

"I promise."

When I got to the car, Tinkie was, thank goodness, out cold. I left the windows down as I drove through the clear night. The frigid air didn't even make her eyelids flutter. When I got to Dahlia House, I was in the process of dragging her up the steps when I heard someone clear a throat. I turned to find Humphrey sitting in one of the rocking chairs.

"Need some help?" he asked.

"No, I think I'll just leave her out here on the steps." Tinkie was a petite woman, but she was deadweight. I was struggling, and he had to ask if I needed help.

He laughed. "It might be easier to leave her there for several reasons. You can hose the steps down afterward."

"If you're going to sit there and crack wise, you can leave." I lugged her limp body up another step. At the rate I was going, it would be dawn before I got her inside.

He sauntered over. "Allow me." He lifted her in his arms and carried her inside.

"Put her on the sofa," I said, trailing behind.

He did and stepped back. "She smells like a distillery, with a back note of something distinctly unpleasant."

"I know." I got some warm, soapy water and a washcloth from the downstairs bathroom and set about bathing her face. Behind me, I heard the tinkle of ice and the splash of liquor. Humphrey appeared at my elbow with a Jack on the rocks.

"For you. A little hair of the dog that bit her."

I rocked back on my heels and took the drink. Tinkie looked awful, and it was only a prelude to what she was going to feel in the morning. "I should call her husband. And her father."

Humphrey put a hand on my shoulder. "No, you shouldn't."

"Why not?"

"Tinkie is a grown woman. She shouldn't have to report to any man. Not her father or her husband. Secondly, you can't patch up her marriage, no matter how much you may want to, Sarah Booth. If Tinkie wants to see her husband, she'll have to call him. The hardest lesson in being a parent or a friend is to step back and let folks learn the lessons they need to learn."

I was amazed. "How much money did all that knowledge cost you?"

"I haven't been in therapy. I learned this from personal experience." Humphrey perched on the arm of the sofa. He took an ice cube from his glass and held it to Tinkie's lips. "My parents rushed to get me out of every fix I got into. If they'd left me alone, I would have had to grow up."

"Tinkie is grown." I watched with fascination as he ministered to Tinkie. She'd actually parted her lips to accept the ice.

"If you truly believe she's grown, then you trust her to choose what's right for her."

I closed my eyes and sipped my drink. He was right, damn him. "Okay."

"Let's go out on the porch and talk."

I followed him out into the night. The sky was a dull black velvet sprinkled with the winkings of a million stars. I stood near the balustrade and felt his arms circle me. He pulled me back into his chest and wrapped his arms around me.

"You're shivering."

"It's thirty-something degrees."

"Are you sure it's not anticipation?"

I smiled. Humphrey had the ego of the accomplished lover. "It's not anticipation. I'm exhausted. And worried. And longing for something that can't be."

"And honest. Maybe too honest." He held me close. "You're more than a conquest, Sarah Booth. You might be the woman who makes me grow up."

Staring into the night, I felt only sadness. "I'd stay a child if I were you. It's a far better gig than being a grown-up."

He laughed, and the touch of his warm breath near my ear made me realize how lonely I was. I stepped from his arms and turned to face him. "Thank you for your help tonight."

"I'm being dismissed." In the soft moonlight, his face showed no anger.

I touched his cheek. "I need a friend. And you've been that."

"How about we skip the serious relationship and go straight for the kinky sex?"

I kissed his cheek. "I'll call you tomorrow."

He went down the steps. "I'm not giving up. I know there's something in my bag of tricks that will turn you on."

I blew him a kiss and walked into the house and the very unladylike snoring of my partner.

* * *

"Oh, God, I'm dying!"

I put the water in the coffeepot and ignored Tinkie's howling. She had come to at about six o'clock, with a roiling stomach and her head pounding against an anvil. She'd refused the glass of water and buttered toast I'd offered her. In another few moments she'd be on her knees in the bathroom.

As the coffee began to perk, I heard the bathroom door slam. I made some fresh toast and poured a glass of orange juice. After a little while, I took them to her.

She sat pale and shaky on the old horsehair sofa. Her hand trembled as she took the toast. "I think I might die."

"No chance of that. You'll recover."

"I have this vague memory of glass breaking."

"Good. When you get the bill from The Club, you won't deny the wreckage."

Her face screwed up, and I got some aspirin. She swallowed them down without complaint.

"Cece is talking to Marilyn and Lorilee on your behalf," I told her.

"Good." She ate a little more toast. "I owe you an apology."

"Not me. Oscar maybe, and a half dozen other people, but not me."

"No, I put you in the middle of my marriage. That's not something you do to a friend. I'm sorry, Sarah Booth."

"I'm sorry you're hurting, Tink. But I know Oscar loves you. And you love him. Remember, the past is a nice place to visit, but it isn't where you want to linger. You have to let it go."

Her jaw set in a stubborn line. "You make it sound so easy."

I knelt beside her. "Tinkie, of all the people in the world, I'm the last one to preach to you. I'm haunted by the past. That's why I know it's so important to let it go." I patted her knee. "Or you could end up like me."

The doorbell rang, and Tinkie burrowed against the arm of the sofa. "If it's Oscar, tell him I died."

I chuckled softly as I opened the door to Cece. She was ravishing in a black slack suit with a faux fur–collared vest embroidered with gold. Her stiletto boots clicked across the floor as she unerringly zoned in on Tinkie.

"Well, well, if it isn't the vandal of high society." She tapped her toe, completely unsympathetic to Tinkie's sorry state.

"Go away," Tinkie croaked.

"I'm here for an interview. And to think, I turned down working for a really big newspaper in New Orleans so I could interview my friend about a drunken hair-pulling in Zinnia, Mississippi."

Tinkie forced herself upright. "If I recall, it was only a few weeks ago that I stood by you when you tackled a supermodel in the middle of the biggest high-society ball in the Southeast."

Cece grinned, her perfect white teeth glistening in the dim morning light. "How true, dahling. Birds of a feather and all that." She sat on the sofa. "Gather round. I had the most interesting night. I almost came over here, but I feared one of you was sleeping it off and the other was merely sleeping."

"What happened?" I knew she'd been with Marilyn and Lorilee, respectively. It must have been a grueling night, but if Cece had gone without sleep, I couldn't tell it.

"Lorilee was the bitch I've known for years, but Marilyn . . ." She tapped her finger on the sofa arm. "Marilyn was very informative. Were you aware that Lorilee's husband, Charles, was arrested last year for attempted murder?"

Tinkie and I shook our heads. "No." We were all ears.

"It's a rather strange and bizarre story and follows

closely on the heels of Lorilee's lust for the weed-eater boy."

Cece, knowing she held her audience captive, looked around. "A Bloody Mary would be nice."

I made three and forced one into Tinkie's hand. It was minus the raw egg, but I thought it might revive her. "Now tell us," I demanded of Cece.

"About three weeks after Charlie caught Lorilee with the boy, Lorilee was out in her yard, running the weed eater." She smiled. "Poetic justice, isn't it?"

I made a threatening gesture.

"Okay, okay. Lorilee was weed eating around the garage when the lawn tractor suddenly shot out of the garage, riderless, and nearly ran her down. Because of the noise of the weed eater, Lorilee didn't hear the tractor until it was almost on her. The only thing that saved her was a faucet. The tractor hit it and was diverted at the last minute."

"The tractor started on its own?" I found this too strange.

"Spontaneous starting?" Cece was having way too much fun. "I've heard of that when people live under high-voltage power lines.

"Death by mower." Tinkie was at last smiling. "Now that would have been a real mess. Talk about compost."

"That's disgusting." But I couldn't help laughing. "But even if the mower started by itself, how did it get gas?"

Cece had the answer. "I checked out the police report in their hometown. It appears the gas pedal was stuck at full throttle. If the damn thing had hit Lorilee, it would have flattened her and kept on going."

"Spontaneous starting and a conveniently stuck gas pedal? I'm just not buying that this was accidental."

"Hence the fact that Charlie was charged with attempted murder," Cece reminded us. "Lorilee dropped the charges when there were no fingerprints found on the mower. None. Not even hers."

"And the police let it go after that?"

Cece nodded. "I'm certain they felt it was all set up by Lorilee in an attempt to put Charlie on the defensive if he sued her for divorce."

"That's too crazy even for Lorilee." I looked at Tinkie.

"Do you think there was—" Tinkie was cut short.

"A note?" Cece finished. "Absolutely. That's why Lorilee charged her husband with attempted murder. She had written evidence that someone had threatened her."

"Does Lorilee still have the note?" I asked.

Cece shook her head. "I'm not sure. Marilyn didn't know that, but she did know that Quentin had found out about the arrest for attempted murder. Lorilee was livid. Charlie almost divorced Lorilee about the weed-eater boy and the false arrest, but then he backed off. Quentin was just about to drag it all out in the open again." She grinned. "It would have been the end of Lorilee's marriage for sure."

"And good motive for murder." Tinkie rose unsteadily to her feet. "I need a shower."

"Indeed, you do," Cece agreed. "While you're cleaning up a bit, I'm going to make more Bloody Marys." She grabbed the decanter of vodka and headed to the kitchen, pausing at the door. "By the way, Marilyn and Lorilee have agreed to drop the charges against you. You can thank me later."

"How did you do it?" Tinkie asked.

"I pointed out that I might pick up where Quentin left off and write a second tell-all. They chose not to be a chapter."

"I didn't realize they were that smart," I said as I got a notepad and followed Cece into the kitchen. While she found celery, olives, and the other ingredients, I made a few notes to myself.

"Did you know that Genevieve Reynolds received a

threatening note, and then her mother was accidentally killed?" I wrote that down.

"Killed how?"

"Crushed by books. The note said Genevieve would die under the weight of her own intelligence."

Cece stirred the drinks and put them on the table. "May I make some cheese grits?"

"Go for it." I listed Marilyn Jenkins's name. "Marilyn's mother was killed by falling rocks while she was acting like a slut."

I had Cece's undivided attention. She held the bag of grits in her hand, but she stared at me.

"The note to Quentin said she would pay for dragging her family's name through the mud. And now we find out that Lorilee was almost killed, and she received a note, too. We need to find out what it said."

Cece put the grits in the pot and turned down the heat before she picked up the telephone and dialed The Gardens's number. "Lorilee Brewer," she said in her imperious tone.

In a moment she continued. "Lorilee, whatever did that note say when you were threatened?"

There was a pause. "*'Like wheat before the scythe, you will be cut down for your lust.'* Very interesting. Uh-huh, thank you." She hung up and turned to me. "What's going on?"

Tinkie returned looking half-alive. She took the drink Cece had prepared without comment.

"There's another death we need to look into." I glanced at Tinkie. "We need to go to West Memphis. Belinda Loper."

"The hairdresser?" Cece was intrigued.

"Right. We need to find her sister, Jolene."

Cece refilled her Bloody Mary from the pitcher she'd made. "So Genevieve Reynolds, Lorilee Brewer, Quentin, and possibly Belinda Loper all received notes? This would make a fabulous story."

"And clear Allison," Tinkie said. The beverage had obviously restored her brain function.

"But it also means that the killer is still on the loose," I pointed out just as the doorbell rang.

We all jumped, and it was Cece who leapt up first and ran to the front door. There was no sign of a person, but a small package had been left on the porch. As we approached, we realized the package was moving.

Humming, actually.

"It's a bomb!" Tinkie grasped our hands and pulled us back into the house. "Call the bomb squad."

I looked at her as she slammed and locked the door. "We don't have a bomb squad."

"Then call the sheriff's department!"

"Brilliant idea," Cece agreed, whipping out her cell phone and placing the call.

Before anyone could stop me, I rushed out the door and kicked the package as hard as I could. If it was a bomb, it wasn't going to blow up Dahlia House. The package flew across the lawn and landed in the driveway, rattling against the oyster shells.

We took our positions, peering out the front windows, waiting for help to arrive.

16

Within six minutes we saw flashing blue lights headed toward Dahlia House. Acting sheriff Gordon Walters must have jumped in the patrol car and floorboarded it. The glance I shared with Tinkie told me we were both impressed.

"Nothing like seeing the boys in brown jump to it," Cece drawled. None of us made a move as the patrol car skidded to a halt ten feet from the package, which I now noticed was pink and wrapped with a red bow. I suddenly had a very bad feeling.

"My, my," Cece said as Coleman Peters stepped out of the car and walked toward the package.

I unlocked the door and yanked it open. My bare feet slapped across the porch as I ran toward Coleman. "No! Don't touch it!" I yelled.

"My God, she thinks he'll be hurt," Tinkie cried, and I heard her running after me. Halfway across the lawn, I felt her arms tangle in my legs as she tackled me with a flying leap. I went down with a hu-ff-ff.

"Don't move!" Coleman ordered just as Gordon and Dewayne drove up in a second car. Gordon was wearing what looked to be a catcher's outfit covered by a Kevlar vest.

"Stand back, Sheriff," Dewayne said. "I'm equipped to handle it." He bypassed everyone and ran to the box.

He stared at it, bending closer. "It's not ticking. It's humming."

I swallowed and made no effort to dislodge my legs from Tinkie's grasp. We both lay in the grass, she in her attire from the night before and I in my flannel pajamas. I put my face down in the winter-dry blades and prayed that the ground would swallow me up.

"Just a minute here," Gordon said, tearing off the bow. "If this is what I think it is." He lifted the box lid, pushed aside the layers of tissue paper, and pulled out a humming vibrator. It was very lifelike.

"Good lord," Coleman said.

"It's the Elvis," Cece screamed, rushing over to it. "Watch." She hit another button, and the vibrator began to gyrate.

Cece pointed it at me with an accusatory glare. "You always had a thing for Elvis."

With as much dignity as I could manage, I said, "That does *not* belong to me."

Coleman's blue gaze raked over me, and though I wanted to cringe, I didn't. I wasn't responsible for the things left on my porch.

"There's a note," Cece said.

I wanted to beg her to shut up, but I merely arched my left eyebrow.

"It's handwritten, and it says, '*Warm up with The King; I'll be by later tonight.*'" Cece looked at me. "It's signed Humphrey."

"Humphrey Tatum?" Coleman asked.

"He has a thing for Sarah Booth," Tinkie said softly. "He just won't give it up." She assisted me to my feet.

I couldn't speak. My tongue was paralyzed. I could only look at Coleman and wonder why he hadn't called me. Not even once. And here he was back in town and back in uniform.

"I guess the bomb scare is over," Coleman said. He cast one unreadable look my way, walked to his car, and got in.

Unable to do anything else, I stood frozen. He was leaving.

Tinkie edged past me and walked to the patrol car. She lowered her head to speak directly to him, but her voice carried back to me.

"What in the hell is wrong with you?" she asked him. "Are you in town, or are you moving?"

He gazed straight out the front window, ignoring me. "I don't know," he answered. "That's the whole problem. I don't know what to do." He stepped on the gas and shot down the shell drive, the faintest wisp of dust trailing after him.

Cece still held Elvis as she walked over and put an arm around me. "This is a very expensive model," she said, handing it off to me. "Whatever else you say about Humphrey, he gives top-of-the-line gifts."

"Right," I said as the Elvis jerked in my hand. "Right."

Tinkie put her arm around me and gave me a squeeze. "I need to get home. Sarah Booth, we'll head to West Memphis after the reading of the will and lunch. That is if you aren't . . . busy." She winked at me.

"That's uncalled for."

"Where's my car?" She turned around in the driveway, ignoring me.

"At The Club," Cece said. "I'll take you to retrieve it. I have to get to the paper. After all, dahling, I'm on dead-line."

Since no one wanted to stay and talk with me about Coleman's odd behavior, I got a shower, dressed, and went to the jail to visit Allison. There was an ulterior motive: Coleman was bound to be in his office.

But, of course, he wasn't, and Dewayne would barely meet my gaze when I walked in.

"Where's Coleman?"

"Had some business to finish up," Dewayne said to his boots.

"Where?"

"Didn't say."

"When will he be back?"

"Didn't say that, either."

I could see Dewayne had no intention of being helpful, so I pushed it. "Where's Connie?"

"Connie?"

He could act like he didn't know the sheriff's wife, but I knew better. I arched both eyebrows and waited.

"He didn't—"

"Say," I finished for him. "I need to see Allison."

He seemed relieved to unlock the door to the jail, and as soon as I stepped through, he slammed and locked it behind me. Dewayne was taking no chances.

Allison perked up as soon as she saw me. "Humphrey said you'd uncovered some leads." Her face betrayed her hope. It was interesting to see that Humphrey was attempting to comfort her, even if it was with mostly false hope.

"I need to ask you about the notes Quentin received, and I had these photos printed up from some disks I found at your cottage." I handed her the pictures of their wedding preparations.

She gave a little cry as she realized what they were and sank down to the floor of her cell to hungrily look at them.

Since I wasn't in a hurry, I watched her flip through them twice, stopping to study certain pictures as tears dripped off her chin.

"I miss her," she said, wiping her eyes with the sleeve of her shirt. "When you find the person who killed her, it won't change that she's gone. I'll still be suffering."

"I know." And I did. Truth couldn't undo loss.

"What leads have you found?" Allison asked.

I told her about the notes and the other deaths. She was an intelligent woman, and right behind comprehension was concern. "Then the killer is still out there."

I nodded. "That would be true."

"Who is it?"

"I don't know," I had to admit. "Were Quentin's notes mailed to her?"

"Yes. Out of Memphis."

I jumped at that. "Memphis?"

She nodded. "I remember distinctly, because we both tried to figure out who we knew in Memphis who might threaten us."

"And who did you come up with?"

"The Loper girls, but the first note came before Quentin even considered putting Belinda and Jolene in her book."

"You feel the notes weren't book related?"

She thought about it. "Yes and no."

"Go on."

"Yes, because they each refer to paying for what's been written, and no because they weren't linked to anything specific involving the book."

"And you don't believe Jolene Loper wrote them?"

She shook her head. "No. Not the Jolene Loper I remember. Her idea of a note is one of those tacky cards with the words already printed."

I touched her hand on the bars. "We are trying, Allison."

"My brother says he's impressed with you."

I dropped my gaze. "Humphrey has a unique way of showing his interest."

"I know. He's worked so hard to prove he's a deviant that he may have convinced himself." Her gaze held mine.

"But I remember him differently. I was younger. He was gone most of the time, but when he did come home, he would smile at me, and I felt like someone loved me."

I didn't have to ask Allison if she'd heard from her parents. Dewayne would have told me had the Tatums visited. She was alone, except for Humphrey.

"The reading of the will is at ten."

"Are you going?" she asked.

I nodded. "Me or Tinkie." I didn't intend to tell her that my heart lay at the board of supervisors meeting, where Coleman was due to show up.

"If you see Miss Carrington, would you tell her to please stop by and see me?"

"Sure. She's your biggest defender."

She handed me the photos. "Give these to her. She took them. I told her she had a good eye."

I took the photos and put them in my purse. I'd drop them by The Gardens after the reading of the will. Right now, I wanted to find Coleman before either meeting began.

Dewayne unlocked the door at my knock, and I checked Coleman's office before I left. He was nowhere to be found. Outside, the sky had begun to cloud over. November storms were often cold and damp. I buttoned my jacket and headed to the roadster. There was one place Coleman might be where I could talk to him. I followed my instinct and drove to Opal Lake.

It was a much better ride on horseback, but I didn't have time to go home and saddle Reveler. I drove fast, the dead leaves skittering over the pavement behind me as I blasted down the highway.

Opal Lake was a small, round lake tucked in a state recreation area. It was a parking place for high school kids, and for a few of us older adults. It was not an official rendezvous location for me and Coleman, but more than once we'd found each other there.

This time I was in luck. I saw his old pickup before I saw him sitting under a sweet gum tree.

"Sarah Booth," he said, rising as I walked toward him.

My first impulse was to slap him. Hard. Right in the face. Restraint cost me a lot, but I gritted my jaw and held my temper.

"Your face looks like the sky—stormy weather."

I couldn't read him. He was acting all down-homey, like I was a casual stranger. "What is going on with you? You show up at my house and act like I'm a stranger."

The mask dropped, and for a split second, I saw his pain. Then he was composed again. "I'm trying hard not to walk over there and take you in my arms."

My own heart rate jumped. I'd hoped that my sexual feelings for Coleman had been tamped down. But they hadn't. I wanted him instantly, and I read the want on his face, too.

"Why haven't you called?"

"Connie tried to kill herself last week. She's in a hospital, tied in a bed. They have to restrain her. They're running all kinds of tests."

"I'm sorry." I forced myself to say the words. I was sorry. For Coleman. For Connie. For the situation. And for myself. We were all losers.

"I think about you every minute of every day. And then I look at Connie, and I think she's paying the price for the fact that I don't love her anymore."

"Perhaps if she'd acted in a more lovable fashion."

He shook his head. "I blame myself."

"And me? Do you blame me, too?"

Before I could blink, he had me in his arms. "I don't blame you for anything, Sarah Booth." He kissed my forehead and pulled me against him.

He smelled of cold and sunshine and woods. I closed my eyes and leaned my head against his chest. A wave of sadness engulfed me, and I clung to him. For a moment, I thought my heart would break.

"It's okay," he whispered. "I see you. I hold you in my arms, and I know that it's going to be okay."

At last I had control of myself. I pushed lightly, and he released me. The wind off the little lake had grown colder as the clouds blotted out the weak sun. I looked into his blue eyes.

"What are you going to do?"

"I'm going to sell the house. The medical bills are piling up. Insurance covers a lot of it, but not all."

"And your job?"

"I'm coming back to work."

I couldn't help the smile. "Thank goodness."

"I don't have a choice. I need the money, and I can't take it if I don't earn it."

"And Connie?"

"The doctor says he wants to keep her isolated for two weeks. Then we'll reevaluate. There's just no telling what she told him."

That was true. Connie was a manipulative, conniving bitch. "And you're meeting with the supervisors to . . ."

"Tell them I'm back on the job."

"Where will you live?"

"I haven't figured all of that out."

It was on the tip of my tongue to offer Dahlia House. It was plenty big. We could both live there and never bump into each other. But I knew that wouldn't be the case. We were both walking a thin line, and if we were physically together, we wouldn't be able to resist each other.

"My feelings are hurt, Sarah Booth." His smile was tired. "I've been gone less than a month, and you already have a new beau. Humphrey Tatum. A man who gives interesting gifts."

"This from the man who has a wife. A pregnant wife." My smile took the sting out of the words.

He looked out at the lake. "If Connie were well, I'd divorce her so quickly, her head would spin around."

"I know." That was Coleman's curse. And mine, too. To abandon a sick and mentally ill wife was unacceptable. It was easier to live with unrequited love than guilt.

"The doctor said he'd have the tests back in by Monday. Once a positive diagnosis is made, I'll have a better idea where I stand. Connie's not right mentally. She's . . ." He stopped.

"I'm glad you're back at work."

"Me, too. Maybe we can have lunch and talk about the Tatum case."

"Sure—" But my answer was interrupted by the querulous ring of my cell phone.

"Sarah Booth Delaney, where are you?" Tinkie had recovered and was back in form.

"I'm on my way—"

"They're going to read the will in about sixty seconds."

She was aggravated, but I held the trump card. "Maybe you could drink something and then vomit everywhere, you know, give me a chance to get there." Out of the corner of my eye, I saw Coleman shake his head, but he was smiling.

"Where are you?"

"On the way."

"It doesn't sound like you're driving. There's no wind rushing and all of that. What's going on?"

"I'll tell you when I get there." I shut off the phone and pulled my car keys from my pocket. "Duty calls. The reading of the will."

"I'll see you after the supervisors' meeting."

"I'll count on that." I drove out of the woods before I did something both of us would regret.

By the time I got to Jocko Hallett's office, the sky was gunmetal gray, and a brisk wind was blowing the remaining leaves free of the trees and sending them pell-mell through the air. I ran into the building, propelled by the wind.

Tinkie was waiting for me in an outer office. "They won't let us in," she said testily. "And Oscar has gone out of town on a business trip, and I don't know where."

"He's probably aggrieved that you didn't go home last night."

"I would have, if I'd been in any condition to drive."

I patted her knee. "Who's inside for the will reading?"

"Umbria and her husband. And Humphrey, as well as the lawyer."

"A nice cozy gathering."

"I hope they have a professional cleaning company lined up. I have a feeling blood is going to flow."

There was nothing for it but to have a seat and look through the stack of investment and travel magazines. Jocko's clientele was better heeled than I was. I couldn't afford investments or travel. I scanned the photographs of golden Tuscany and tried to eavesdrop on the loud voices coming from the conference room behind me.

The door opened, and Umbria stormed out, followed by Rutherford. They glared at Tinkie and me and fled the office.

Humphrey came out, his normally debonair façade mildly ruffled. He turned to speak to Jocko.

"The will is ironclad?" he asked.

"T's crossed and i's dotted," Jocko answered. He adjusted his four-in-hand tie, which I thought was a little much for Zinnia.

Jocko spoke to Humphrey, but he addressed all of us in his bass-baritone. "I didn't draw this will up, but Linda Feinstein knew what she was doing. Umbria can bitch and moan all she wants. Allison inherits. Everything."

To my surprise, Humphrey didn't seem elated. His face showed only concern. "The will was sealed?" he asked.

"Yes. I opened it myself."

Tinkie and I stood. Humphrey shook his head as he gazed at us. "This won't look good for Allison."

"Maybe not," Tinkie said. "But all is not lost. Sarah Booth and I have some leads."

I nodded agreement while keeping an eye on the lawyer, who was looking at Tinkie like she was the main course of an expensive menu.

"Mrs. Richmond," Jocko said. "May I have a word with you?"

"Me?" Tinkie was surprised.

"Your husband called this morning. He's hired me to represent him in divorce proceedings."

Tinkie paled. "This is a joke, right?"

Jocko stood taller. "Absolutely not. Oscar is hoping for—"

He didn't get to finish. Tinkie was out the door like a shot.

17

Zinnia's Main Street was jam-packed with cars and shoppers as the pre-Thanksgiving sales began to draw folks in for holiday shopping. I maneuvered through the congested streets, looking for Tinkie's Caddy. I'd already checked Hilltop, and the maid told me Tinkie had come home, checked through the house, and roared away again, sending a spray of gravel flying that cracked one of the front windows.

I also gleaned the fact that Oscar had stayed up all night drinking and had left the house in a thunderous rage and without breakfast. Too late. I should have telephoned Oscar and told him Tinkie was safe at my house. We'd really pissed him off, and I wasn't certain what the consequences might be.

Worried for my friend, I drove out to The Gardens to give Virgie her photographs. I went straight to her room, and when the door creaked open at my knock, I walked in.

There is a distinctive scent that goes with being a proper older lady—floral sachet mixed with a light talc. It is a heady and, sometimes, frightening smell for younger women who fear they may never reach the pinnacle of propriety. I thought of my mother, who always smelled of sandalwood incense and something else dark and mysterious. And Aunt Loulane, who was proper but more of a vanilla extract kind of woman. Virgie was lavender.

"Miss Carrington?" I stepped into the room and glanced around. A slip dangled over a chair, and two sensible shoes lay as if she'd walked out of them. Virgie must have left the room in a big hurry. If she knew I was looking at this disarray, she would be embarrassed. A proper lady never left undergarments lying around.

To my amusement, there was also a pair of oversized muck boots. I couldn't imagine Virgie, in her cashmere twin set and silk skirt, wearing muck boots, but she was, like Gertrude Stromm, an avid gardener.

That was probably where she was. I backed out of the room and pulled the door shut and went to find her among the vivid mums. She was kneeling in khaki slacks and a harvest-hued sweater, a flush of exertion on her cheeks as she dug a well-established buck vine from the middle of a flower bed.

She wiped her forehead with her arm. "Gertrude told me I could have some amaryllis, but this damn vine is making it difficult. Is there something I can help you with?"

"I'm not in a rush. Please, finish what you're doing. Allison sent you some pictures." She attacked the vine again, and in a moment she pulled out a huge tuberous root. She removed stout leather gloves and took the pictures, her face falling into sadness as she looked through them.

"They seemed so happy."

I motioned to a bench beneath the oak, and we took a seat. "Miss. Carrington, I don't want to upset you, but Tinkie and I have unearthed several deaths that may not have been accidental."

"What?" She put the photos beside her leg. "Who?"

"Quentin, of course, was murdered. We also believe Genevieve Reynold's mother was murdered."

"Who would do such a thing to Betty? I didn't know her well at all, but she seemed perfectly delightful. She loved her daughter. Besides, this can't be true. She died in an accidental fall."

"Maybe not." I told her about the shelf in the library.

"Who could mastermind such a terrible thing? And why target Mrs. Reynolds?"

"I believe the murderer intended to kill Genevieve." I told her briefly about my suspicions regarding Mrs. Jenkins and Belinda Loper. "We don't have substantial proof, yet, but when we find it, we're going to be able to clear Allison totally."

"That is such a relief." She picked up the pictures and pointed to one. "Allison wanted roses and calla lilies. Quentin wanted poinsettias. I was able to forge a compromise." A tear traced down her cheek. "You can't begin to imagine how hard this is. I loved those girls like they were my own. Better than their own parents loved them. I saw such a future for Quentin."

Virgie suffered the loss of Quentin as if she were blood, and I felt for Virgie. She wasn't a woman who enjoyed pats and hugs, so I stood up and offered my hand. "We'll find the person who killed Quentin. You have my word on it."

"Where is your partner?" She dried the tears from her face with the back of her hand.

"Tinkie is running down a lead." I glanced around. I'd hoped Tinkie might be at The Gardens, but she was nowhere in sight. I needed to find her. She wasn't the kind of person to do something rash, but she was carrying a heavy load—guilt, remorse, anger, fear, and now what had to feel like betrayal.

"What kind of lead?" Virgie asked.

"Oh, the biggest one." I stepped away. "I'll be in touch."

"Let me know as soon as you find something."

"I'll do that," I promised as I turned and hurried to my car.

I drove through town several times again, hoping to see Tinkie's vehicle at Millie's; or the Cut and Curl; or at her salon; or the coffee shop; or even the library. Tinkie had vanished.

I drove past Jocko Hallett's office on the off chance she'd gone there to kill him. The parking lot was empty. In a last ditch effort, I drove to the bank. I needed to talk to Harold, anyway.

My heart dropped when I scanned the bank parking lot and didn't see Tinkie's car. I'd hoped she'd gone to Oscar and begged forgiveness. Now it was up to me.

I parked and went inside, asking for Harold. I was ushered into his private office. While his secretary brought in a tray of coffee and Scottish shortbread, I watched him pace the room, his dark brow furrowed.

"Oscar has lost his mind," he said as soon as the door closed behind his secretary. "He's divorcing Tinkie."

"I know. I was with her when Jocko dropped the bomb that Oscar had hired him."

"This is insane!"

"I know."

He paced some more. "They love each other."

"I know."

"So Tinkie pitched a drunk. Who hasn't? I've seen Oscar so tanked that Tinkie had to support him."

"I know." I'd become very good at saying that phrase with sincerity, and for the moment, Harold didn't want or need another response.

"What in the hell is wrong with Oscar?"

"I don't know."

Harold sat down across from me and poured the coffee. "What are we going to do?"

"I don't know that, either." Tinkie's lump was a heavy

secret as I stared into Harold's pale eyes. "I'm worried about her."

"I'm worried about them both." He offered the short-bread, and I shook my head.

"I'm going to talk to Oscar."

"Good." He stood up. "You may be able to talk some sense into him."

It was my experience that sense could never be talked into anyone. Still, there was nothing else for it. I rose, too. Harold opened the door and stopped. "Good luck," he said.

As I walked across the marble lobby of the bank, I felt all eyes on me. Business stopped as everyone watched me tap lightly on the door to Oscar's private office.

"Come in." It was a command, not an invitation.

I opened the door and stepped in, closing it firmly behind me. The look he gave me almost boiled my blood.

"What do you want?" He rose slowly, and I could smell the alcohol from where I stood. His suit was rumpled, his hair uncombed.

"Oh, Oscar," I said, walking to his desk.

"Get out of here. This is your fault."

I had his number, though. "Tinkie is afraid." I spoke softly. "She's terrified, and if she's going to get through this, she's going to need both of us."

"She's determined to kill herself, and I for one am not going to sit around and watch."

I walked around his desk and captured his hands in mine. Though he pulled them away, I held on. I was trading on the fact that he was too much of a gentleman to fight with me.

"Tinkie's not going to die." I looked him right in the eye. "I've lost everyone I ever loved. But not Tinkie."

"She has a lump in her breast, and she won't go to the doctor."

"I know." I held his hands tightly. "I know all about it."

"She's committing suicide, and I won't be party to it."

I gripped tighter, until I lost the feeling in my own fingers. "She's not going to die, Oscar. Tinkie believes the lump is healed."

"By some miracle." His tone was scornful. "Wouldn't that be wonderful, if we could just wish bad news away?"

Only yesterday I'd been urging Tinkie to see a surgeon, but suddenly I understood. "Oscar, this isn't about Tinkie's lump. It's about your fear."

He looked at me as if I'd grown a second head. Before he could react, I pushed him into his chair and sat on the edge of the desk, blocking him.

"You have to love Tinkie enough to allow her to seek the type of treatment she feels is best."

"But she'll die."

I put my hands on his shoulders. "You don't know that."

"Cancer is—"

"Tinkie was never diagnosed with cancer."

"But it's a lump."

"And it could be anything. Benign. Some kind of fatty tumor. A fibroid. It could as easily be nothing as something terrible. You and I, both of us, have jumped to the worst possible conclusion. We're wrong. Dead wrong."

He stared into my eyes. "You're saying Tinkie is right to ignore the lump?"

"I'm saying she has a right to do what she wishes, and we should support her."

"You're as crazy as she is." He tried to stand, but I pushed him back down.

"Maybe I am, but I know if we don't stand by Tinkie, we're both going to lose her."

"All I want is for her to get the damn thing biopsied. Is that so wrong?"

I shook my head. "You want to protect her because you love her."

"Yes!"

"But you have to love her enough to support her choice."

"Even when it's wrong?"

I smiled. I'd finally come to understand. "We don't know that it's wrong. Or right. Only Tinkie knows that. She's the one who must bear the consequences of her choice, so it's her right to choose."

Oscar slumped in his chair as if the air had been let out of him. "I want to fight this. I want to take action."

"I know." I cleared my throat. "There's something else."

He looked up at me. "What now?"

"Tinkie says she can't have a child. I think the whole breast lump–doctor business is tied together."

He looked out the window onto a bustling downtown Zinnia. "She blames me. Did she tell you that?"

"Blame is easy to hand out but hard to get rid of."

"I wasn't ready to be a father."

I stood up and walked around his office, taking in the photographs of Sunflower County from the 1920s. To my surprise, I saw Dahlia House, resplendent with fresh paint and pots of flowers. "You and Tinkie have to figure this out together." It wasn't the most original advice, but it was true.

"There's nothing I can do to make it up to her."

"So you've quit trying?" I looked at him. "I never figured you for a quitter, Oscar."

He looked down. "I would change it if I could. I would go back and change it." He shaded his eyes with his hand.

"Maybe that's all Tinkie needs to hear."

"It won't change anything."

"Except she'll know you hurt as much as she does."

"And that's going to fix everything?"

"It's a step in the right direction." I walked back to him and rubbed his back. "Tinkie feels alone. She feels isolated with only her broken dreams and a future that looks pretty lonely."

"She'll never be alone as long as I'm alive."

I hugged him. "Now you need to tell her that."

He stood up. "Do you know where she is?"

"I was hoping she was here, but I didn't see her." My worry returned. "I've looked in all the usual places. We were supposed to go to West Memphis this afternoon."

Oscar frowned. "Did you check The Club?"

"No. I have tried her cell phone, and she isn't answering."

"I'll drive out to The Club. I want to talk to her."

"Good. I'm going to head on to Memphis. I need to talk to Jolene Loper."

He held the door, and we left the bank together. I'd never doubted Oscar's love for his wife. Now he had to convince her of it.

I followed him out of the parking lot, and when he turned to go to The Club, I headed north. It would have been a better trip with Tinkie as a companion, but she needed to focus on her marriage. I could handle an interview with a beautician's sister.

The brown cotton fields stretched out on either side of the road as I headed north. Almost a year had passed since I'd come home and started to work as a private investigator. In that time I'd solved five cases and gained and lost sixty pounds in five-pound increments. I was still wearing the same black jeans and driving the same car. I'd been engaged and unengaged, involved and abandoned. One of the best things that had happened was my partnership with Tinkie.

As the roadster covered the miles, I thought about the past. It was a dirty pleasure with me, and I indulged. Growing up, I'd never considered there was another world other than the Delta. The land was part of my subconscious. My parents discussed it as if it were a family member, and with their deaths, I had become custodian. It marked me and shaped me in small, indefinable ways. The longer I stayed in Sunflower County, the more I would belong to the land.

My drive paralleled the river, and even though I couldn't see it, I knew it. Brown and lazy looking, the Mississippi was strong. The man-made levees contained it, for the moment. But the river's whim could change everything for miles around.

The photographs in Oscar's office had shown cotton being readied for shipment downriver to New Orleans. Down to the mills, where city labor had turned the fiber into thread. Now machines did the work.

At last, I hit the outskirts of Memphis and headed west, toward Arkansas. West Memphis had been the boomtown for the blues. The greats, like Howlin' Wolf and Muddy Waters, had played in juke joints. Time had changed everything—for better and for worse.

The beauty salon I sought was another half hour away, and I watched for my exit. From what I'd learned, Jolene had taken over the salon after Belinda's death.

The shop was called Shear Excellence, and once I was off the interstate, it wasn't hard to find. In fact, it was the only salon I'd ever seen advertised on five billboards. The ads themselves were interesting. Sexy blondes, redheads, and brunettes posed in provocative positions, with the line "Let us 'do' you." Subtlety was indeed a dying art.

When I spotted the shop at last, I was agog. It was huge, more like a Wal-Mart of hair. Belinda Loper must have been raking in the dough. I got out and walked inside. A teased young girl looked at me with contempt. "We don't take walk-ins," she said, "and we're booked through January."

"Is Jolene Loper in?" I forced a smile.

"Ms. Loper is busy. Like I said, we don't take walk-ins."

I smiled and walked past her.

"Hey! Come back here!"

I ignored her shouts and kept walking past chair after chair of stylists working on hair. There were bleach jobs, perms, cuts, blows, curls—everything that could be done to hair. I kept walking, with the young receptionist snipping at me like a rabid Chihuahua.

I spied a door at the end of the salon and opened it without the least hesitation. I was met with a squeal.

"Damn nation! That hurt!"

I rounded the corner and came upon Jolene Loper holding a strip of wax and what had once been someone's very personal hair. A woman reclined on a table covered by a sheet.

I slammed the door in the Chihuahua's face and leaned against it.

"You said it wasn't going to hurt. You're a damn liar." The woman shifted up on her elbows so she could see who'd entered the room. "Hey, if you're here for a bikini wax, don't! It hurts like hell."

"Fashion is supposed to hurt." Jolene dropped the wax into a trash can and snapped off latex gloves. "Quit whining, Beth Anne. If you want to compete with the girls on Montgomery Street, you're going to have to update your act."

"Update is fine. Having my skin torn off is not." Beth Anne swung her legs down and sat up. She was a beautiful woman, if a little overly made-up. "Who are you?" she looked at me.

"A private investigator."

Jolene turned slowly around. "I know you. You're from Zinnia. What are you doing here?"

"I need to talk to you, Jolene. About your sister." There was no easy way to say what had to be said. "I'm working on a case—"

"I paid Belinda's back taxes and all of that."

I shook my head. "It's about her death. About how she died."

Tears formed in Jolene's eyes. "It was horrible. When she didn't answer her cell phone, I came here looking for her. I found her. She'd convulsed on the floor. It was gruesome."

Beth Anne found her jeans and pulled them on. "We were all just plain horrified."

I gave up on trying to be delicate. "I think Belinda may have been murdered. Did she receive any kind of threatening note before she died?"

Jolene's eyes narrowed. "There was a note."

My heart beat faster. "What did it say?"

She frowned. "She put it in her office somewhere. It might still be there."

"Let's take a look."

She opened a door that led to a small office. Sitting down at the desk, she began to pull out drawers and shuffle through the contents. I watched, praying she would find the note.

"Here it is!" She drew out a plain white page, just like the notes Quentin had received. Typed in the same font were the words *It's a great day to dye!*

I looked over the note to Belinda. "Did she ever report this to the police?"

She nodded. "She did, but no one took it seriously. I mean she's a stylist. D-y-e."

"When did she receive the note?"

"Last March. About a week before she inhaled the dry peroxide. She'd gotten another one before that. Something to the effect that her business was in poor taste." She shook her head. "We've heard that all our lives. Poor taste. But that's no reason to kill someone, is it?"

I didn't say anything, but I saw it on her face. She knew. Her sister's death was not an accident.

18

As I drove home, I felt as if a year had passed since I went to the reading of Allison's will. I tried repeatedly to call Tinkie on her cell phone, but there was no answer. She had it turned off. I could only hope that Oscar had found her and that they were together, ironing out the hurt and pain of their relationship.

My fingers hovered on the cell phone pad, and at last, I dialed.

"Sunflower County Sheriff's Office," Dewayne drawled.

"Is the sheriff there?"

"Why, hey, Sarah Booth," he said. "Coleman was here, but he left about ten minutes ago."

"Do you know where he went?" I tried to sound nonchalant.

"Couldn't rightly say. You want me to tell him you're looking for him?"

"No."

"Need some help handling that dangerous bomb you received?"

A flush crept up my neck. "No. Not tonight. See ya, Dewayne." I hung up fast.

Millie's was still open when I hit town, so I stopped for a burger. Most of the tables had been cleared when I sat down, but to my surprise, Marilyn and Lorilee were having dinner at a table in the front. In a far corner, Harold sat with a cup of coffee and some papers.

I'd barely taken my coat off and sat down when Lorilee came over. "Why, Sarah Booth, I heard you had a terrible scare."

Everyone in the place stopped eating to listen.

"Drop it, Lorilee. I need to talk to you about something serious."

"You're the only person I know who could confuse a vibrator with a bomb. Makes me wonder if you'd know what to do with the real thing."

Cutlery was on the table, and I wondered if a stainless knife would work as effectively as a wooden stake. "I'm not an expert in battery-operated toys like you."

Marilyn had risen from her seat, but she didn't move. She only stood and watched.

"I heard you and Tinkie and that newspaper person were all cowering in the house while your gift vibrated around the driveway." She laughed. "That must have been a sight to behold."

Before I could respond, Harold stepped to my side. "Lorilee." He oozed charm. "I haven't consulted your financial statements, but I have a tip for you—invest in sex toys rather than young boys. It's far less expensive in the long run."

Harold assisted me from my seat. "Let's go to my place."

"You, too, Harold?" Lorilee's face contorted in a sneer. "What does she have that fascinates men so?"

"Perhaps it's her kindness, Lorilee. Something you have none of, so are therefore doomed to a life of loneliness."

We left without a backward glance.

Once out in the night, I kissed his cheek. "What a gallant rescue."

"Nothing better than to slay the fire-breathing bitch. Are you still hungry?"

"Yes."

"I have some pheasant soup I made yesterday."

Harold was a gourmet cook, and I appreciated his talents. "That would be lovely."

"Follow me." He got in his Porsche and led me to his home.

When I turned down Harold's oak-lined driveway, I stopped. Rope lights had been wrapped around the tree trunks and limbs, creating a fairyland. I remembered Harold's Christmas party last year. He was a man's man with a great sense of the magical.

He was waiting for me on the porch when I pulled up at the house. "Are you having another holiday party?" I asked.

"Yes. But I keep the lights up year-round." He smiled. "I have a remote. I turned them on for you."

He led the way to the kitchen, and while he heated the soup, I sliced bread. We sipped a dry red wine as we worked. When everything was prepared, we sat at the small kitchen table. "Much cozier than the dining room," I said. The large table there seated twelve.

"Oscar never came back to work today."

"I never found Tinkie." A flicker of concern washed over me, and he must have read it on my face.

"They have to work it out alone."

"I know."

He smiled. "You're a loyal friend, Sarah Booth."

"Tinkie is more than just a friend. She's like a sister to me."

"You've changed her. She's stronger, more confident. You've been good for her."

"Oscar may not feel that way." I ate a bite of the dark pumpernickel bread. "They love each other. It's just that Tinkie's hurting."

Harold picked up my hand and held it gently.

"And you're hurting, too."

I squeezed his fingers. "Have you heard from Rachel?"

"Yes. She's in Mexico."

"Is she going to open some salons with a Latin flavor?"

He laughed. "She's an amazing businesswoman. She combines financial savvy with an unerring ability to know what the public will pay for."

"And you miss her."

"Tremendously."

"Call her."

As if the phone company did my bidding, my cell phone rang. I jumped for it, pulling it from my coat pocket, knowing it was Tinkie.

"Sarah Booth, dahling," Cece drawled, "I've found something that may interest you."

It wasn't that I didn't want to talk to Cece, but I'd so hoped it was Tinkie. I struggled to hide my disappointment. "What did you find?"

"Where are you? I want to show it to you."

"I'm at Harold's." I watched his expression as I talked. He was curious.

"I'm on the way," she said.

Before I could respond, she hung up. I closed the phone and looked at him. "Cece has something to show me, and she's on her way here."

He laughed. "An impromptu party. I'll set another place."

Cece was knocking at the door before I could pour the wine. "The lights are *magnifique*." She breezed in waving a sheaf of papers, took the glass of wine I offered, and slid out of her coat. "Look at these." She thrust the papers into my hand.

"We were just having some soup and bread," Harold said, holding a chair for her.

I took my place and studied the newspaper clippings

about the tragic death of Marilyn's mother, Karla. Cece had pulled up the clips from the Birmingham newspaper, which covered the freak accident in great detail.

Cece's attention had fallen on the soup, and she attacked the food with great gusto. "Harold, this is delicious. I'm impressed. I'm doing a column on holiday food for the Thanksgiving issue. I'd love to feature you."

Ignoring Cece's chatter, I read the articles. I was on the third story when I found what I wanted. Birmingham police officer Clyde Marshall talked about the threatening note that Karla Jenkins had received only the week before her death. *The penalty for fornication is stoning.*

I grabbed Cece's hand. "Thank you, Cece. You found the note. Marilyn's mother was definitely murdered." The full impact hit me, and I grasped Cece's hand in mid-swallow of soup.

"There's a serial killer on the loose."

Cece rolled her eyes. "Why do you think I rushed over here, dahling?"

I left Harold with orders to call Rachel. Were I not in the middle of a case, with a horse and a hound to care for, I would have been on a flight to Acapulco. Harold was just being hardheaded.

Even though it was after eleven o'clock, I tried Tinkie's cell again. Still no answer. I drove by Hilltop, but the house was dark. Maybe they were home, sleeping.

When I got to Dahlia House, I stepped over a small package in front of the door. I'd had it with Humphrey and his wicked surprises. I kicked the bow-laden box hard enough to send it careening into the shrubs by the side of the porch. I wasn't going to be suckered yet again by the mad humper.

When I got to the barn, Reveler was miffed at his late dinner. He turned his butt to me and ate. Sweetie, too, was pissed. She came out, sniffed my leg, and squatted to pee.

No one was happy to see me. I slipped in the back door and fed her some meat loaf, hoping to win her over. No such luck. She ate and went to sleep in the dining room.

Exhausted, I tiptoed up the stairs. I didn't have the strength for a confrontation with Jitty. She'd be mad, too.

I stepped onto the second-floor landing, expecting to hear her voice. There was only silence. I hurried to my bedroom, shucked off my clothes, and slipped beneath the quilts. I was asleep almost before I could turn off the bedside light.

My sleep was tormented by the dream cries of a baby. I awoke the next morning to the ringing telephone. Squinting against the late morning sun, I answered.

"Sarah Booth, this is Tammy Odom."

Tammy, also called Madame Tomeeka, was an old friend with psychic abilities. "What's wrong?" I wasn't psychic, but I could detect worry in her voice.

"Where's Tinkie?"

"At home." On second thought, I added, "Isn't she?"

"I had the strangest dream. Tinkie was . . . afraid."

"Have you talked to her?"

"No, that's why I'm calling you. I tried to call her this morning, but she didn't answer at the house or on her cell phone."

This wasn't good news. Tinkie wasn't the kind of person to make her friends worry. "I'll go over to her house."

"Will you call me?"

"As soon as I know something."

I'd just replaced the telephone when it rang again. Coleman's low tones made me catch my breath as he said my name.

"Have you seen Tinkie lately?" he asked.

"No. I'm getting worried about her. I'm on my way over to Hilltop to see Oscar."

"Don't bother. He's standing right here. She didn't come home last night, and he's beyond frantic."

"Shit." It wasn't a ladylike expression, but it pretty much summed up the situation. "I'm on my way to the sheriff's office. Keep Oscar there. I want to talk to him."

"Hurry. He says he's going home to call the governor. He wants the National Guard to help hunt."

"Detain him." I hung up the phone, grabbed some clothes, and rushed out of the house. Sweetie Pie gave me a condemning look, and Reveler bucked and went running to the back of his pasture. I couldn't help it. I had to find Tinkie.

I floored it as I sped to the courthouse. It was Saturday morning, a busy time for downtown Zinnia. My high-speed passing created a tide of ill will, as pedestrians shot me the finger and shook fists at me. Too bad.

By the time I ran into the sheriff's office, I was panting. Coleman nodded at me, but I turned my attention to Tinkie's husband. "Oscar!"

He took one look at me and almost cried. "Did she say anything to you?" he asked.

This was touchy. I drew him into Coleman's office and shut the door. "I never spoke with her, Oscar. Did you talk to her at all yesterday?"

He shook his head. "She called me yesterday morning, before I talked to you. I didn't take her call. I was mad."

I put my arm around him. "I know. I know."

"You were with her. Did she say anything?"

This was going to be hard. "The last time I saw her, we were in Jocko Hallett's office. He told her you'd hired him for the divorce. She was pretty upset."

"I didn't mean it. I never intended to divorce Tinkie. I was just mad, and I wanted to hurt her the way she'd hurt me."

"We have to figure out where she went. Once we find her, you can talk to her, and everything will be okay."

"Happily ever after" wasn't my normal prognosis on

relationships, but I did believe it for Tinkie and Oscar. They were meant for each other.

"I've called everywhere. Now her father is terribly upset."

"He hasn't heard from her?" I'd hoped Tinkie would call her daddy.

"Not a word." Oscar sat down in a chair and put his face in his hands. "This is all my fault. Tinkie's been impossible. I've been worried for weeks, but I shouldn't have reacted in anger."

"It takes two to tango, Oscar. This can't *all* be your fault. But enough whining, let's find her." I opened the door and signaled Coleman in.

He stepped into the doorway, and though I was worried sick about Tinkie, I couldn't help but feel a thrill. He was back. No matter that he was married, at least we could see each other, talk, solve cases. Find Tinkie.

"We're both worried." I gave him a rundown of what had occurred, leaving out the baby issue. Coleman had enough pregnancy problems of his own, and it was Tinkie and Oscar's secret, not mine.

"You've checked all the usual places?" Coleman asked.

"I don't know where she could be," Oscar said. "I've tried her friends, her family, her usual haunts."

I remembered Madame Tomeeka's dream. I didn't want to say anything to Oscar, but I needed to talk to Tammy. "I'll check around. Call me on my cell." I darted out the door and drove through town like a bat out of hell for the second time.

Tammy met me at the door before I could knock. Her house smelled of cedar and a roast that bubbled in the oven. The scent was so homey and comforting that I felt my shoulders begin to relax.

"Sit down," she said, and the expression on her face made me tense again. Tammy was not a charlatan. She had a serious link to another plane, and though many people came to her for a reading of their future as an entertainment, I knew she had a gift.

"Tell me."

"I'm worried." Her hands rubbed each other on top of the table. "In the dream, Tinkie was afraid. She was in a glass, or something like a bell jar. She kept putting her hands against the glass and pushing, but it wouldn't move. She called out, but no one could hear her."

"Did you have a sense of where she was?" If I'd been concerned about Tinkie before, now I was terrified. There was a serial killer on the loose, and we'd been tracking him or her.

Tammy shook her head. "It's confusing. The dream was so vivid. There were rulers all around her and shelves and shelves of books. Like a library. There was a table of cutlery, like knives and forks and things."

Dreams were never straight-up informative messages. Library shelves could mean anything from knowledge to decoration. Tinkie had a huge library at her home. As did Genevieve Reynolds. And Harold. And me, for that matter. Lots of older homes had libraries that were the accumulation of generations of readers.

"Is there anything else?"

She worried her hands again. "That's all I remember. Except Tinkie was wearing a navy suit and a white blouse with a bow tie."

"She's been wearing the uniform of the well-bred lady for several days now. It's the case."

Tammy nodded. "It didn't suit her."

I had a call to make. "Thank you, Tammy. I'll let you know as soon as I find her."

"If I have another vision, I'll call."

I hugged her tight. "Day or night."

I jumped in the roadster and burned rubber as I left. Cell phone in hand, I dialed Oscar. I didn't give him a chance to even say hello.

"Did Tinkie get any kind of note?" I asked.

"Note?"

"Like a threatening note. Like someone telling her to stop snooping. Something like that." I tried not to let on to Oscar how concerned I was, but my voice gave me away.

"You think someone has kidnapped her because she's snooping?"

"Oscar, did you check your mail?"

"I'm at home. Let me see."

There was the sound of papers shuffling. I was headed toward Hilltop at ninety miles an hour.

"There's nothing here except magazines and bills. Have you checked your mail, Sarah Booth?"

I did a 180 in the road and pointed the roadster toward Dahlia House. "No," I said. "I'll call you if I find something."

On the way home, I dialed Coleman. "This could be serious," I said. I told him about the notes and my theory about a serial killer. There was a long moment of silence.

"If this is true, Sarah Booth, Tinkie could be in real trouble."

"The killer always sends at least one note. Oscar says nothing came to Hilltop. Let me check my mail." I tore down the driveway, creating a cyclone of fallen sycamore leaves in my wake. As I skidded to a halt at the front door, I said, "I'll call you in a minute."

A week's accumulated mail was piled on my desk, and I went through it at lightning pace. Bills, bills, bills, a few advertisements, and more bills. Not a single strange envelope. I breathed a sigh of relief and then remembered the package on my doorstep. Humphrey. Was it possible Humphrey was the killer?

I dashed out the front door and jumped the balustrade to land in the huge azaleas. It took a little rooting around, but I found the package. It was white with a white bow. I opened it quickly.

There was nothing inside except a single sheet of white paper. My hands trembled as I unfolded it. The laser-printed words were crystal clear. *Poke your nose where it doesn't belong and it'll get chopped off.*

I staggered back against the porch. My heart was thrumming. The threat had been made against me, but it was Tinkie who'd been taken.

Legs wobbling, I went inside to call Coleman.

19

Coleman poured a hefty portion of Jack over ice and handed the glass to me. To my shame, my hand was shaking so badly, the bourbon sloshed over my fingers. I put the glass down and tried to breathe.

"She's going to be okay." Coleman knelt in front of me, his forehead furrowed. "You have to get a grip. Tinkie is going to be fine."

It was a nice sentiment, but Tinkie was missing, and a murderer was still at large—a murderer who'd warned me about my nosiness. "Why didn't I read the note last night?"

"Sarah Booth, stop it!"

The harshness of his tone was as effective as a slap. I gulped in some air and sat up straight. He was right. Wallowing in guilt and doubt wasn't going to help anyone.

"Okay." I inhaled again. "Okay, what can we do?"

"All of the victims you've named received more than one note, is that right?"

I tried to think. "We're not certain about Karla, Marilyn Jenkins's mother. There was only one mention of a note in the newspaper article."

"It appears to me that the killer kills as a last resort. Once the victim has been warned and the warning unheeded, then he or she feels forced to kill."

"Most serial killers are white males in their thirties." I'd read a few profiler novels. Tinkie might accuse me of not being a reader, but it wasn't true.

Coleman actually smiled. "Perhaps we can find Hannibal Lecter and ask him for some tips."

My smile was shaky, but it was there, and it was rewarded by a gentle touch on my cheek. Coleman knew not to push it, though. Too much kindness and I'd crumple in a heap of self-pity.

"So what should we do?"

"Begin to figure out what all the victims had in common. We can't jump to the conclusion that Tinkie is in danger at all. It could be that she's simply gone away to think through her marriage."

"If that's the case, I'm going to kill her when I find her."

"I'll help." He stood up. "Karla Jenkins, Quentin McGee, Betty Reynolds, Belinda Loper. We have to find the common thread."

"They're all women."

"A good point. But there has to be something else."

"If Tinkie is in trouble, this is a change in the killer's method. This would be the first time one person received a note and a second person was . . . involved." I couldn't say hurt or killed. "I believe Betty Reynolds was killed accidentally. Genevieve was the target."

"Now you're thinking, Sarah Booth." He paced the parlor. "I agree. The dowels on that shelf were deliberately cut. The killer expected Genevieve to replace the books she'd taken down."

Though I would normally bask in Coleman's praise, my heart was too frozen with fear for Tinkie to bask. "We have to find her."

"Tell me Tammy's dream again."

I told him about the glass, the sense of a bell jar, of Tinkie crying out but not being heard.

"Is there any place like that?"

I shook my head. I'd already given it some thought. "Like a small solarium or sunroom, maybe. There's one at Hilltop, but Oscar would know if she was there."

"I'll take the note for fingerprints, but so far the killer has been very careful. There weren't prints on the shelf or on any of the other notes."

"This killer is careful and clever."

"And resourceful, if Quentin's death is any indication. He or she bides his time until the murder can be set up exactly as he wants it."

We were triggering each other. "The killer punishes. Death is the ultimate punishment."

"Punishes for perceived crimes? Injustices?"

It struck me with such force, I must have looked like a beached guppy. "For social infractions!"

His eyes widened. "Dragging her family's name through the mud!"

"Crushed by the weight of her own knowledge—that's arrogance or pride."

"A good time to d-y-e. A slam at the things Belinda Loper was doing in her salon. Things that might be thought of as immoral."

"Oh, my God! I'm nosey. I'm tending to others' business. So the killer takes my best friend and partner."

Coleman picked up the note, which he'd placed in a plastic bag. "Let me get this checked. We may get lucky."

I was torn between pushing him out the door and begging him to stay. I didn't want to be alone, but the fingerprints were more important than my fears.

"Hurry," I said as I walked him to the door. "Call me as soon as you hear anything."

"What are you going to do?"

"Get with Cece and see if she knows of any houses with solariums."

He stepped toward me, then stopped. "I don't want you to be alone. Stay with Cece."

"What about Oscar?" I stepped closer to him. I wanted the comfort of his touch, nothing more. Because of the man Coleman was, he made me feel stronger, better. I wanted to lean my forehead against his chest and let him hold me, just to share his strength. But I would not.

"The less Oscar knows, the better. For the moment." He circled me in his arms and pulled me against him. I resisted, but only for a second. Right or wrong, this was what I wanted, what I needed. I felt the strength of his chest, inhaled his scent, remembering our so very brief moments of physical contact. "I'm worried about you, Sarah Booth."

"I'm okay." There was nothing else to say. "We'll find Tinkie, and we'll find the killer."

"I'm going to make some calls to West Memphis, Rosedale, and Jackson and see what I can find out about the Loper, Reynolds, and Jenkins 'accidental' deaths."

I stepped back from him and walked outside. The cold air brought me to my senses, and I managed a smile for Coleman. "Tinkie. That's all that matters right now."

"After we find her, we need to talk, Sarah Booth. There are things you need to know. About my situation."

My heart rocketed around my chest, but I hung on to my smile. "After we find her."

He waved and walked to his car. I waited until his patrol car was at the road before I drove to the newspaper and the busy, busy typing of Cece Dee Falcon, society editor.

"Do you have any photographs of Harold, hopefully doing the wild thing?" she asked, without looking up. She kept typing with one hand and held the other out for the cup of coffee I always brought. "Harold gave me his recipe for pheasant soup, but he refuses to let a photographer stop by his house and snap him. I need a photograph. What can you come up with?"

"Cece."

The tone of my voice froze her. She stopped typing and looked up. "What? What's wrong? Is it Sweetie Pie?"

"It's Tinkie."

Cece was made up with all the latest fall colors, but her skin tone faded to a pasty white. "What's wrong with Tinkie?"

"She's missing. I'm afraid she may have been kidnapped by a serial killer."

Cece looked at me, shifting her head so that she got me from several angles. "You're not kidding, are you? Because if this is one of your practical jokes, I'm going to break all of your fingers."

"It's not a joke." I sank on top of a stack of old newspapers that cluttered the only half-empty chair in her office. "She's been gone since yesterday morning. Oscar is frantic. I'm—" A sob caught me unexpectedly. I looked up and saw the compassion in Cece's face. It was my undoing. My next words were lost in a wail. I stood up, arms hanging at my sides, and just blubbered. My terror was paralyzing.

Lucky for me, Cece isn't short on courage. She dropped the blinds in her office so the curious reporters couldn't see in, sat me down in her chair, and lifted my chin so that I looked into her eyes. "If you don't stop it, dahling, I'm going to take your picture and put it on the society page. Too bad Halloween is over."

Cece never made idle threats. I managed to choke back the wailing, but I couldn't stop the tears. Cece handed me several tissues and sat on the edge of her desk. "Go on and cry," she said with a sigh. "The worst thing you can do is bottle up emotions."

About five minutes passed before I could manage to collect myself. "Thanks, Cece."

"Don't mention it. *The Crying Game, The Crying Room,* what's the difference in a town like Zinnia?"

I matched her wispy smile as I wiped the last of the tears from my face. "I'm sorry. My emotions just caught up with me."

"Tell me all about it."

So I did. I went through everything, including my last conversation with Coleman. "Can you make some calls to the newspapers in Rosedale, Jackson, and West Memphis? The reporters who worked the case may have details that were never put in print. Then we need to make a list of every building we know that has a solarium . . . maybe an Internet check, if that's possible."

"Yes and yes. My only regret is that while the serial killer was on the job, he didn't finish what he started on Lorilee Brewer."

"That's right." It was a tidbit of information I hadn't recalled. "Maybe Lorilee heeded his warning?" I felt something click in my brain. "She's the only one who escaped, isn't she?"

"The only one we can put our finger on. Of course, we have no idea who else has been threatened and who complied with the threats." Cece's perfect eyebrows arched. "Shall we pay Lorilee a visit?"

"I'd rather spend an hour with a viper."

"Oh, Sarah Booth, where is your sense of adventure? Come along with me, and we'll interview her. I assure you, she'll answer every question you want to ask."

I followed behind Cece as she led the way out of the newspaper. "How can you make that promise?"

Cece threw a dazzling smile over her shoulder. "For Tinkie, I'm quite willing to bring out the big guns. Just wait and see."

*   *   *

Since Cece was ready for action, we decided to leave the computer research until after our interrogation of Lorilee. I drove while Cece reapplied her China Rouge lipstick and freshened her make-up.

We arrived at The Gardens, and Cece led the way unerringly into the bar, a room dominated by dark wood, crystal, and mirrors. Lorilee sat alone drinking a Bloody Mary.

"How many notes regarding your grass-stained knees did you receive?" Cece asked as she slipped into the chair beside Lorilee.

"Whatever are you talking about?" Lorilee glanced over at me with complete disdain.

"Dahling, I'm working on my Sunday spread. How interesting that you've graced Zinnia with your presence for almost a week. That's worthy of a story. Of course, I'll have to dig up the past. Let's see, how old was that child? Thirteen?"

The color fled Lorilee's face. "You're as bad as Quentin."

"And I'm still alive and writing." Cece tapped her bright red fingernails on the table. "And I'm waiting, which lends itself to creative imaginings."

"If I tell you about the note, will you promise you won't print anything about me in the newspaper?"

To my amazement, Lorilee was a pushover when it came to bad press. I drew up a chair and sat down to listen.

"I promise that your story will wane in my interest." Cece signaled Gertrude to bring another round of drinks.

"Are these two women bothering you?" Gertrude asked Lorilee.

"No. Just bring the drinks." Lorilee looked at Cece. "I want it in writing."

"How boring." Cece drew a pad from her purse and scratched out three lines of an agreement. She signed it and held it so Lorilee could read it. "Now tell us."

"What difference does it make?"

Cece leaned in so that her face was only inches from Lorilee's. "It means a lot to me. So talk."

"I got a note telling me something to the effect that I'd be punished for fooling around with an underage boy. I thought it was amusing and probably written by the young man's high school girlfriend. So, I didn't stop." She stirred her drink with a celery stalk. "About a week later, someone rigged the riding lawn mower to start via remote. It came right at me—chased me, in fact. I was almost killed."

"What did the police say?"

"Something about spontaneous starting. They say it happens sometimes around high-voltage power lines."

"Do you live under a power line?" I was having difficulty believing that people were so foolish.

"No, of course not. Charlie and I wouldn't live by such an eyesore. Charlie was threatening divorce. The police believed he tried to kill me, to get out of any alimony. I convinced Charlie to give me a second chance, and then I convinced the police the lawn mower incident was an accident." She ate her celery stick in one large bite.

"Tell us about the notes you received," I pressed.

"Note." She was bored and didn't bother to hide it.

"Just one note?"

She looked at me as if I'd grown horns. "One was all it took. I got the message."

"And you broke off the relationship with the boy?"

She sighed heavily. "After the lawn mower incident, I did. The boy had grown rather . . . demanding. It was best to break it off before it got public and ugly."

"So how did Quentin find out about it?"

"That bitch Genevieve dug it up somehow. Bank transactions or something. She followed the money that I put in an account for Jos—the boy."

"You wouldn't happen to have kept the note?" I asked.

"Are you insane? What? You think I'd frame it to remind Charlie of the whole incident?"

She had a point. "How long ago?"

"Last March. Listen that's the whole story."

Cece looked at me. "Was the note mailed to you?"

She thought about it. "Yes. From Memphis. I remember it was in the mail when Charlie brought it in. He thought it was an invitation to a party."

"And you never wondered who'd sent it?" I was frankly amazed. Lorilee was the kind of woman who would have turned heaven and earth to find the person responsible for her fall.

"Oh, I tried to find out, but how could I? It was typewritten. There wasn't a clue." She drained her drink and signaled for another one. "You know. It was just like the one Tinkie received."

Neither Cece nor I moved. Dust motes spiraled in the open window. There was the clink of ice in glasses.

"What's wrong? Didn't Tinkie show you the note?"

"When did you see Tinkie?" My voice was normal.

"Yesterday evening."

Lorilee was stupid but cunning. I didn't want to give anything away. "At The Club?"

Her gaze narrowed as she studied me. "What's going on? Tinkie didn't tell you about the note?"

"Where was Tinkie?" My voice must have carried an implied threat, because Lorilee looked down at her empty glass. "She was here. She'd come to talk to Marilyn about something."

Cece and I rose in unison. "Do you remember what the note said?" I asked.

"She didn't tell you." There was satisfaction in her tone. "Why don't you ask her? Did you two have a falling-out?"

Cece, who had large, strong hands, grasped the front of Lorilee's blouse and twisted. "You'd better pray that we get a chance to ask Tinkie. Now if you know what it said, tell us."

She shook her head, afraid to say anything. "She didn't show it to me. She told me about it. She was upset. She said she'd figured something out, but she didn't say what."

Dread chilled my spine. "She said she figured something out?"

Lorilee nodded. She was too smart to show her superior attitude. "That's all I know."

Cece let her go, and we left, headed back to the car. For a long moment we sat in the shade of the beautiful oaks in silence. Finally, Cece reached across the seat and touched my arm. "Do you think she figured it out?"

I nodded. "Why didn't she call me for backup?"

"It would seem that both of you got notes at the same time. Do you think that means that the killer will come after you?"

"I don't care."

Cece patted my arm. "You have to care. If we're going to find Tinkie alive, you have to care."

I looked at her but saw only a quick montage of Tinkie, laughing and tossing her glitzed hair, holding Chablis in her arms, ordering up French toast and coffee at my kitchen table. Tinkie, whose joy and verve for life had made mine so much better.

"Let's work on those newspaper articles."

"Sarah Booth, would you consider putting something in the newspaper saying you were withdrawing from the case?" Cece watched my profile as I backed out of The Gardens and headed back to the *Dispatch*.

"Do you think I should?" It was an angle I hadn't considered.

"It might buy some time. If you simply say you're retiring from private investigation, then maybe the killer will stop. I mean, if it's true that Lorilee stopped with the weed-eater boy and she never got another note, this might be a way to stop the killer from hurting Tinkie."

It was possible. "But Lorilee wasn't taken hostage."

Cece didn't say it, but we both knew if Tinkie had seen the killer's face, there was nothing I could do that would save her.

"Let's put the story in the paper," I agreed. "It can't hurt, and it might help." I pulled up in front of the newspaper. Cece started to get out, but I grasped her hand. "Why do you think Tinkie didn't call me and tell me she'd figured it out?"

Cece didn't hesitate. "She was trying to save you, dahling. Remember all the other times she's saved you? Now's your chance to pay her back."

She got out of the car and walked to the newspaper door. "Aren't you coming?" she asked.

"Yes." I answered her question and my own. Yes, I would find Tinkie and save her.

20

Cece's ability to do a global search of Southeastern newspapers for a specific topic was awe inspiring. The *Memphis Commercial Appeal* covered Belinda Loper's death as a type of Ripley's Believe It or Not! item: BEAUTICIAN DYES INHALING DRY PEROXIDE. Too cute to pass up. Because of the humorous angle, there appeared to be no real investigation. Belinda was found on the floor of her shop, poisoned to death by the chemicals normally found in a beauty parlor. No other papers even covered it.

Karla Jenkins was a different matter. She got coverage around two states and in national real estate journals. Her death was treated with sympathy and a kind of "Eek! That could happen to me" horror.

Her body was found beneath several rocks that had fallen from a steep hillside in an exclusive neighborhood in Birmingham, Alabama. The coroner's examination showed death by a sudden blow to the head. The rock, of course. There was no reason to regard Karla's death as foul play. Other than the strange fact that the body was nude, with the exception of a pair of Victoria's Secret pom-pom stilettos. The police deduced, accurately enough, that Karla was planning on enjoying a tryst when a small avalanche tumbled down the hillside and killed her. There was no evidence that anyone started the rock slide, and no great attempt was made to find her tryst partner.

"I guess the police viewed it as one of those incidents 'when good sex goes bad,'" Cece said.

I put a hand on her arm. "While you're doing this, I need to talk to Marilyn."

"Call her." She waved at her phone. "I'll look for Genevieve's mother's obit. Rosedale only has a weekly, so I'll check around the area."

"Thank you." I blew her a kiss as I sat at her desk and picked up the phone. Information gave me Marilyn's home number, and with a bit of finagling, I managed to get her housekeeper to give me her cell number, which I dialed.

She answered in what sounded to me to be a fearful tone.

"Marilyn, I need to talk to you."

"Have you seen Tinkie? She was supposed to meet me for breakfast. She never showed."

"Tinkie may be in serious trouble." Where I hadn't wanted to tell Lorilee the time of day, I didn't mind sharing this information with Marilyn.

"I've been so worried. She told me about the note."

I was momentarily stunned. "She did? What did it say?"

"She didn't tell you?" Marilyn asked.

I managed to control my temper. "I haven't seen Tinkie. Please, tell me what the note said, if you can remember."

"Oh, I remember," Marilyn said. '*Birds of a feather flock together—then die together.*' Those are the exact words. I'm terrified for her. You know, Mother received one of those enigmatic notes before she died."

I knew. It made my heart squeeze painfully in my chest.

"Did your mom receive more than one note?" I hoped she'd say six or eleven or thirty.

"I don't recall but one." Marilyn paused. "There could have been more, but I only found that note after the fact. Mother had stuck it in one of her drawers."

"Typewritten?"

"Yes."

"How long before she was . . . died?"

"About two weeks, judging from the postmark."

"Mailed in Memphis?"

"Yes, how did you know?"

I ignored her question. "Was Tinkie's note mailed?"

"No, it was hand delivered. She found it tucked in the windshield wiper of her Cadillac."

"Do you know where she was going when she left you?"

Marilyn considered her answer. "She was very excited. She said she'd figured something out and that you were going to be so proud of her. That's all I remember."

Her words were like small stones striking my soul. Tinkie didn't have to do anything to make me proud. Especially not risk her life. "Where were the two of you?"

"At The Gardens."

"And after she left, what did you do?"

"I went to my room for a rest. Lorilee is driving me insane. I had to get away from her, so I left word at the front desk that I had a headache and was not to be disturbed. You know, I'd rather not have a friend than have to put up with her."

"Have you received any notes?" I heard the thrum of my pulse in my ears as I waited for her answer.

"One."

It was clear she was reluctant to talk about it, but I had to push. "What did it say?"

"*Ashes to ashes and trash to trash—you will be canned.*"

"When did you get the note?"

"About three weeks ago."

"What have you done?" Three weeks had passed, and Marilyn was still walking around unharmed. She had to have done something.

"I called up the chemical company and told them I wasn't interested in selling my land to them."

I bit my lip. "You took immediate action to cancel that plan?"

"I'm not an idiot, Sarah Booth. Mother was murdered. I knew it, though I couldn't convince the police. Mother flaunted her sexual conquests. She was shameless, having sex in houses she was supposed to be selling. She disregarded that note, and she died. I wasn't going to be next."

"Thanks, Marilyn." I had to get off the phone. I hung up and turned to Cece. She held up several sheets of paper she'd printed.

Her voice was angry. "Mrs. Reynolds's death was ruled accidental. No one even examined the bookshelf. It was treated as a freak accident, just like all the others."

"I hope Coleman has more success than we did," I said.

"Maybe we should pay him a visit." Cece picked up her coat as I filled her in on everything I'd learned from Marilyn.

Coleman's news was even grimmer than what I'd learned. He closed the door to his office as he told us that the investigations into all three murders had been slipshod. "It was assumed that the women had no enemies. The authorities were never told about the threatening notes," he said.

The fact that his gaze slid from mine every time we connected told me a lot about how worried he was for Tinkie.

"Marilyn and Lorilee both said Tinkie figured something out. That she was very excited." I took a deep breath. "Do you think she confronted the killer?"

"So quickly? That would imply the killer is in Zinnia," Coleman said.

"I know. But Tinkie's note and mine were hand delivered."

He nodded. "The question is, do we believe the murderer is a resident of Sunflower County or a visitor?"

"Visitor," Cece said without hesitation. "This all came to town with Quentin. Before she arrived, we'd never heard of these notes or any of it."

I nodded agreement. Coleman smiled. "On the surface I'd have to agree, but there's not enough evidence to view that as a fact."

"My gut tells me that whoever is responsible for all of this blew into town for Quentin's funeral." I couldn't sit still. "That's where we need to start looking."

Coleman sat on the edge of his desk. "I agree. It's where *I* start looking. Sarah Booth has already been threatened. Cece, I don't want to have to assign a deputy to watch over you. It would be best if you both took a little vacation."

"Are you insane?" I jumped to my feet. "Tinkie is in danger. I'm not going anywhere."

Coleman only looked amused. "I figured you'd say that. So I'm going to assign Gordon and Dewayne to watch you."

"I don't want a bird dog on my tail. The deputies should be out looking for Tinkie."

"I can't afford to lose you, Sarah Booth. So we'll do it my way."

I didn't have a choice. I looked at Cece, who was studying her feet and trying hard not to smile. She thought it was amusing. "If Tinkie did figure this out, she must have found out something I don't know. I intend to find out what, and I don't want one of your deputies interfering."

"There's a fine line between interfering and protecting," Coleman said. "I'll tell them to stay on the protecting side."

He wasn't going to change his mind, and I wasn't going to get any support from Cece. "Do you have any leads?" I asked.

"Nothing you don't already know. She was last seen at The Gardens B&B."

I nodded. "Cece and I will follow the solarium clue and see what we can turn up."

Coleman stood up and came to me. He didn't care that Cece was sitting right there. He drew me to my feet and circled me in his arms. "I'm not trying to thwart you, Sarah Booth. I'm trying to protect you and find Tinkie."

His arms were warm, but his words were cold. I stiffened and stepped back. "Tinkie is in this because of me. If something happens to her, it's my fault. Keep that in mind when you try to corral me."

I walked out, and Cece hurried after me.

"That was cold, Sarah Booth. The man is only trying to protect you."

"And you were *such* a support system." I kept two paces ahead of her.

"Because I agree with Coleman and what he's trying to do."

We got in the car, and as I adjusted the rearview mirror, I saw Gordon Walters pull in behind us in the patrol car. Coleman had put words into action already.

"What about solariums?" I asked.

"The Memphis paper did an article several years ago on the resurgence of sunrooms. I can look it up if you'll drop me at the newspaper."

"I'll be glad to." I eyed the attractive leopard-print hat she was wearing. A plan had come to mind.

Wheeling into Dahlia House with Gordon not-so-subtly on my tail, I saw the bright purple ribbon on the package that was leaned against the front door. I sighed. Humphrey

had struck again, or at least I hoped it was Humphrey. I'd
have to open the package to be certain.

I darted up the steps and snatched it up as I stepped inside and closed the door. Gordon parked behind the
roadster and kicked back in his seat for a wait. I had an
urge to go out and fuss at him, but he was only obeying orders. It was Coleman I was mad at.

I tore the ribbon off the package and dumped the contents on the parlor floor. At first, I didn't comprehend
what all the red and blue Lycra meant, but as I untangled
arms and legs, I saw the emblem of Wonder Woman.
There was even a cape. I shook out the costume and
watched the note drift to the floor.

*Women call me the "man" of steel. Let's bump superpowers!
Humphrey (Call me right away. I have news.)*

I put the costume back in the box and tapped the note
on my palm. Humphrey might have a lead. It was worth a
try. I made the call and waited for Gertrude Stromm to
connect me to his room.

"Why, Sarah Booth," he said. "Did I finally hit on your
weakness? Superheroes."

"What news do you have?"

"Allison had a visitor this morning."

"The Easter Bunny?" I was aggravated.

"No, Miss Carrington. She stopped by to say good-bye.
She said she had to get back to the school, that she'd gotten some calls and was needed at home."

"That's the big news?" My temper sizzled. What a de-
ceptive move.

"There's more. I'd like to deliver it in person."

"The only thing you're ever going to deliver in person
to me might be a pizza. What's the big news?"

"Testy, testy." He laughed. "Call your source at the hospital. Umbria Clark's husband, Rutherford, was taken in
by ambulance about half an hour ago. He'd been stabbed

in the chest, and I heard he was singing like a bird, telling all of Umbria's dirty little secrets."

I was surprised; it was a great lead. "Thanks, Humphrey."

"How about a date?" he asked.

"You can't be serious."

"Very. We could stage a kinky little scene where you find a necklace of kryptonite and bring me to my knees, if you get my meaning."

I didn't bother to respond. I hung up and ran out the door. I didn't care if Gordon followed me to the hospital.

Doc Sawyer's gaze pierced me as he sat behind his desk and waited. "Now tell me the truth. No foolishness."

"Tinkie is missing."

"I thought as much."

Doc had a million sources—far more than I did—but I was curious about this one. "How did you know?"

"Harold called about an hour ago and asked me to call in something to calm Oscar. In all of my years of treating the Richmonds, I've never known Oscar to need a sedative. I knew it had to be bad. How long has she been missing?"

It wasn't jeopardizing the case to talk to Doc. He'd taken care of both me and Tinkie when we were children. "More than twenty-four hours."

He didn't have to say that the longer she was gone, the less likely it was that she'd come back alive. "So what are you looking for here at the hospital?" he asked.

There were ethics and laws, and I was going to ask Doc to violate a bunch of them. "Rutherford Clark was brought in here. I heard he was stabbed and that he was talking a lot."

"All of that is true."

"Did you hear what he said?"

Doc considered. He got up and poured a cup of his terrible coffee. "I heard a good bit of it. I was the attending physician in the emergency room."

Thank goodness. Now all I had to do was pry the information out of him. "Doc, if Umbria McGee Clark is the killer, she may be holding Tinkie alive. What did Rutherford say?"

"A lot of things." He paced the small office. "You've put me in a spot, Sarah Booth."

"I know."

"I could lose my license."

"I could lose my partner. I'm not being melodramatic."

He sat back in his chair and looked out the small window onto the emergency room parking lot. One scraggly pine grew by the potholed tarmac. It wasn't much of a view for a man who'd dedicated fifty years to medicine, but it was his view. I was asking him to put all those years in question.

"Rutherford was stabbed in the chest. The knife penetrated to the scapula, but I'd say it wasn't a serious attempt on his life. In fact, he's saying he fell on the knife."

"Could he have?"

Doc chuckled. "No, he was stabbed. Most likely by Umbria."

My pulse increased. Umbria had become a very good suspect, in my book. "What did he say?"

"Only that Umbria had threatened to divorce him. He was rambling, cursing, bemoaning his fate for marrying an heiress who would never inherit, that kind of stuff."

"Why did Umbria stab him?"

"I'm not clear about that. It was a heated argument. There was an issue about Rutherford having other girlfriends."

"I'll say. He has a lust for bimbos." I thought about my bar fight with his lady friends. "But surely Umbria has known about the girlfriends for years. He didn't exactly make a secret of it."

Doc shook his head. "I was in there when Umbria came in. It was one of the strangest things I've ever witnessed."

"Tell me."

"She bent over him on the table, and I think her hand slipped up between his legs. I couldn't be sure, you understand. I was across the room. But something was going on. Anyway, the strangest look passed over his face—a combination of terror and awe."

"What did she say?" I didn't know if this would help my case, but I was just flat curious.

"She told him that if he did one more thing to cause her public shame, she would rip off his testicles and serve them to him for supper."

"Yow-zer!"

"Exactly what I thought."

"I guess she's had enough." I didn't blame her. I would have done worse than threaten my husband if he'd gone around with women he bought with my money.

"I guess the thing that caught my attention was that Umbria was more afraid than angry." Doc dropped his Styrofoam coffee cup into the trash. "Umbria was afraid of something."

"Do you know what?"

He shook his head. "She left after that. She didn't stay to see how Rutherford was going to be, and she didn't ask. I got the impression she didn't care if he died."

Again, I understood that emotion, but I didn't say anything. Doc was worried about something. "How is Rutherford doing?"

"He's too stupid to die." He sighed. "He wants his cell phone so he can call his women to come play cards with him."

"He isn't very bright. I wonder why Umbria married him."

"Now that would be the question of the week."

"It just became a burning issue." I didn't have any other lead to pursue, so I picked up my purse, kissed Doc on the cheek, and headed to The Gardens. If Umbria was still in town, that's where she'd be staying.

21

"I guess I'm going to have to call the exterminator. The bugs have come crawling back," Gertrude Stromm said as I paused in front of the desk.

"What room is Umbria Clark staying in?" I ignored her rudeness. I'd deal with her later, when I had Tinkie to help me.

"I don't give out that information to busybodies."

I took a deep breath. "Gertrude, please tell me."

"Why should I?"

I leaned very close to her face. "Please don't make me do something we'll both regret. Just tell me the room number."

Her gaze shifted to her little pigeonhole desktop. Room 22 was missing. I ran down the hall to the room, passing the open door to Virgie Carrington's empty room. I didn't blame her for heading back home. Things in Zinnia were getting deadly.

I tapped politely on Umbria's door. She yanked it open with a growl. "What do you want now? I'm not stealing your towels!"

Her face changed from annoyance to downright anger

when she saw me. "Get away from me. You're working for that woman who killed my sister."

Stepping into the room, I forced her back, closed the door, and leaned against it. "Tell me, Umbria, do you really believe Allison killed Quentin?"

Her face told the story. Though she recovered quickly, I saw the truth. She knew Allison was innocent, yet she was willing to let her stew in jail because Allison had inherited the spoils that Umbria coveted. Not all of Miss Carrington's carefully applied polish could change what Umbria was.

"You know she's innocent!" I moved in for the kill. "The question is, *how* do you know she's innocent?"

"Get out of my room before I call the sheriff."

"Coleman will be delighted to talk to you." I took a seat on the trunk at the foot of the bed. "Who stood to inherit if Quentin died before she reached the age of twenty-five?"

Her gaze darted around the room, and I knew she was looking for an escape route. I was too close to the only door. She could run and lock herself in the bathroom, but she couldn't escape.

"You were the one who stood to gain everything, weren't you?"

"What difference does it make? Quentin inherited, and she left every dime to that little tramp Allison." Her face shifted to a sneer. "Maybe all that money will buy her a nice cell at the Mississippi State Penitentiary, or wherever they cage women felons."

"You know she's innocent, Umbria. How can you let an innocent person go to prison?" I knew it was because she was a greedy, heartless bitch, but I wanted to hear her say it.

"Why should I care what happens to her? She doesn't care anything about me."

Now that was an interesting statement. "Why should she care about you?"

She turned away. "Quentin has always hated me. That hate just rubbed off on Allison. They both spent all of their time figuring out ways to screw me out of what was rightfully mine."

I saw it then, the mentally ill way in which everything revolved around Umbria. Everything was constructed to appease or torment her—at least in her own mind. Quentin wouldn't have been able to order eggs for breakfast without Umbria assuming it was to somehow prevent Umbria from having eggs.

"Where is Tinkie?" I didn't care about tricking a confession out of Umbria. I didn't care about any of it. I'd been remiss in not pursuing Umbria as a suspect. I'd known all along about her philandering husband, the inheritance, her place as favored child. All of that, plus her paranoid complex, made her the perfect killer.

"Why should I know where Tinkie is? I'm not her keeper. She's nothing to me."

"Umbria, I'm going to ask one more time." I kept my voice level, but I rose to my feet. "What have you done with Tinkie?"

"Done?" She frowned at me. "Are you insane? I haven't done anything with Tinkie Richmond. You've deliberately misconstrued everything to somehow blame me, and I don't even know for what."

"When was the last time you saw Tinkie?"

"Yesterday morning." She grabbed her suitcase from against the wall. "I'm going to start packing, if you don't mind. I have to get on my way back to Greenwood. I have an appointment with my masseuse."

"Where did you see Tinkie?" I watched her closely, expecting her to pull a knife from amongst her undies.

"Here, at The Gardens. I'd just received a very upsetting note, and she bought me a drink."

A chill swept over me. "An upsetting note?"

"What, are you going deaf now? That's what I said. I got this threatening note about Rutherford, and I told Tinkie about it over a drink."

"Do you still have the note?" I could barely swallow.

"Here!" She reached into the suitcase and pulled out a sheet of the now familiar paper. The typewritten note said: *Control and decorum are the wife's duties. Your husband's deeds reflect on you.*

"Is this why you stabbed Rutherford?"

"It has yet to be determined that anyone stabbed Rutherford. The last I heard, he fell on a knife. But I take the note to mean his behavior reflects poorly on me and my family."

"So you put a stop to it."

"That remains to be seen, doesn't it? But I did scatter that little covey of quail." She grinned wickedly. "I took a shotgun filled with rock salt and peppered their asses. My daddy taught me to be an excellent shot. I don't think those girls will be back."

Rock salt wouldn't kill them, but it would burn and sting. I hated to admit it, but I had a moment of admiration for Umbria. "When did you receive the note?"

"The day after Quentin's funeral. It was in my mailbox here at The Gardens. I knew it was directed at Rutherford, and I knew if I didn't act on it, something terrible would happen."

"How did you know that?"

She frowned. "You ask a lot of nosey questions, Sarah Booth. I'm surprised you haven't gotten a note."

I must have looked like a gaffed fish because she nodded. "You did get one, didn't you? Well, you'd better fix whatever the note talks about. Back in school, several of the girls got notes."

"Back in school? At the Carrington—"

"Yes, where else. The notes were about conduct and

comportment. Lisa Belk got one about wearing her skirts too short, and when she didn't lower her hem, someone went in her closet and cut all of her clothes into shreds."

"She wasn't hurt? Her clothes were just shredded?"

"That's right. My note was about . . ." She turned away from me and walked to the window. "About boys. I was sleeping with several."

"And you stopped?"

"I stopped doing it close to the school. I was more careful."

"Other girls got notes?"

"A few. Lisa's was enough to straighten up most of the girls."

"Who wrote the notes?"

"They were never signed. Some busybody, like Genevieve, was always tattling on us, though."

"What did Virgie say about the notes?"

"She was very sorry and offered to pay for Lisa's wardrobe, and I think she did buy her some new clothes. I don't remember that. I just remember that the girls in our class were more wary. It sort of put a damper on the entire year."

"Thanks, Umbria." I was ready to go. I had to make a call, and I didn't want her to overhear me. "Can I have that note?"

She looked at it with distaste. "Why would you want it?"

"Evidence."

She hesitated. "Why should I help Allison? She has everything."

I didn't bother trying to explain to Umbria yet again the ethical issues of an innocent person in jail. I snatched the note and ran out the door. To my surprise, I collided into Gertrude Stromm, who'd been eavesdropping at the door. I leapt her like a hurdle and kept running, leaving the two squawking women behind me.

* * *

As I drove toward Dahlia House to fetch Sweetie Pie, I tried to call Coleman. His phone rang and rang, which prompted me to beat my phone on the dash of the car. It didn't make him answer, but I felt better. Then, I called Oscar.

"I may know where Tinkie is."

He sounded like a man surfacing from ten thousand feet below the ocean for a gasp of air. "Where?"

"The Carrington School for Well-Bred Ladies."

"Why would she be there?"

"Because Virgie Carrington is our killer."

"Sarah Booth, that's ridiculous. She's an old lady."

That was the crux of it. I'd completely overlooked her as a suspect because she was "an old lady." But she wasn't. She was in her sixties, and I'd seen her gardening. She was strong as an ox. "There's one thing all of the suspects, except for Tinkie and me, have in common. They were all graduates of the school. They all got notes. They all were engaged in socially inappropriate conduct."

"Tinkie is never inappropriate."

I applauded Oscar's loyalty, but he was living in a dream world. "Oscar, Tinkie's a private dick. She's inappropriate."

There was a pause. "Virgie wouldn't hurt her?" It was more of a question than a statement.

"Maybe, maybe not. I have to find Coleman, and I know just how to do it."

"I'll meet him at the office."

"Good. I'm heading to the school."

"Absolutely not!" He sounded very masculine and bossy. "You'll wait for Coleman."

"Oscar, you aren't my husband or my father. I'm going after Tinkie. I owe her about three 'saved from the jaws of death' rescues."

"Sarah Booth, Coleman is going to be very upset with you."

He was right, but what else was new. Coleman was often upset with me and vice versa. "I promise not to act rashly and endanger Tinkie."

"Be careful." And as much as Oscar worried for his wife, he was also worried for me.

"I promise." I hung up and wheeled down the drive to Dahlia House. Gordon was conveniently behind me, and I dashed to the patrol car.

"Virgie Carrington is the killer. I think Tinkie's being held at the school. You have to find Coleman, right away, and tell him to meet me there."

Gordon hesitated.

"Find Coleman. If Tinkie's hurt and you don't—"

He drove off, scattering dirt and leaves behind him.

I ran up the steps. To my aggravation, another package was propped against the door. Something about the size of silk ropes or a blindfold. I kicked it aside and rushed into the house, calling Sweetie as I ran upstairs and did a quick costume change into basic black. Virgie didn't approve of women in pants, but if I was going to do some ass-kicking, I didn't need to be hampered by a skirt.

Coming back down the stairs with Sweetie bounding beside me, I remembered my error in not opening a package and retrieved the one from the front porch. I tore the blue ribbon off it and pulled out a book. *Women on Top.* There was a note. *Pick out your favorite fantasy, and I'll make it come true.*

The package was, indeed, from Humphrey. I dropped it on the porch and ran to the car with Sweetie on my heels. We took off, the fallen leaves a trail spiraling behind us.

It was dusk when I arrived at the Carrington School. Even though I'd never attended, I knew exactly where it was. Everyone in the Delta did. It was a stately mansion set back off the road, on about three hundred acres of what would be termed "grounds." The price of Virgie's tuition allowed her to maintain a full lawn crew, and the place was beautiful. Live oaks draped with Spanish moss dotted the landscape. The sun was setting, tracing fiery fingers through the mossy limbs as I drove slowly down the driveway.

Virgie was one smart cookie, and I needed a foolproof plan. Now that I was at the school, I realized perhaps I'd come unprepared. The last thing I wanted to do was to put Tinkie in more danger than she already was. I absolutely refused to believe that Tinkie was injured. In order to save her and protect myself, I needed a good plan.

I could pretend that I'd stopped by for a chat. That might throw her off guard enough for me to hunt for Tinkie. Or I could pretend I was there for a chat and turn Sweetie loose to find Tinkie, which was probably the fastest method.

Or, I could do reconnaissance around the building while I waited for Coleman and Oscar. That seemed a good place to start. Maybe Sweetie would even let me know which part of the school Tinkie was being held in. Then I remembered Tammy's dream. Tinkie was in a solarium or sunroom. That shouldn't be too hard to find, since it would have to be on the outside of the house.

The school was constructed as a squared-off U, with classrooms flanked by dormitories on either side. Virgie's house was at the open end of the U. I scouted around the classrooms and dormitories just to be certain there was no solarium there. None. I moved on to her house.

The school was quiet, too quiet, and I wondered if the girls were on break. It was that time just before Thanksgiving when some schools began their holiday break. I couldn't imagine being twelve years old and living at a school rather than at home with my parents. Some girls would prefer it, but it would have been a terrible punishment to me.

If there were young people in the building, I saw no

sign of them as I slipped past the last segment of dormitory and on to Virgie's house, which was lit up like a fairy mansion with its leaded-glass windows. In a word, magnificent.

The house had been built with a three-foot crawl space beneath it, which put the first-floor windows beyond my ability to see inside. Sweetie pranced beside me, oblivious to the danger we faced. I saw an old magnolia tree beside the house and decided that was the best vantage point to view the western side. "Stay," I whispered to Sweetie, who lay down at the base of the tree.

I began the torturous job of hauling myself up the tree. As a child, I'd loved to climb trees. I'd spent many an afternoon climbing the tallest oaks around our house, daring the boys to climb as high as I could. What had been wrong with me?

By the time I got fifteen feet up the tree, I was trembling with exhaustion. Somewhere in the intervening years from childhood, I'd developed a real discomfort around heights. Luckily, I was still going up and had no need to look down. A problem would arise when it would become necessary to reverse my efforts.

I had a clear view of a sitting room, which was empty; a library, which seemed empty; a music room, also empty; the kitchen, which was empty; and part of a huge solarium. I focused my attention there. This room was unlit, and it took a lot of eyestrain to detect wicker furniture, a swing, what looked like a Ping-Pong table, and a lone figure, hands pressed against the glass.

Tinkie! She was alive! She wasn't dead! I'd refused to even think of her as hurt, and there she stood, seemingly okay.

"She's there. Tinkie's in the house," I whispered softly to my hound. But Sweetie wasn't there. To my horror, I saw her loping across the lawn to the back entrance.

"Sweetie!" I was afraid to call her loudly. "Sweetie!"

In typical fashion, she completely ignored me and dashed to the back steps that led to the solarium. She bayed loudly, demanding entrance.

I saw the figure press against the glass. Sweetie had given herself away, but she'd also let Tinkie know that help was on the way. Tinkie looked up and scanned what she could see of the yard, looking for me. This time, I was the cavalry.

A front light snapped on, and Virgie Carrington stepped out on the porch. "What is all that commotion?" she called into the darkness. In one hand was a flashlight, and in the other a gun.

My heart rose in my throat as I watched Sweetie bound around the house and head for the front steps. The dog would never expect anyone to hurt her. She had free rein at Dahlia House and Hilltop, and expected it everywhere she went.

She flew up the steps and directly at Virgie. Virgie pointed the gun, but before she could fire, Sweetie ran right over her, knocking her to the ground. Sweetie rushed into the house, barking and baying.

Quick as a flash, Virgie was on her feet. She hurried back inside. The front door slammed closed.

Now she had my partner and my dog.

22

I had pinpointed where Virgie was holding Tinkie, which was important to any rescue attempt. What I couldn't begin to say was what she'd done with my hound. Virgie didn't strike me as the kind of person who would be agreeable to the idea of dog hair in her home.

I clambered down from the tree, happy to feel terra firma beneath my feet. I didn't have time to bend and kiss the earth; I had to distract Virgie. And the best plan was simply to knock on her door and try to worm my way into her home. She couldn't hurt Tinkie or the dog if I was there to stop her.

My car was down the driveway, which would alert Coleman and Oscar when they arrived. I walked up the front steps and rang the doorbell, bold as you please.

The door opened wide, and Virgie smiled at me. "Sarah Booth Delaney, what are you doing here? Don't you know it's rude to pay unexpected calls on people? A little sophistication would make your life so much easier."

I couldn't be certain, but I thought I detected a certain tightness of the skin around her eyes. "I do know it's rude, Virgie, and I apologize. I need your help."

Her smile widened. "Come right in."

I stepped into the foyer and heard the door slam and lock behind me. Virgie was a bit overly conscientious about her safety. She stepped in front of me and led the way to a parlor on the other side of the house. There was no sign of Sweetie Pie anywhere.

"This has been an interesting night," she remarked as she showed me into a wing chair. "I was planning on reading a novel and going to bed early. So what brings you to my school?"

"My partner has gone missing, and I'm worried about her."

"Tinkie? Missing?"

I had to hand it to her, she was a good actress. She seemed genuinely concerned. "She disappeared yesterday, after I got a note warning me about my nosiness."

Her face furrowed into a frown. "That's terrible. Did Tinkie get a note, too?"

"I'm not certain." The old fox was trying to figure out how much I'd put together. "I was hoping maybe you'd talked to her before you left Zinnia. She was at The Gardens, talking to Umbria."

"Umbria!" She threw up her hands in disgust. "What a waste of time and money she's turned out to be."

"Did you hear that someone stabbed Rutherford?"

A smile touched her face. "Oh, really? Is he dead?"

"It wasn't a fatal wound. He's going to recover, but word on the street is that Umbria plied the knife, and he's too afraid of her to rat her out."

Virgie's expression was one of sorrow. "I never understood why Umbria married him. She could have had her pick of decent men."

"She was one of your most promising students, wasn't she?" I had to keep her talking. Coleman and Oscar would arrive soon. All I had to do was occupy her until they did.

"Umbria had such potential. She understood how powerful she could be as the woman behind the man." She paced back and forth behind the sofa. "She got it! But she could never apply it. She always found these worthless men. If Rutherford Clark had one ounce of honest ambition, he could be governor of the state, with Umbria at his side."

"I've only met Rutherford once, and it was another 'p' word that seemed to occupy all of his attention." I had to find out how stable she was. If she was, indeed, killing people over social infractions, how would she react to a little verbal vulgarity?

She didn't hesitate to show her disapproval. "No lady ever alludes to that word. Sarah Booth, I'd always heard that your mother raised you as a heathen, but surely she taught you that when you belittle the female gender with crass and vulgar references, you lessen all women."

"Sorry." I tried to look contrite. She was hanging on pretty well. I didn't think she was going to flip out and come at me with a knife. Then again . . . "Would it be possible for me to use your ladies' room?" I rose.

Momentary annoyance flitted across her face. "This way."

I followed her to a bathroom off the hallway. I had no doubt she'd stand guard while I did my business. I flushed the toilet, ran the water, went through the motions, the whole time trying to frame the layout of the house in my mind.

When I left the bathroom, Virgie was waiting in the hall, her black skirt and pale pink blouse perfectly crisp. "Your home is lovely, Virgie. Might I have a tour?" I smiled.

"Another time. I'm truly not prepared for a guest. Now that you've refreshed yourself for travel, I think it best that you leave."

I hadn't expected this turn of events. Proper ladies

were supposed to be gracious above all else. I frowned.
"I'm sorry. Might I have a glass of water before I go?"

"Are you deliberately delaying your departure?"

She hadn't moved, but there was a change in her posture. I had to remember that she'd lured Quentin McGee into a cotton field and killed her, not to mention starting a landslide. She was physically competent.

"I'm sorry," I said. "It's just that I'm thirsty, and I thought well-bred ladies always offered a guest refreshments. Even an unexpected guest."

"Of course, you may have a glass of water. I'll bring it to you in the parlor."

I could almost hear her teeth grinding as she led me to the parlor door. I walked inside and took a seat until her footsteps faded down the hall.

I had a minute, maybe two. Even though I'd listened closely, I was distressed that I hadn't heard a whine from my hound. Sweetie had gone into the house and seemingly disappeared. What had Virgie done with her?

I tiptoed across the hallway and through the formal dining room into a back stairwell. The temptation to run up the stairs was great, but I was afraid if Virgie knew I was loose in her home, she'd hurt Tinkie.

"Sweetie," I called softly. "Sweetie." Dogs have hearing six times more sensitive than humans. Of course, that doesn't mean they come when they're called.

I didn't even hear a toenail click on the wooden floor. Damn. I unlocked a window in the dining room, tiptoed back across the hall, and was seated in my chair when Virgie returned with a glass of water on a silver tray. There was a napkin and nothing else. She was going to perform the ritual, but with a minimalist approach.

I took the glass and thanked her, sipping daintily. "Are you on a well?"

"Yes, we're on a deep well." If she hadn't been such a lady, her leg would have swung in annoyance.

"The well at Dahlia House is over two hundred feet deep, and the water is pure, like this."

Virgie perched on the edge of the sofa and watched the level of the liquid in my glass. She wanted me gone, but she couldn't tell me to hurry. She was biding her time.

I put the glass on the napkin on the side table. "I can see you have a lot to do, so let me get right to the point."

"What point?"

At last I had her attention. "I wanted to talk to you about the murders."

"Murders? Plural? Who else has been killed?"

"You haven't heard!" I leaned forward in perfect gossip mode. "It's been discovered that several women received threatening notes and then later met with foul play. Well, it wasn't actually ruled as foul play until I put it all together." My intention was to take the focus off Tinkie and put it on me. Virgie would have a hard time overpowering me.

"Why, Sarah Booth, I didn't realize you were such a good detective. Tell me everything you discovered. Would you care for some coffee and some homemade fruitcake?"

I'd turned the tide. She was eager to hear what I'd found out. I smiled. "Fruitcake would be lovely. You know, as soon as I find Tinkie, I'm going home to Dahlia House to make my traditional fruitcakes. All of this detective business has gone too far."

"You're quitting?"

"Indeed. Cece is running a story on my 'retirement' tomorrow. To be honest, I may have jeopardized Tinkie's life with my desire to solve cases. At least, that's what the note I received implied."

"And you're just going to give it up?"

"When it comes to a choice between Tinkie and a career, it's easy to pick Tink. It's not even a choice."

"Let me get that coffee." She was up and across the room before I could blink. I figured I had five minutes and took off for the staircase. I hurried through the upper floor but didn't see or hear a trace of Sweetie. She had to be on the first level, maybe with my partner.

I hurried silently back down the stairs, pausing to look at the family portraits that lined the wall of the dining room. The Carringtons were a very proper family, but a smile wouldn't have broken any rules of etiquette that I knew.

I was back in my chair when she brought in a bigger silver tray, this one laden with goodies. I had to hand it to Virgie: she had all the accoutrements for a proper Southern lady—silver, china, linen napkins, the whole deal. "Please, help yourself," she said as she poured coffee for each of us from a silver pot.

The fruitcake was laden with bright green and red cherries. Fruitcake is one of my favorites, but I hadn't just fallen off a turnip truck. I suspected Virgie of being a serial killer. I wasn't about to eat her fruitcake. I took a slice and pretended to nibble as I tucked it in the folds of my napkin. "Delicious."

"I'll share my recipe with you. You know, Sarah Booth, if you worked on your homemaker skills just a little, you could probably find a man who could keep you in style."

I forced a smile before I sipped the hot coffee. "I guess that's something I'll have to consider now that I've retired as a private investigator."

"So tell me what you learned."

This was where I'd have to tread carefully. I didn't want to reveal too much, but I wanted to string her along. And where the hell were Coleman and Oscar? I'd been in the house at least twenty minutes. They should have arrived by now. I was counting on Coleman's big fist hammering on the front door.

"Marilyn Jenkins's mother, Karla, received a note warning her of her bad conduct before she was killed." I pretended to nibble a bit more fruitcake. She'd laced it with bourbon, and it did make my mouth water. Instead, I finished my coffee.

"Karla Jenkins died in a freak landslide. I read it in the newspaper." Virgie was watching me closely.

"The death was ruled accidental." I didn't want to put her on the defensive by telling her the case was going to be reopened.

"What else?" She poured me another cup and topped hers off.

"Genevieve Reynolds's mother died in another freak accident. There was a note involved there, too."

"Have you linked the notes with the deaths, or is it just a coincidence?"

"I don't know. I suppose it's none of my business anymore." The room spun, and I shook my head. I was exhausted. I downed the last of my coffee. "Of course, I don't have a clue what the sheriff will do."

She smiled like the Cheshire cat. "Oh, I don't suspect he'll do much of anything."

I tried to focus on Virgie, but she kept moving around the room. My stomach was suddenly queasy. Something was wrong, very wrong. I tried to stand and heard the sound of breaking glass. I took one step toward Virgie and was surrounded by darkness.

The sound of footsteps awakened me. Someone was walking back and forth, back and forth. I came around slowly, wondering where I was and who was with me. I was lying on a cold, uncomfortable wooden surface. When I tried to move, I moaned.

"Sarah Booth!" Tinkie touched my forehead. "You're okay! I was afraid the old bat had poisoned you."

"Tinkie?" Something about Tinkie was coming back to me. She was in danger. I was supposed to save her. I took a breath and forced myself into a sitting position. I had messed up bad.

"Did she hurt you?"

"You ate the fruitcake, didn't you?" Tinkie asked. "We are the only two people in the world who could be poisoned by fruitcake. No one else would eat it."

"I didn't eat it. I knew better. But I did drink the coffee. Who puts drugs in coffee?" I did my best to gather my wits. "Are you hurt?"

"She wouldn't dare hurt me. As soon as she comes back in here, we'll jump her." She bit her lip. "There's a small problem, though. She has a stun gun."

"Did she use it on Sweetie?" A blast from a Taser could kill a hound.

She shook her head. "I saw Sweetie outside. That's how I knew you'd come to rescue me. I waited and waited, but I never saw or heard anything until Virgie dragged you in the door and dumped you. What happened to Sweetie?"

"The wicked witch lured her into the gingerbread house and has probably put her in the oven." How could I have been so stupid as to drink something from a known murderer? I needed to hang up my license.

"She probably fed her some of that Seconal-laced fruitcake, and Sweetie is snoozing away in one of the back rooms."

One thing about Tinkie, even in the direst situations, she always thought of the best possible outcome. "I can only hope she's okay. I shouldn't have brought her, but she did track you down. She went straight to the back steps."

"She's a great dog." Tinkie sank onto the floor beside me. "We'll get out of this."

"Coleman and Oscar should arrive any minute." I'd been thinking that for the last forty minutes. Where were they?

"They know I'm here?"

I nodded. "We were a little behind you, Tink, but we finally figured it out. Virgie was the common factor in all of the deaths. The women were her pupils. I guess she decided if she couldn't teach them how to behave properly, she'd just bump them off."

"Except for us. We were never her students."

"Which may be the only reason we're both still alive. She's not responsible for our behavior. We aren't her failures. She simply wanted us to leave her alone."

"She's still going to kill us. She can't afford to let us go."

Although Tinkie looked on the bright side of things, she was a realist. We were dead meat.

I heard a slow step, slide. Step, slide. I thought of every horror movie in which the malformed monster steps out of the darkness. That was my talent—to remember every terrifying event of a spooky show. Tinkie's fingers dug into my arm, and we quaked together. The steps passed our door and continued on.

"Who was that?"

I rose to my feet. "I think that was Virgie dragging my dog." Fury replaced the fear that had gripped me. "We need to get out of here."

"We need a gun or a knife or a tool of violence." She stood up, too. "I never thought I could hit an old lady on the head, but I'm telling you, I could give her a headache that would last until next June."

I understood completely. Searching the solarium for a weapon, I suddenly remembered Tammy's dream about Tinkie. I thought it was worth at least a mention, so I told her about it.

"That's so strange. For the first few hours I was here, I could see girls leaving the school. Only a few of them, in their black skirts and white blouses. I beat on the windows and tried to get their attention, but they couldn't hear me. I had the distinct impression that I was in a glass of some type."

"That's how Tammy described it."

"Sometimes she's just plain creepy with her gift," Tinkie said as she gave a small cry of joy. "Here's a pen."

"Now there's a deadly weapon if ever I saw one."

"Be sarcastic, but if wielded with enough force, I could puncture her lung."

"Or give her a small ink tattoo." I put my arm around Tinkie. "I'm only kidding. The pen is the best weapon we have so far. Let's keep looking."

We searched in the darkness, rejecting the pillows from the wicker furniture, but I did manage to wrest a leg off the coffee table. It wasn't exactly heavy, but if I swung with enough force, I could stun her.

"When she opens the door, I'm going to step out from behind it and whack her in the head." It wasn't a very original plan, but we were limited by our resources.

"When she falls to the floor, I'll straddle her and hold the pen at her throat." Tinkie was determined to put that pen to use.

"Fine." I hoped once I hit Virgie, she'd go down all the way. But there weren't any guarantees when dealing with a homicidal septuagenarian. I just had one more thing to add. "Where in the hell are Coleman and Oscar?"

"Maybe they won't come. Oscar was pretty angry with me."

Now was my chance to return so many of the good deeds Tinkie had done me. "We should have called him when you were going to spend the night. He worried all night long."

Even across a dark room I could see her stiffen. "Tinkie, if you had a child, think how worried you'd be if he or she stayed out all night."

"The difference, Sarah Booth, is that I'm not a child."

"But you also aren't in the habit of staying out all night. Oscar thought something tragic had happened to you. We should have called."

"I'm not going to apologize."

I chuckled. "At this point, I don't think it matters. He'll be so glad to see you alive that he'd agree if you wanted to do burlesque."

She sank into one of the wicker chairs. "That's the problem. I don't want Oscar's permission, tacit or explicit. I'm going to make my own choices in life from now on."

"Even if it means worrying the people who love you?"

She thought about it. "Maybe."

"Tinkie, the whole time you've been gone, Oscar has been afraid you were in trouble, and look, you are. There are factors that make it reasonable for him to worry. The work we do for one. And he's worried about your breast lump." I figured I might as well dig up the whole potato patch.

"He has no right to say a word. It's my breast. My lump. My choice."

"And his heart." Tinkie was kind and considerate. Why was she being such a hardhead? "If something happened to you, it would kill Oscar."

"We risk that every day. Everyone who loves risks losing their heart every minute of every day."

She was right, but there were degrees. "What would it hurt to go to a doctor? What would it hurt?"

"If he tells me the lump has grown, I might lose my faith that it will go away. I just need some time."

That was it in a nutshell. She needed time to feel her way through the situation, and Oscar and I wanted immediate action. We were all wrong. "Will you consider something for me?"

"Maybe."

"If we get out of this, take it as a sign that we're both intended to live long, full lives. Make an appointment for February with a surgeon to have the lump biopsied. If it's gone by February, you won't have a worry in the world."

A long silence stretched across the dark room. All around us the world was quiet.

"Okay, I'll do that. I'll make the appointment for February fourteenth, Valentine's Day."

"I think Oscar will take that as a true gift of love."

There was the sound of footsteps approaching our door, the steady clatter of Virgie's sensible but feminine shoes. I took my position behind the door, and Tinkie turned in her chair so that she was silhouetted by the light in the yard.

We held our breath as we waited for the door to open.

23

The door opened slowly, and no one stepped through.
"Sarah Booth, get out from behind that door, or I'll
have to hurt you."

Virgie was one sharp cookie. There was no point pretending. I edged out, away from her reach, and went to
stand beside Tinkie. If I couldn't catch her by surprise,
Tinkie and I would try to overpower her.

"What are you going to do with us?" Tinkie asked.

"Even more important, what did you do with my dog?"

"You shouldn't try sneak attacks when you have a dog
with your name and phone number on the tag," Virgie
said. "It gives away the endgame."

She had played me like a fiddle. I'd underestimated
her, and now I was as much a hostage as Sweetie and
Tinkie.

"What are you going to do with us?" Tinkie repeated.

"I don't know," she said. "It depends. I can't let you go.
I have no faith that you'd keep your mouths shut. And
don't pretend you don't know all about it. You both ended
up talking to me, which tells me you figured it out. Now
whom did you tell?"

"No one." We said it too quickly.

"The truth," she said, stepping into the room a foot or two. She had the Taser in her hand. "You might as well tell me, or I'll get it out of you the hard way."

I squeezed Tinkie's shoulder to give her strength.

"You want to know who we told? We told all the authorities between Memphis and Jackson," Tinkie said matter-of-factly. "Your goose is cooked. You might as well let us go."

It was a bold stance, but one without proper backing.

"If that's the truth, I might as well kill you both. I can only be executed once, you know."

Spoken in true serial-killer style. She was right, though; she had nothing to lose by killing us. We would be victims five and six, or maybe fifteen and sixteen. There was no telling how long Virgie had been conducting her own Darwinian efforts to stamp out the socially inept gene pool.

"We might be of use to you." I stepped in front of Tinkie. If she was going to attack us, Tinkie might have a chance to get away.

"But not as much use as I would be." Tinkie stepped in front of me.

I rolled my eyes and leaned down to whisper, "I get one chance to save you."

"You had your chance." She held her ground. "And you blew it."

Tinkie's one flaw as a partner was that she liked to rub things in.

"Stop it. And stay back, or I will Taser you into a jerking puddle."

"That's not a very ladylike threat." I stepped in front of Tinkie. "Where's my dog?"

"She won't be chasing any more coons," Virgie said.

I made a grab for her, but she was quicker. She slammed the door on me, and I heard the dead bolt turn.

But I'd also heard the doorbell chime. Coleman had arrived at last.

Tinkie and I took turns listening at the door, in the hopes of hearing some sign that help was on the way. There was only silence, though.

We sat in the wicker chairs and waited, helpless to act to save ourselves or the Pie. I was seriously worried about my hound.

After a half hour had passed, I stood up to pace. "What's taking them so long?"

"Are you sure they understood?"

I thought back through my conversations with Oscar. "I'm positive. He didn't want me to come by myself, because of the danger. I ignored him because I wanted to get to you. Then I told Gordon, and I'm sure he had a clear picture of what was going on."

Tinkie slapped her forehead. "Sarah Booth, we are dense! Coleman doesn't have any jurisdiction in Coahoma County. He's the sheriff of Sunflower County!"

The truth of her words was like a bone in my throat. "Surely that won't slow him down. Doesn't he have probable cause or something to that effect? Can't he just break in and worry about the consequences later?"

"Not if he wants a good case against Virgie."

Tinkie leaned back in her chair. "We may be here a while, so you might as well get some sleep. What time is it, anyway?"

I checked my watch to discover it was after ten. My life was slipping away, minute by minute, and I needed to check on Sweetie. I didn't believe Virgie had killed her—drugged her, yes. But not killed her. Sweetie loved food, so she would have eaten fruitcake laced with tranquilizer without batting an eye. The dose Virgie gave me had knocked me flat, and I outweighed Sweetie by at least sixty pounds. She could be out for hours.

"I know you're worried about Sweetie," Tinkie said. "I

wish there was some way we could get out of here and check on her."

"Me, too." But I'd been all over the room. The windows didn't open. They were huge slabs of glass fitted into the walls. The outside door had been locked by someone standing on the steps. The room was, for all practical purposes, sealed like a tomb.

"Maybe that wasn't Coleman at the door." Tinkie tucked her feet up under her. "It was probably some school business or something. No one has come to help us, and we're going to die here. Even if Coleman has to go through another sheriff's department, it shouldn't have taken him this long."

Her doom and gloom were interrupted by a sound outside the door. Footsteps approached down the hallway.

"Listen." I held up a hand. "Let's pretend to be asleep."

We draped ourselves appropriately over our chairs and played possum as the door unlocked and Virgie stepped into the room.

"Your rescue team has come and gone," she said. "Coleman Peters and John Adams, the Coahoma County sheriff, just left. They never even mentioned your name, Sarah Booth. Only Tinkie's. I threw them a false lead, and they're off to New Orleans, baying like green hounds."

"Virgie, they saw my car."

"Really? Where did they see it?"

"Parked near the road, in your driveway."

"Funny, they didn't say anything at all about your car, Sarah Booth."

My worry ratio tripled. "They had to see it."

"Unless someone moved it."

"But I have the key." I reached into my pocket only to find emptiness.

"While you were taking your little snooze, I borrowed your key and moved the car. Or should I say hid the car."

I hadn't realized how much I was counting on Coleman

seeing my car until she took that hope away from me. For all Coleman knew, I'd fallen off the edge of the world. And if they concentrated their efforts on finding Tinkie in New Orleans, Virgie would have time to kill us and chop us into flushable bits.

"You look a little defeated, Sarah Booth."

"Not at all," I lied.

"I never intended to hurt either of you." She stood in the doorway as she talked, the Taser in her hand. "I want you to know that. Since you weren't my girls, I had no obligation to make you toe the line. I only meant to stop you."

"And it was the notes to us that finally made us see what was happening. Had you not threatened us, we wouldn't have figured it out," Tinkie said.

"Ironic, isn't it?"

Virgie could afford to be intellectual about it all since she was on the non-shocking end of the Taser.

"I'm not going to ask you for understanding—"

"But I do understand." Tinkie rose slowly to her feet. "I see it clearly. You've devoted your entire life to shaping these young women into remarkable creations. You gave them an education, social graces, strategies, introductions, and a sense of social propriety. You gave them all the best of you."

I almost applauded. Tinkie deserved an Oscar—a real one and a gold one. I held my breath to see if Virgie had bought the performance.

"You do understand."

In the moonlight coming in through the many glass windows, I could see that Virgie had relaxed her stance a tiny bit. Tinkie's understanding was soothing her.

"We both do, Virgie. Maybe me a little more than Sarah Booth, who has always traveled her own path. But as a wife, the partner of a man whose business depends on propriety, I do understand. There are values that are reflected in conduct and grace. There is also the fact that good manners improve life for everyone."

Virgie held out her empty hand, palm up. "Imagine a world without manners. What you'd have is rudeness and chaos. I've seen it all falling apart. With the breakdown of our communities has come the total disruption of our families. We're a society of anonymous commuters."

Even I had to agree with some of what she was saying, but I wasn't going to open my mouth. Tinkie was doing a brilliant job and needed no help from me.

"Well put," Tinkie said.

"I worked so hard on these girls. I put everything into helping them. And when they graduated, they went out into the world as representations for my school. Their bright lights reflected back on me. They were the validation of all my hard work."

Tinkie stepped a little closer. "And when their conduct was reprehensible, what reflected back on you was unacceptable."

Virgie nodded. "I tried with the notes to warn them back into line."

"You started with the notes even when they were at the school, didn't you?" Tinkie asked.

"Yes. For the most part, it was effective. Every few years I'd have to take it a step further, but usually it required only the destruction of some personal property or a note on a blackboard embarrassing the offender. That's the job of society, to hold a person to standards."

"But who sets those standards?" I asked.

"When I first opened the school, it was easier because there were community standards. For the past twenty years, I've been spitting into the wind. Young women won't abide by standards when they receive no credit for them, and no censure for breaking them. Unless there's a consequence."

I had a moment of concern for myself. Virgie made sense in some weird kind of way.

"That's when I had to up the ante," she said.

And I realized again how completely insane she was. It was one thing to rue the loss of manners and grace in society and quite another to kill people who violated your individual rules of conduct.

"Murder is a pretty high ante." I took a step away from Tinkie. If Virgie was coming after us with the Taser, the farther apart we were, the better it would be.

"There was no other punishment. There is no public humiliation, no shame. No shunning or exclusion. People rob, steal, extort, lie, fornicate, produce illegitimate children, fail to pay child support, and no one would ever think to exclude them from a club or group." She shook her head. "What's left other than murder?"

"Maybe it isn't up to you to stop them." I said it in the gentlest way possible, but the effect was impressive.

Virgie seemed to swell with anger. "That's the problem. No one wants to assume the responsibility. So I did. I said I would hold people accountable, but only those people who I knew had been taught better."

"Then Tinkie and I are off the hook."

I should have kept my mouth shut. Maybe a few months at Virgie's school would have done me good. She looked at me with such utter contempt that I felt it.

"Your mouth, Sarah Booth, is going to be the death of you."

With that, she slammed the door shut. Tinkie and I were prisoners once again, with an enraged and insane warden.

Dawn broke over the grounds of the Carrington School for Well-Bred Ladies, and I shook Tinkie awake.

"There's someone under the trees," I said.

She sat up, rubbed her eyes, ran her fingers through her completely unmussed hair, and examined the lawn shaded by huge oaks. "There!" She pointed to the place where I'd seen movement.

"Can you tell who it is?" Perhaps it was time to put vanity aside and get some contacts. Then again, if I were dead, I wouldn't have to worry about vision choices.

"I can't be sure, but it looks like . . . Humphrey."

"Humphrey Tatum?" That was impossible. Why would Humphrey be here at the school?

"Yep, that's who it is."

"Can you tell what he's doing?" I squinted and saw the blurry image of a man moving among the trees. The sun was behind us, so we had pretty good light.

"Looks like he's walking around, taking in the air, as some would say."

"Great. Are you sure he doesn't have one of the students out there with him?"

Tinkie laughed. "Humphrey is too smart to sample jail bait. I think he prefers a more experienced partner."

"I think he prefers something breathing."

Her laughter was louder. "You're too hard on him, Sarah Booth." She leaned closer. "You'd better be careful, or you'll end up being the Virgie Carrington of sexual mores."

That was a cut to the bone, and I grabbed my chest and fell over my chair. "You've wounded me mortally."

"Better me than Virgie." She sighed. "What are we going to do?"

I'd been thinking about it off and on all night. "I'm not certain. If she was going to kill us, wouldn't she have already done so?"

"Maybe she thinks she can use us for bartering."

"She may think that, but we know it won't work." I had a thought. "Maybe we can make her think it'll work."

Tinkie's eyebrows lifted. "We'd better do something, or I'm going to starve to death. My stomach sounds like a roller rink."

She was right. I was hungry, too. Virgie had made no effort to feed us anything since the fruitcake. "We have to be careful, or she'll lace the food with something."

Tinkie sighed. "Then our only recourse is to escape."

I nodded for her to look out the window. Humphrey was sauntering toward us like a man without a care. He came up to the window and waved, ignoring our pantomimed gestures of captivity.

Though we pounded on the glass and screamed his name, he didn't pause. He kept walking right beside us, hands in his pockets and chin in the air as he apparently whistled a merry tune.

"You're right, Sarah Booth. The man is a complete idiot." Tinkie sat down in a huff, examining her fingers. "I broke two of my nails, and he didn't even try to comprehend what we were trying to tell him."

"What's he doing here?" The answer to that question could be either good news or very bad. It might also explain why we were still alive. Virgie might be waiting for the arrival of her partner in crime, if that was what Humphrey was.

"What's wrong with you?" Tinkie put her finger in her mouth and attempted to chew her nail smooth.

"Nothing." There was no point in making her feel dread, too. "I wish we could hear what was happening."

She stood up and paced to the window. "What kind of glass is this, anyway?"

"Expensive."

She picked up one of the wicker tables and smashed it into the glass. The table fell apart in her hands, but the glass was untouched. "I want out!" She attacked it with her fists. "Let me out of here before I go insane."

I grasped her fists and tried to hold on to them. Tinkie was surprisingly strong. "Hey, let it go. This won't help anything, and you'll break another nail."

She struggled, but with half the will. At last, she

stopped, and I held her tight against me as she cried. "I want to go home," she said.

I had wondered what her feelings were about Oscar, but I hadn't asked. "Home to Oscar?"

She nodded. "I thought I hated him. Maybe I did, but it was only a passing emotion. The love is deeper and stronger."

"I know." I patted her shoulder as I held her. Tinkie was far stronger than I and also more fragile because she dared to risk everything. "Click your heels together three times, and say the magic words."

Tinkie closed her eyes and clicked her heels three times. "I want to go home. I want to go home. I want to go home."

I was so busy watching Tinkie, at first I didn't see the door of our prison slowly creak open.

24

"Ladies!" Humphrey Tatum stepped through the doorway with a million-watt smile. "What a predicament you find yourselves in."

I'd never known what to make of Humphrey, but now I did. He didn't have whiskers and a tail, but he was a rat, nonetheless. He was in cahoots with Virgie. He'd hired us only so that he could keep tabs on what we were doing. Tinkie and I exchanged angry glares.

"Humphrey Tatum, you are a low-life scoundrel." Tinkie put her hands on her trim hips and walked right up to his face. "You are lower than the underbelly of a snake. You are viler than castor oil. You are . . ." Polite words failed her, and she simply slapped the stew out of him.

Humphrey stepped back and rubbed his cheek. "I hope Sarah Booth isn't as passionate in her anger."

My thought was to kick him in the tender place, but I restrained myself. We had to think, not react. "How deep are you in this?" I asked.

He did something strange with his eyebrows, like a rabbit eating. "Up to my ears. Virgie and I are partners."

He kept his back to the doorway and his face to me. His

face twitched again. Something was wrong with him. Maybe he'd run out of his medication.

"What are you going to do with us?" Tinkie demanded.

"I don't know."

Great, the man with all the sexual plans had no idea what to do with his hostages. "Why did you do it, Humphrey?"

A sad look touched his face. "We were losing everything at Tatum Corner. Quentin, and her *legitimate* marriage to me, was our last hope. Al threw a monkey wrench into those plans."

"Your sister is going to prison. The woman she loved is dead." I wanted to slap him cockeyed.

He shrugged nonchalantly. "I have to admit, I wasn't in on the plan to kill Quentin, but once the deed was done, I saw a golden opportunity with Virgie's help. We'd say Quentin died before midnight, and then I'd bump off old Rutherford. Umbria would be free to marry me, and we could divide the spoils."

"Umbria's in this, too?" I wasn't shocked; I was disappointed with myself. I'd dismissed Umbria far too quickly. I'd underestimated her intelligence and deviousness; I'd cast too small a net.

"With Allison facing a prison term, what will happen?" I kept my voice level, like a curious stranger.

"If the will stands—there is some thought that if Allison is convicted of Quentin's murder, then Quentin's will can be invalidated—but if the will stands, Allison will have to appoint someone to manage her money while she's in prison. That will be me, the noble brother who tried to save her."

Tinkie moved to stand beside me, her face pale. "What about the other murders? Were you involved in those, too?"

"I'm a Johnny-come-lately on those. I had nothing to do with them." His eyebrows shifted up and down dramatically. "Virgie is a genius, isn't she?"

"What is wrong with you?" I snapped. "Take your antipsychotic meds, and stop twitching!"

He chuckled, but there was a brittle sound to it. "Such a card, Sarah Booth. If only you'd married me, then you'd be free right now."

"Right, one prison for another."

Tinkie poked me in the ribs. "He's not talking about marriage because he desires you. A wife doesn't have to testify against her husband."

Unbelievable, but my ego took a painful pinch. "So that's what all the gifts were about? You didn't want me. You wanted to muzzle me!"

"I thought something leather would be the quickest way to your heart."

"Tell us what you want, and then get out." I found it bitter that I'd ever been flattered by the attentions of such a shallow man, but the facts were staring me in the face. Humphrey was the worst kind of cad.

"Give up on Coleman and say you'll marry me, Sarah Booth. I'll talk to Virgie about Tinkie. I'll try to work it out so that both of you live."

"Coleman is coming." My jaw jutted out of its own accord.

"I personally gave Coleman the number of a room booked in Tinkie's name at Audubon Place. Number 945. I told him you'd discovered it and left for New Orleans about ten last night. Of course, I made the reservation, but he doesn't know that."

I sat down, my legs suddenly rubbery. Humphrey had too many specific details. It wasn't just a bluff. My hopes had been staked on Coleman and a rescue. Now we were lost. There was nothing we could offer to entice Virgie to let us go. Eventually, Coleman would arrest her for the murders she'd committed, but she was right. She could only be executed once, no matter how many people she killed. Humphrey was in the same boat: he could kill the two of us at no extra penalty.

"We're stuck here." Tinkie plopped down on the sofa. She'd obviously come to the same dark corner as I had.

Humphrey cocked his head. "Since you've admitted defeat, Sarah Booth, care for a little fun?" He reached into the pocket of his sports jacket and drew out black lace panties and a bra. "We could play Victoria's Secret model interview."

I jumped to my feet. "You are despicable."

"No, Sarah Booth, I'm merely a pragmatist and a man doing his best to *protect* his interests."

"Go away." I sank back into my chair. From beneath the weight of my defeat, I tossed one parting shot. "I can't believe Virgie, Miss High-and-Mighty-Let's-Murder-Folks-Who-Break-My-Rules, would actually hook up with a pervert."

"I guess Virgie takes the broader view of bedroom activities," Humphrey said, not the least disturbed by my ire. "Who the heck knows what she may be into." He held up a hand to stop our comments. "Virgie has said that I can have your hound, Sarah Booth. I just want you to know that she'll be well taken care of. Should you hear a commotion, don't fret. The dog is mighty loyal to you, and I had to tie her up, but I'll make sure she's safe when the time arrives." He tossed the underwear onto the sofa.

His laughter remained behind in the room as he closed and locked the door.

"We're in big trouble." Tinkie sat across from me. "I hope you have a plan, Sarah Booth, because I'm all out of ideas."

Tinkie finally fell into a light sleep. The skin beneath her eyes looked bruised, and I thought about all of the things she'd confronted in the last few weeks, from her arguments with Oscar to her breast lump, and now this. We weren't in imminent danger, but we'd been through a rough night. Worst of all was the loss of hope in Coleman and Oscar's rescue.

I had no reason to believe anything Humphrey the Humper said, except for the bald fact that Coleman hadn't burst through the door. It was possible he'd come to the school and Humphrey had convinced him we'd gone to New Orleans. Still, Coleman wasn't stupid.

So where was he?

As the shadows outside our glass prison began to shorten toward noon, I thought about a lot of things. My romantic life had been a mess of impulses. I'd never balanced my heart and my head. Maybe Jitty, with all of her court pretensions, was right. Maybe I should've had a plan. But how did one plan for true love?

The DGs approached marriage like a battle strategy. All the small skirmishes of sex and seduction led to the ultimate goal of marriage to a man who could provide. My mother had taught me that financial security wasn't the pinnacle of existence, but for some of my friends, it had become the bedrock of their marriage. With my attitude that true love would come strolling, complication free, into my life, I'd accomplished only pain.

Coleman suffered because of me. He had obligations and commitments, and I hovered out of his reach. He'd said he wanted to talk to me, and I felt the numbness of what he might say—that he was leaving Sunflower County forever. Because of me.

Now maybe he wouldn't have to.

That thought was so depressing, I rose from the sofa and went to the window to look out at the tree-shaded back lawn, which gave way to an open field and then the cotton fields beyond. Sunlight glinted on something metal near the oak where I'd first seen Humphrey.

I stared, trying to figure out what I was seeing. Vanity be

damned, I needed glasses. I made a vow that if Tinkie and I escaped, the first thing I'd do was make an appointment with an ophthalmologist while she made one with a surgeon. There would be no arguing or procrastination. Like the captain of the starship *Enterprise*, I would simply "make it so."

Movement at the oak tree stopped my internal tirade. I caught a blurry glimpse of what looked like a man in brown. I moved to the sofa for a better look, brushing aside Humphrey's odious panty set. The silky undies fell to the tile floor with a tiny clink.

I paused. There was nothing in a panty set that should make a metallic sound. Nothing. I scooped up the lacy web of material and felt it. My fingers instantly found the hard lump in the crotch of the panties. *Oh, Humphrey, you sicko!* Using more care, I untangled the undies and found a key. A key!

"Tinkie! Wake up!" I kept my voice down as the entire scenario with Humphrey replayed through my mind. He'd stood in the doorway, assaying his normal posturing around the room. Then there'd been the bizarre twitching of his face. The room number—945—was a clue to the time of the rescue. His theft of my hound had been a hint that Sweetie Pie was safe. Humphrey had no use for a dog or anything else that required time and attention. He'd been trying to tell us that he was really on our side. He was our deliverer, not our executioner.

"Tinkie!" I shook her shoulder. For someone who slept lightly, she wasn't eager to wake up.

"What is it? Has Virgie come to kill us?" She rubbed her eyes, and when she took her hands down, she saw the key I held in front of her.

I dangled it like a hypnotist. "Let's blow this popsicle stand!"

"If you're waiting on me, you're late." She was on her feet with her shoes on.

I fitted the key in the back door and turned it. The lock clicked free with a minimum of pressure. Fearing an alarm system, I eased open the back door and heard the trill of a winter songbird, the first external sound we'd heard since our imprisonment.

We looked at each other and then flew out the door and began to run toward the oak tree where I'd seen movement. Halfway there, I realized who I was running to, and I put on my last burst of speed as Coleman opened his arms for me.

I hit him with enough force to fell a block wall, but he caught me against him and reached out to drag Tinkie behind the tree with us.

"I was beginning to think she'd killed both of you and Humphrey, too." He squeezed me so hard I thought my ribs would collapse.

"We didn't find the key at first," I gasped. "Humphrey had cleverly disguised it in a pair of panties."

He released me slowly and stepped back so he could examine both of us. "You're okay?"

We nodded.

"Is Humphrey still in the house?"

"I don't know, but Sweetie is."

"Don't worry, Oscar's at the front door right this minute. When you two didn't come out after two hours, we decided to force the play."

"Oscar's going in?" Tinkie gripped Coleman's arm. "We should tell him I'm okay."

"Too late for that." Coleman picked up a rifle from beside the tree. "Now if you ladies will step back out of the line of fire, I need to give Oscar backup."

"He needs more than backup! He's not trained for this." Tinkie was frantic, and I have to admit, it did my heart good to see her so worried about her husband.

"Tinkie, the plan is in effect. There's no changing it now, and we did the best with what we had. There are several Coahoma County deputies waiting just down the driveway."

"Oscar is a banker, not a law officer. We have to stop him." She clutched Coleman's arm.

"It's too late to stop him." Coleman lifted the rifle.

"We'll see about that!" Tinkie wheeled around and started off at a sprint. I didn't wait for a signal from Coleman. I had the longer legs and the more sensible shoes. I tackled her before she'd gotten twenty feet and brought her down with an angry whuff of wind.

"You're my partner!" She thrashed and tried to bite me.

"I'm your best friend." I let my full weight drape across her.

"You're suffocating me."

"That's the idea. Unless you promise to get back behind the tree and let Coleman do his job."

"After all of this big talk about me seeing a surgeon because Oscar loves me, you won't let me protect my husband."

I sighed. "Don't you see, Tinkie? I'm in exactly the same position with both of you. You want the freedom to avoid the doctor, and Oscar wants the freedom to try and save you. Whose freedom do you want me to respect?"

She fell silent, and I rolled off her. Once I was on my feet, I helped her up, and we went to stand behind the tree.

"It's terrible waiting to see what happens." She glared at me.

"Exactly my point. So now you know how Oscar feels." My attention shifted from Tinkie to the back door, which opened. Virgie stood in the doorway with a gun pointed at Humphrey's head. There was no sign of Oscar or Sweetie.

"I want a car and safe passage to Venezuela," Virgie yelled.

"This has become hostage *du jour*." I looked to see what showed on Coleman's face.

"Where's Oscar? I don't see him anywhere. If she's hurt him . . ." Tinkie craned around me for a better view. She had a one-track mind, and it was focused on her husband.

"What are you going to do?" I asked Coleman.

"Whatever is necessary."

The fact that he wouldn't look at me told me too much. He feared Oscar was dead. "Sweetie Pie is in there." I saw in his firm focus on the house that he held little hope for her, either.

Tinkie stood beside me, tears gathering in her eyes. "This is my punishment," she whispered.

My impulse was to shake her, but instead I folded her into my arms and held her tight. "You've done nothing wrong." Over the top of her head, I watched Virgie holding the gun on Humphrey.

"Deputies are covering the front of the house," Coleman said. "I'm going to try and talk her out."

I wanted to stop him, but I couldn't. "Be careful."

Coleman stepped out from behind the tree and lowered his gun. "Virgie, we can all walk away from this."

"Not me. Everything I worked for is gone. I put my life into those girls. I put everything, and they betrayed all of my teachings."

"You have to let Humphrey go."

"He tricked me. He lied to me. He deserves to die."

Coleman walked closer. There was nothing for him to hide behind. He was in the open, moving toward a crazy woman with a gun.

"Where's Oscar?" he asked her.

"He chose the wrong woman."

"That's not his fault." Coleman spoke in a calm, reasoned tone. "Look, I understand how you feel. I know what its like to be disappointed by people. I see it every day in my work." He stepped closer. "Let's talk about this. If I put my gun down, will you do the same?"

"You're trying to trick me." She shifted the barrel of her gun from Humphrey to point at Coleman's chest.

I felt my heart squeeze painfully. Tinkie and I clung to each other, unable to do a single thing that would make a difference.

"I'm not trying to trick you, Virgie. I'm trying to help you." Coleman moved closer. He was only thirty feet away. If she was any kind of shot at all, she could hit him right in the heart.

"No one can help me. I've made my decisions. I'm prepared to do whatever I have to, to get away."

"None of this is necessary." Coleman stepped closer. "We can talk this out. Just put the gun down and give it a chance. What do you have to lose?"

"I'm not going to prison. I won't spend the rest of my life among women with no refinement, with no breeding. I'd rather die."

"I thought you were a woman who enjoyed a challenge." Coleman shook his head. "I thought you were a woman with a spine, but you're like all those disappointments. You just take the easy way out. Things don't go your way and you just curl up and whine."

"How dare you?" She leveled the gun at his chest. "I'm going to die anyway, and I'm going to take you straight to hell with me!"

"No!" I broke free of Tinkie and started running toward Coleman. Tinkie was right behind me, screaming my name.

The barrel of Virgie's gun swung away from Coleman and aimed right at me. I saw Humphrey's face freeze in panic. I put everything I had into running. Coleman was the prize, and I kept my eyes upon him. To my horror, he rushed Virgie. The gun moved off me and sighted on him.

There is no sound as final as that of a gunshot. I heard the shot at the same time I saw Coleman twist, red blooming on his chest.

"Coleman!" I screamed his name. My feet were suddenly bound in concrete. I tried to run, but I was locked in place. "Coleman!"

"Sweet Jesus!" Tinkie cried behind me as she ran toward Coleman, who'd fallen and was stretched on the ground, unmoving.

On the back steps my hound accosted Virgie, knocking her sideways and away from Humphrey. They both tottered on the top step and then fell in opposite directions.

Sweetie Pie cleared both of them as she bounded down the steps. She snapped up the gun that had fallen from Virgie's hand and held it in her mouth.

"Sweetie!" I called, patting my leg in the "let's play" signal. She shook the gun like some captured prey and then brought it to me and dropped it at my feet. When I looked up, Oscar was standing in the back doorway, a pistol trained on Virgie.

"Oscar!" Tinkie cried. Her heart was in that single word. "Thank goodness. Help Coleman." Tinkie snatched my hand and dragged me behind her as she ran to Coleman. He'd fallen on his face, and I could clearly see the bullet's exit hole in his back, where blood seeped out.

"Sarah Booth, get some towels." Tinkie rolled him over, and I heard myself gasp. Coleman was either unconscious or dead. His eyes were closed, and his face was pallid. I felt Tinkie's hand on my leg. "Go inside and call an ambulance. Get some towels. Do it now!"

25

Humphrey took the towels to Tinkie as I gave directions over the phone to the ambulance. I kept my voice calm and rational, until I hung up. My knees buckled, and I dropped into a chair. I felt as if I were still in my glass prison. No sound penetrated the thrumming of my heart and the terrible litany of my brain. *Coleman is shot. He's lying on the ground bleeding. Coleman is shot. He's lying on the ground bleeding.*

I walked back outside and went to him. Kneeling beside him, I held his cool hand as Tinkie and Oscar fought to staunch the bleeding while Humphrey tied Virgie into one of her lawn chairs.

"Big, dumb fool!" she spat. "I hope he dies."

We were too busy to respond to her.

"Press hard," Tinkie told Oscar as the blood seeped through the towel and between his fingers. "Press really hard." She put her hands over his, and I added mine, all three pressing on Coleman's chest, pressing the blood back into his body.

I heard the ambulance, but it didn't register. It was only

when the paramedics physically pulled me back that I let go. Tinkie and Oscar stepped away and let the professionals work. We were all covered in blood.

The paramedics loaded Coleman in the ambulance and careened away to the hospital. We were left with the deputies. And Virgie. I looked at her and felt nothing. Tinkie walked over and put her hands on her hips as she glared down at Virgie.

"You'd better hope he doesn't die."

"Why should I care?" Virgie asked.

"Because if Coleman dies, you have my word that you won't be executed. You'll spend the rest of your life in prison if I have to spend my last penny filing petitions to stay your execution." She stepped back as two deputies untied Virgie and put the cuffs on her.

The Coahoma County deputies were not as personable as Dewayne and Gordon, but they did their jobs. In quick order, two took Virgie to jail, and two others took our statements. Humphrey carried the burden of the story, and he agreed to go to headquarters with them to fill in any gaps.

My first impulse was to head to the hospital as fast I could go, but Oscar detained me. "Give them some time," he said, and I'd only heard him speak so gently to Tinkie. "Stay here for a while, in the sunshine. There'll be plenty of hours to spend in the hospital."

Tinkie, Oscar, Sweetie, and I stood on the blood-soaked lawn of the premier ladies school in the Southeast, listening to what seemed an unnatural silence and waiting for the phone to ring with news of Coleman.

Oscar and Tinkie couldn't keep their hands off each other, and while it saddened me when I thought of the future without Coleman, it also gave me hope.

"I'm glad you're okay, Oscar," I said. "I was worried sick, but Tinkie threw a hissy fit. Don't let her try to pretend she wasn't worried about you. She almost had a cow."

"Quite a feat for a well-bred lady," Oscar said, and even though I thought my heart was breaking, I smiled.

"Coleman's going to be okay." Tinkie put her arm around me on one side, and Oscar on the other. "He is, Sarah Booth. He's a tough man, too ornery to die."

I wanted to believe her, but I was afraid to. So much blood! How could someone live after losing all that blood? It didn't seem possible.

"How did you find Sweetie Pie?" I asked Oscar. We moved to the striped canvas chairs, which made a picturesque setting on the lawn of Virgie's home. Sweetie settled at my feet.

"How about a drink, Sarah Booth?" Tinkie moved to the back steps. "I don't think Virgie's going to object if we sample her liquor."

I nodded. "I don't care what it is, just make it strong."

"I'll get something for all of us," Tinkie said. "Even Sweetie deserves something to calm her nerves."

I didn't know what might calm a hound's nerves, and I didn't ask. Tinkie was in charge.

"I want to tell you about Sweetie." Oscar sat across from me and took my hands in his. "She saved me. You know I adore Chablis, but Sweetie Pie is nobody's fool. She saved me."

"How?" I was merely curious. I'd learned long ago that Sweetie was miraculous, and I would gladly talk about the weather in Timbuktu if I didn't have to think about Coleman.

"I went to the front door as Coleman told me to do. I knocked; Virgie answered and invited me in. She was cool as a cucumber. Coleman had warned me not to be taken in, but she was so cordial and so . . . refined. I was thinking that surely there'd been some kind of mistake. I mean Virgie is in her sixties, and her hair is so perfectly silver and old lady–like, and she wears those pastel dresses and sensible shoes." He shook his head.

"We were all taken in," I said. "So what happened?"

"I went in the parlor, and she brought me some coffee with a slice of fruitcake. I meant to eat only one bite, but it was delicious. I have to say, it rivals those fruitcakes you make, Sarah Booth."

"Don't feel badly about the fruitcake, Oscar. The drug was in the coffee, too."

Tinkie came out with a tray of tall, dark drinks and a portion of roast, carved into bite-sized nuggets, for Sweetie. I took a drink and sipped. A Cuba libre, with expensive rum and a slice of lime. Perfect.

"Oscar, how long did it take for the drug to hit you?" Tinkie perched on the arm of his chair.

"About ten minutes. I hit the floor." Oscar rubbed his jaw where a discoloration was forming. "She may have been trying to kill me on the spot."

It was possible. Killing Oscar would accomplish nothing, but Virgie wigged out. "At first, Virgie used some restraint in her actions, but she completely lost it toward the end." I tried to blink away the image of Coleman lying in the grass. "So when did you find Sweetie Pie?"

"I didn't find her. She found me. Virgie must have dragged me into a bathroom. She didn't bother to lock the door, and I managed to open it and fall halfway out into the hall. I was semiconscious when Sweetie came up." He reached down to pat my hound's head. "Let's just say she forced me to wake up."

"She licked your face." I gave her a kiss on the head. "Sweetie isn't real tolerant of folks who try to nap."

"She wouldn't stop. She kept on until I made myself get up. I was woozy and sick, but there wasn't a chance she'd let me sleep."

"That's my girl." I stroked her long ears as she pretended to doze by my chair. "What happened after that?"

"I heard a commotion, and I crept to the kitchen, where I found Virgie and Humphrey. Everything happened too fast for me to stop it. She accused him of double-crossing her, pulled the gun, and took him to the back door where she tried to negotiate her freedom. I had another spell of unconsciousness."

"And that's when Sweetie saved the day," Tinkie said. "She knocked Virgie off the steps and snatched up the gun so Virgie couldn't reach it. If it wasn't for Sweetie, we might all be dead."

That was true, but if it wasn't for me, Coleman wouldn't even be wounded.

As if she sensed my thoughts, Tinkie knelt beside me. She took one hand, while Oscar held the other. "Sarah Booth, I've learned something very interesting about guilt in the last few weeks."

"What might that be?" She was staring at me so intensely, I wanted to draw back.

"You have to believe me."

I gave a weak smile. "I always believe you."

"I didn't believe you when you tried to talk to me about Oscar and the baby. My need to punish myself was greater than my common sense. And in punishing myself, I also punished Oscar and my friends. I don't want to see that happen to you."

"I'm not much on self-punishment." I spoke the lie with a smile.

"All of us are. I think it's part of the human condition, but I learned something from Doreen Mallory that I forgot until today."

Doreen was our former client who'd been falsely accused of killing her own infant child. She'd also been something of a miracle worker. Even though I'd greatly resisted her attempts to ease my pain, I had learned something from her.

"Things happen for a reason, Sarah Booth. I forgot that when I thought of my baby. Now you have to remember it when you think of Coleman. He came here to do something he had to do—to protect the two of us. He was shot while doing that. But we don't know that if he'd stayed home, something else horrible wouldn't have happened to him."

I rolled my eyes. "Like what? He might have been vomited on while arresting a drunk?"

Tinkie increased the pressure on my fingers. "Sarcasm won't deflect the pain for long. Listen to me. If you don't get a grip on this now, if something does happen to Coleman, you'll carry the guilt the rest of your life. Like I carried the guilt for my child. It almost destroyed me, and it almost got Oscar, too."

"Sometimes people are guilty, Tinkie!" I couldn't stop the rush of angry words. "Sometimes people do things and they deserve to suffer."

"Virgie deserves to suffer. You don't."

"I could have done things very differently, and perhaps Coleman wouldn't even be wounded now."

"You could have done them differently, and he might be dead." Oscar patted my hand. "What Tinkie is trying to make you see is that we aren't omnipotent. We can't know the outcome of our actions, and even actions taken with the very best of intentions sometimes cause suffering. But the only people who are guilty are those like Virgie, who harm others without regard."

"I just want Coleman to be okay." Once I said the words, I couldn't stop the tears. My whole body shook, and there was no more need for words. Tinkie and Oscar wrapped me in their arms, and Sweetie Pie sat up and licked my face. And I allowed them to comfort me.

The Clarksdale hospital was clean and quiet. I sat in the waiting room with a stack of magazines and a diet cola and waited. Tinkie had gone to the gift shop to find something for Coleman to read once he came out of surgery; she refused to behave in a way that implied he might not recover. Oscar had taken Sweetie back to Zinnia.

Both Gordon and Dewayne had called to check on Coleman, but there had been no word from Connie, his wife. Perhaps no one had told her. I kept telling myself over and over that it was none of my business, but it didn't do any good. In my heart, I was Coleman's family. At last, when the doctor pushed through the doors into the waiting room, I stood to hear the news.

"Mrs. Peters," he said, wrongly assuming I was Coleman's wife, "we repaired the damage to his lung and the shattered rib." He paused, and the frown on his face told me he was worried. "The heart wasn't damaged, which is very good news, but he lost a lot of blood."

"But he's going to be okay?" I could hardly speak for the hammering of my heart.

"He's in stable condition now."

"You didn't answer my question. Is he going to be okay?"

He finally met my gaze. "We feel his prognosis for recovery is good."

What was wrong with this man? Double-talk wasn't what I wanted to hear. "Will he or won't he recover?"

He sighed. "We're not gods, Mrs. Peters. We can't see the future. He should heal, but a lot depends on him. On how much he has to live for."

"You're saying it's up to him. He has to want to live." I wondered what the doctor had seen that made him understand Coleman had been in emotional turmoil.

"That's right. He's asleep now, but maybe you'd like to see him. Talk to him a little."

"I would." I glanced around to see if Tinkie was in sight, but she was still buying magazines at the gift shop. "Is he in his room?"

"Recovery. Don't be shocked by his appearance. He lost a lot of blood. Just touch him and talk to him."

I followed the doctor down a green corridor and into a wing shut off by swinging doors. We entered a room with several beds, but only one was occupied. The man in the bed looked vaguely like Coleman. He was deathly pale.

Tears started to my eyes, but I forced them back. Crying would do no good for either of us. The doctor nodded at me, and I walked to the bedside and picked up Coleman's chill hand. I had to fight back the tears for a second time. Coleman and I had never had the luxury of walking down Main Street together, holding hands the way lovers do in movies. Heck, we were a long shot from lovers. We'd kissed, but that was it.

I brushed the fine blond hair back from his forehead, noting the dark circles beneath his eyes. "Coleman," I whispered, though there was no one else to hear me, "you have to recover. I need you."

His breathing was shallow but regular, but there was no sign that he'd heard me.

"Tinkie and Oscar are fine. Virgie is in the Coahoma County jail, and Gordon is making arrangements to have her transferred back to Sunflower County to be charged with Quentin's murder."

I felt the lightest pressure of his fingers. It could have been a muscle spasm, but it made my heart jump painfully in my chest. "Sweetie Pie is just fine, too. Humphrey wasn't injured. Everyone is okay. It's up to you now to get better."

In the movies, the camera would close in on Coleman's face, and his eyes would open slowly. He would be fuzzy for a moment, and then recognition would begin. He would turn to me and smile and say, "I've always loved you, Sarah Booth." And I would cry and kiss him, and somehow, magically, he would produce an engagement ring from the folds of the hospital bed and say, "I've been carrying this around for weeks now and could never find the right time to ask you to marry me." And I would say, "Yes, of course. As soon as you're well," and he would say, "No need to wait for that. Let's call one of the ministers visiting the sick in the hospital." And miraculously, the door would open, and Father Smith would be standing there in his Episcopal collar, and he would perform the wedding on the spot.

But this was real life, and Coleman's eyes remained closed, his breathing shallow, and if he had the power to squeeze my fingers, he didn't do it.

I leaned down and kissed his scraped cheek. "I love you, Coleman." I had to tell him that. I'd never said it before, not when he was conscious. I'd never been willing to risk all that it meant. Now, I couldn't help myself. "I've loved you for a long, long time. It doesn't matter whether you can love me back or not, it's just something I want you to know."

I kissed him again and stood up just as the sound of high heels tapped into the recovery room. Tinkie came toward us, her arms laden with magazines, books, candy, and flowers. Had I not recognized the sound of her heels, I might not have known who she was. She was completely hidden by her spoils.

"I'm going to take all of this to his room," she said, easing it down on the foot of his bed to rest her overtaxed arms. She took a good look at him and gave me a nod. "He's a little peaked, but I've seen worse."

"The doctor said they'd repaired everything. It's up to him to want to recover."

Tinkie walked to the other side of the bed and picked up his left hand. She squeezed it tightly. "Coleman Peters, you'd better get well. I won't have any malingering on the job. Folks around Sunflower County need you, and I know one particular private investigator who can't make it without you." She kissed his hand and put it back on the bed.

"I never thought I'd see Coleman so . . . still."

"He said the same thing about you, Sarah Booth, when you were shot. He was hovering over you just like you're doing with him. You probably don't remember it, but you were pale, too. You looked so thin lying on that emergency room table. We were all afraid you'd die, but you pulled out of it just fine, and so will he."

I'd never appreciated Tinkie's optimism more than now. "Thank you, Tinkie."

"Coleman will thank me, too, when he comes to." She picked up her purchases. "I'm going to take these on to Room 43. Why don't you stay here with him until they move him? Then we'll decide what we should do about going home."

"Sounds good to me."

I sat on the foot of his bed and watched the nurses come back and forth to check him. They told me there was no fresh bleeding, which was a good sign. They changed out the blood transfusion bag and gave him another one. Drop by drop, they were replacing what had leaked out of him. Surely it would soon make a difference, and his color would improve.

An hour later, two orderlies came to wheel Coleman to his room. His condition had not improved at all, but the nurses who'd checked him said it wasn't uncommon. He'd been heavily sedated for the surgery.

I wasn't soothed, but I could only follow his gurney past a nurses' station and closed doors. The doctor was standing in the hallway with Tinkie, and there was an intimacy between them that reminded me of Tinkie's former flirtations with handsome men of the medical profession.

They looked up at me and both smiled. "Coleman is holding his own, Sarah Booth. That's good. Very good. Each hour that passes gives him a better chance."

"Your husband is a strong, healthy man," the doctor said, and for the first time I noticed his name, Larry Martin. He patted my shoulder. "He may stay sedated until tomorrow. Now would be a good time for you to go home and get some rest. We'll take good care of him."

Dr. Martin pulled a prescription pad from his pocket, jotted a few words, tore off the sheet, and handed it to me. "Mrs. Richmond has told me a little of what transpired. I've written you a script for a few light sedatives. Have it filled and try to sleep. Believe me, when Sheriff Peters does wake up, you're going to need all of your patience to deal with him. He doesn't strike me as the kind of man who'll be easy to manage while he recovers."

I took the prescription and put it in my pocket.

"Thank you, Larry," Tinkie said, standing on tiptoe to kiss his cheek. "I really owe you."

She took my arm and propelled me down the corridor before I could protest. In truth, I was suddenly exhausted. I'd had almost no sleep the night before, and the day had been a horror-movie blur.

"I should stay." It was a feeble protest at best.

"I'll take you home. Tomorrow you can come back and entertain him."

"Are you sure there's going to be a tomorrow?" Tinkie wouldn't fib to me about this.

"Larry was concerned right after the surgery, but Coleman has had two pints of blood, and he's holding his own. It's looking much, much better." She pushed through the doors to the parking lot. "I called the sheriff's office with a progress report. Gordon told me the deaths of Belinda Loper, Betty Reynolds, and Karla Jenkins have been re-opened based on our investigation. A reporter from the Memphis *Commercial Appeal* wants to interview us."

"I don't want to talk to anyone." I sank into the passenger seat of my car. Tinkie had the keys and refused to yield them.

"That's today. Wait until tomorrow. I think a photograph of the two of us at Coleman's bedside would play well. We'll have more cases than we can shake a stick at."

"You are the optimist, aren't you?" Something was up

with Tinkie. She was her old bubbly self. "Did that doctor give you some kind of happy drugs?"

"Absolutely not."

"Then what's wrong with you? You're positively perky."

"Sarah Booth, I'll tell you all about it tomorrow, after you've had a chance to rest up."

26

I sat in the barn, listening to Reveler munch his grain. For the first time since Coleman had been shot, I felt my heart settle to its normal position. Sweetie Pie curled at my feet in the hay, and I leaned back against a bale and closed my eyes, inhaling the lingering scent of summer that had been baled in the dried grass. The hospital would call me as soon as Coleman regained consciousness. The doctors and nurses were still under the misimpression that I was his wife, so they swore they'd call. All I could do was wait. And hope that everything would be okay.

"Not everyone you love is going to die."

There was the rustle of silk, and I didn't have to look to know that Jitty had joined me. Never before had she left Dahlia House to venture to the barn. Jitty, with her elegant wardrobe and otherworldly beauty, was not interested in farm life.

"Slow night at court?" I asked, keeping my eyes closed.

"The intrigues of society pale beside the needs of family."

I sat up and looked at Jitty shimmering in the dim barn light. Her gown was truly spectacular, a pale champagne with gold stitching. "I'm okay," I assured her. "You look ready for an audience with the king. Why don't you go on about your business? I'm truly fine."

"Pride is the most dangerous of all the sins, Sarah Booth."

She'd called my bluff, so there was no point lying. Jitty knew me too well, and she could hear the hurt in my voice. "Okay, I'm as fine as I can be with Coleman lying in a hospital bed."

The ball gown rustled provocatively. "Let's take a walk."

Jitty had never been one for voluntary exercise. I rose slowly, forcing Sweetie to stretch and yawn. "Where are we going?"

"You'll see."

She may have left the court behind, but she was still mysterious. I supposed it was the prerogative of a ghost. I followed her out of the barn and into the chill night. I noticed the Christmas garland I'd used to decorate the banister of the back steps. The holiday was only a couple of weeks away, and I hadn't bought the first gift.

Instead of heading to the house, Jitty turned beside the barn, directing me toward the back pasture. My curiosity was piqued, and I fell in step beside her. It would do no good to beg her for information. Jitty had all the time in the world and wouldn't be hurried.

We followed along the fence, our way lighted by millions of stars and a half-moon strong enough to cast shadows. It was a beautiful, crisp night, and I inhaled the cold air.

"When your mama was worried or tired or unsettled, she'd come out here," Jitty said. "She had a special place where she said she could think more clearly."

I hadn't thought of that in a long time. My mother was a great one for tramping over the land when she was upset. She often said the land was where she found the things that were important, and that a walk over the property cleared her head. My mother had loved Dahlia House and all the land surrounding it with deep passion. When I'd first come home from New York City, I'd almost lost the property to the bank. I'd understood then how much my mother cared for this place, because I felt that love, that connection, as real as blood. Now, strolling beside Jitty, I felt it again.

Walking among the moon shadows cast by the trees, I put aside my fear and felt the comfort of the land. Here was where I belonged. When all else failed, this land was still here, alive and growing, sustaining.

"I knew you'd feel better out here," Jitty said.

"How did you know?"

"It's always worked this way for the Delaney women."

Now that was an interesting twist. The land had been in my father's family, yet it was my mother who'd fallen under its spell. "Only the women?"

She shook her head. "Not only, but most deeply. When things were at their worst during the War Between the States, there were times when Alice wanted to quit. She could have gone back to Charleston, West Virginia, where she had a sister. But she couldn't leave this place. She'd dreamt the dream of the land, and she couldn't leave."

"Is that why you're here, Jitty?"

"This was never my land." She chuckled softly. "No, I stayed for Alice. I loved her like a sister. And now I stay for you."

As we walked side by side, I considered the gift of her presence. She nagged and tormented and prodded, but I'd come to count on her being at Dahlia House. In a sense, she was my family.

"Thank you," I said.

"Keep walking. There's something for you to see."

We passed the family cemetery, the stones cold and gray in the winter night. This is where I thought we'd stop, but we didn't. We walked in silence until we came to a grove of old oaks, limbs spreading out to touch the ground. Acorns crunched underfoot, and the air was cold and pure.

I'd played here as a young child, drawing lines in the dirt to outline my "house," and building roads and dirt towns to gallop my plastic horses over and through. Sometimes, I'd leave my toys, and when I came back the next day, they would be moved, as if some other child had played with them.

"This is the fairy spot." I smiled as I said the words.

"I thought you might remember," Jitty said.

"I loved it when Mama brought me here. In the cool shade."

"This was one of her favorite places on the entire plantation. She found a lot of comfort here."

"She'd let me play while she sat on that tree limb." I pointed, and for a moment I almost saw her, dark hair tied back in a scarf, red lips smiling when I told her about the fairies. She never felt the need to refute my stories, had never tried to make me toe the line of acceptable beliefs. She'd always encouraged me to play and dream. My smile matched the ghost of hers.

"It's a very special place," Jitty said. "There's not a lot of difference between fairies and ghosts."

"Your point is well-taken." I took a seat in the crook of a swooping limb. "Why did you bring me out here?"

"Your mama was a remarkable woman."

"She was, but we didn't have to come out here to agree on that." Jitty normally preferred to have our discussions in the comfort of the house.

"She's never left you, Sarah Booth."

The lump in my throat was instant. "Oh, but she did. She and Daddy both." I'd been twelve when a car accident had claimed their lives.

Jitty shook her head, beautiful pearl earrings dancing in the moonlight. "No, she's here with you now. Both of your parents are here."

The tears I'd bottled up for so long began to fall. "I want them to be alive." And then I realized the genius of Jitty's walk. "I want Coleman to live. I can't bear it if anything happens to him." I was sobbing outright.

"Whatever happens with Coleman, you'll be okay."

I was instantly furious. "That's not good enough. I'm tired of losing everyone I love. I'm tired of death. I'm sick of the pain. Coleman would be in his office, tending to business, if he hadn't tried to save me."

Jitty sighed. "Loving someone means allowing him to be who he is, Sarah Booth. Coleman did what he wanted to do. It's not your place to judge him or yourself."

"Coleman can be whoever he wants, as long as he's alive." I would give him up. I would let him go, if only he wouldn't die.

There was sadness in her voice. "Death is only an extreme form of change."

"Call it by any name you wish, but it is an ending, a conclusion to being here with me. My parents are gone. Coleman is seriously wounded. He could die, and then he'll be gone from me."

Jitty walked slowly through the clearing, turned, and came back to me. "He's going to be okay."

There was something in the way she said it that chilled me. "Okay? What does that mean?"

"He'll survive the gunshot."

"Survive?" Jitty was playing coy at a game I didn't understand.

"He'll recover from the wound."

I felt the pressure of additional tears. "Are you sure?"

She nodded.

"Thank goodness." Relief swept over me like a gentle wind. "Thank goodness."

"The bullet didn't strike you, Sarah Booth, but you were wounded nonetheless. Keep that in mind. You have to heal as much as Coleman does."

"I'll be fine as long as he's okay."

Jitty only stared at me a long moment and shook her head. "Coleman will not die."

We started back toward the lights of Dahlia House, walking side by side. I could tell by the furrow in her brow that she was worried. "I'm okay," I assured her.

We made it to the barn in silence. "You are the hard-headedest woman I've ever met," she said at last.

"You promise Coleman will be okay?"

She nodded. "Quit worrying about him. There are other things you should turn your attention to. I've learned some things at court."

"I'll bet. What? Excess is best?"

Her smile was sad. "Hardheaded and sarcastic to the end, aren't you?" Her stare became a challenge. "Change is inevitable, Sarah Booth. The art of living is not merely to accept change, but to embrace it. The revolution is coming."

I thought about the little I knew of the French Revolution. It had been a bloody coup fueled by the hunger of the people and the excess of the court. The common man had been aroused to overthrow the monarchy. A lot of people had died. "Don't linger at the ball too long, Cinderella. You'll come home with your head in a basket."

She flickered dimly. "Remember, change is inevitable. It's part of living. Even royalty must bend to change." And then she was gone.

I awoke to the pounding of tiny fists against the front door—and kicking. Tinkie was impatient. Or I'd been deeply asleep. I'd taken one of Dr. Martin's little magic sleeping pills, and I'd turned into a log.

"I'm coming!" I grabbed a quilt off the bed and wrapped it around me as I ran to open the door. Tinkie, dressed in a faux fur–trimmed sweater and leather pants, rolled her eyes as she walked past me.

"It's about time, Sarah Booth. I was freezing my butt off waiting for you to get up and open the door. What's for breakfast?"

I was so glad to see Tinkie, safe and sound and hungry, that I didn't bother to point out that I'd been in a drug-induced coma because I was worried about Coleman. "How about egg sandwiches?" The pickings in my refrigerator were pretty slim since I hadn't been to the store in two weeks.

"Sounds great. There's probably some cheese tucked away in the fridge somewhere, too." She preceded me into the kitchen and started to put on a pot of coffee. I sat at the table.

"I haven't heard a word from Coleman." With Jitty's assurances and Dr. Martin's magic pills, I'd fallen into such a deep sleep that I'd forgotten to worry.

Tinkie turned and frowned. "That's strange. They called me about an hour ago and said they'd called you first."

"How is Coleman?" To heck with the technicalities.

"Up and hungry. He's going to be just fine. In fact, if you'll put some clothes on while I fix breakfast, we'll drive over to visit him."

"Yes!" I danced around the kitchen, my quilt cape flapping behind me. Tinkie tried to look disturbed, but then she smiled.

"This is going to be a wonderful Christmas, Sarah Booth. Just you wait and see."

I didn't have a single doubt. Coleman was going to be fine. Tinkie and Oscar were back on track. Sweetie Pie was circling the table, hoping for a scrap of something to fall her way. Not that her bowl was empty, but human food was always preferable.

"Shall we call Cece?" Tinkie asked.

"Sure."

"Then why don't we just go to Millie's for breakfast, and we can drive to Clarksdale from there."

"Sounds like a plan. Have some coffee, and I'll be changed in a jiffy." Well, not exactly a jiffy. I planned to apply a little make-up, at least. If Coleman was recovering, I didn't want to frighten him back into unconsciousness.

I sprinted up the stairs, turned on the shower, and dragged my favorite black jeans and a jade sweater out of the closet. In a moment I was soaping and scrubbing. I finished in record time, tied my hair back with a scarf that matched my sweater, and bounded down the stairs to meet Tinkie at the door.

"Should I call Coleman?" I couldn't wait to talk to him.

"I think a visit would be better. He can just open his eyes and see you staring down at him, all aquiver for his recovery. That'll be his dream come true."

I slapped her shoulder lightly as I walked around the Caddy and got in the passenger seat. "Where's Chablis?"

"She's with Oscar." When she said her husband's name, her smile softened.

"Things okay in that department?" Her expression told me enough, but I wanted to hear her say it.

"Things are good. We had a long talk last night, and we resolved some issues that had been between us a long time."

"Oscar is somebody." Never in my wildest dreams had I thought that one day I'd be defending Oscar Richmond, wealthy banker. But there was more to Oscar than met the eye. The depth of his love for Tinkie had touched me.

Tinkie spun down the driveway and turned toward Millie's. She glanced at me. "I have something to tell you."

The way she said it made my heart flutter. "What?"

"While you were in recovery with Coleman, I scheduled an appointment for a breast biopsy with Dr. Martin. He's going to do it Wednesday."

"Thank you, Tinkie." I reached across the seat and squeezed her hand. "Thank you."

"I'm perfectly healthy, but I owe it to Oscar and you and my friends to put your minds at ease."

"You don't owe it to us, but I'm glad you're doing it." I felt as if I'd been released by some heavy weight.

"I know I'm perfectly fine, so there's no reason not to do this."

I didn't care how she'd rationalized it as long as she took care of it. "I'll drive you over."

"Oscar's going to do it."

I nodded. "Perfect. Once that's taken care of and we get Coleman home, life will settle back into a normal pattern."

She laughed. "You are an optimist, aren't you? The only normal pattern around you is chaos and lots of danger."

Although I didn't react, her words cut me to the quick. What she said was true. In the past year, I'd found myself in several life-threatening situations, and wherever I went, my friends tended to follow.

"Did I say something wrong?" She pulled into the parking lot at Millie's and stopped the car.

I shook my head. "I have a lot to think about."

"About Coleman getting shot?"

I nodded. "I rushed out to Virgie's to save you because I wanted to show you I could come to the rescue. It was my fault Coleman got shot."

Her laughter was full and merry. "You are such an egotist, Sarah Booth."

In the space of twelve hours, I'd been called hardheaded by Jitty and now an egotist by Tinkie. What was this, Kick Sarah Booth Day? "Why would you say that?" I asked.

"Because it's true. You think everything that happened is because of you. Coleman was there to save me, too. I'm not chopped liver, you know."

It was true. Had I not even been involved, Coleman would have risked himself to save Tinkie. Even though she'd insulted me, I felt marginally better. "But you wouldn't have been held hostage were you not working with me."

"Maybe, maybe not. I might have started a PI agency on my own. Or I might have insulted Virgie in some other way. But that's not even the point, Sarah Booth. Sometimes you are so dense!"

Add dense to the list of insults. "What is the point?"

"You are a vital part of my life. And Coleman's. But you aren't the sun that we revolve around." She circled her finger around her head. "It isn't all about you. How can it be that you made me see that about my breast lump, and Oscar see it about his concern for me, but you can't see it yourself!"

"But if I'm responsible—"

"Good lord!" She sucked in her lip and let it pop out in a gesture that made men so weak-kneed they had to sit down. "If I was nominated for a medal for solving this crime, you'd never consider thinking that you were somehow responsible. You don't try to assume credit for my actions, so for goodness' sakes, don't try to assume the blame."

Tinkie had a way of making things clear to me. "You're right."

"The same is true for Coleman. He chose to be there. He chose to provoke Virgie to give Humphrey a chance to escape. He made a choice and acted on it. You're simply not involved."

"Okay." I felt a good bit better. In fact, my ego had shriveled, and my appetite had returned. I was starving. "Let's eat and then go see Coleman."

"At last, you say something with merit." She got out of the car and led the way to a back table at Millie's, where Cece was already waiting for us.

"Dahlings," Cece said, waving her coffee cup. "Congratulations! I've been fielding calls all morning long from newspapers across the nation. Everyone wants an interview with the two daring private eyes who nabbed a serial killer."

Millie brought two steaming mugs of coffee and gave both me and Tinkie a hug. "Good work, ladies. The Delta is a safer place now that that homicidal maniac is behind bars."

"Thanks," Tinkie and I said in unison as we sat down.

"I got a statement from Coleman's doctor this morning," Cece continued. "He's going to make a full recovery. No permanent damage at all."

My grin went from ear to ear. "That's wonderful. When can he come home?"

"Tomorrow."

"That's even better." I had a sudden vision of him installed in my bed at Dahlia House while I made chicken soup and kept him warm.

"We're going to visit him when we finish here," Tinkie said.

"So, tell me everything." Cece brought a pad out of her purse. "True crime is not generally the province of the society pages, but I'm going to angle the story at two female private investigators." She frowned at me. "Sarah Booth, if you'd just upgrade your wardrobe a bit, I could make this a fashion article."

"Not a chance. I'm happy being an unfashionable investigator."

Millie took our orders, and we laughed our way through breakfast. It was wonderful to be with my girlfriends, to be safe, to know that Tinkie was taking steps to keep herself healthy. To know that Coleman was recuperating.

The front door of the café opened, and Humphrey walked in. Tinkie waved him over. "We never got a chance to thank you," she said as he took a chair between us. "You saved our lives."

"It was nothing." His face flushed only a little. "I knew I had to get you out of the house somehow. Virgie had completely flipped. She was irrational."

"She almost killed you." I handed him the cup of coffee Millie brought. "You're quick on your feet."

"I'm even better in a horizontal position." He looked right at me. "You've underestimated me since you've known me. I wish you'd give me a chance."

His words caught me off guard. I hadn't expected him to be serious, especially not about a relationship with me. "Humphrey, my heart is taken."

Sadness touched the corners of his mouth. "I know. You're in love with the sheriff."

There wasn't any point in denying it. "It's complicated."

"Indeed, it is. Coleman Peters is married."

"I know."

"His wife is a nut case," Millie said. "Certifiable. He's been tied to her by obligation, but that can't go on forever. Once she has the baby, Coleman can file for custody of the child and then divorce Connie."

Humphrey sipped his coffee. "It sounds as if you've got it all neatly planned."

Though he was trying to hide it, I sensed disappointment in Humphrey's tone. I reached across the table and took his hand. "Nothing is planned. But I do love Coleman. I love him enough to let him decide what he should do."

Humphrey finished his coffee and stood. "Ladies, I want to thank you all for your help. My sister—"

"Where is Allison?" I interrupted. In all of the hullabaloo, I hadn't even questioned where she'd gone once she was released from jail.

"She's at The Gardens." He held up a hand. "Sarah Booth, your impetuous nature might be fun in bed, but it's annoying when I'm trying to tell you something."

I rolled my eyes. "Speak."

"Allison wants to invite all of you to a small gathering tonight at seven at The Gardens. Please say you'll come."

"We wouldn't miss it for the world." Cece spoke for all of us. "Would an interview with Allison be out of the question?"

"I could arrange it," Humphrey said, crooking his arm for Cece. "Let me escort you." He shot a look at me. "I'll see you tonight, Sarah Booth. Remember, there's still time to change your mind."

27

Whether she needed to see the doctor or not, Tinkie stopped off by Dr. Martin's office for a "chat" while I walked down the long corridor to Coleman's room alone. Tinkie was the kind of friend who would make up an excuse to give me a few private moments with the man I loved—even though I was a coward and preferred her to be with me.

On the drive over, I'd thought about some of the last words I'd had with Coleman. He'd wanted to talk to me about something. Something important. Something that most likely involved our future, either separately or together.

With each step, I drew closer to my fate. It wasn't a comforting feeling. I was almost at Coleman's room, and I slowed. My courage was failing me.

I heard the sound of padded shoes behind me, and I turned to find a nurse wearing a surgical mask, hurrying toward me, a strange look in her eyes. I felt a sick sensation. "Is Coleman okay?" I asked.

"You bitch!"

I never saw the hand until it smacked into my face. My vision blurred.

"I'm going to show you what happens to a husband stealer!"

I was too busy ducking to get a good look at her face, but I had no doubt who it was. Connie Peters had finally put in an appearance, and she was pissed.

"I'm going to make you sorry you ever thought about stealing my husband. I'm going—" Her diatribe was interrupted by a grunt as she took another swing at my head.

"Hold on, Connie!" I managed as I dropped to the floor, rolled, and narrowly avoided a kick she launched at my midsection.

"You destroyed my marriage. You tantalized my husband. You bitch!"

Several nurses had gathered to watch, but no one lifted a finger to try and stop the mayhem. "This woman is psychotic. Do you think you might grab her?" I asked a stout-looking orderly. He only shook his head.

"You're on your own," he said. "She looks dangerous."

I dodged another swing and dove into her midriff, my head down. I clasped my arms around her and clung like a burr. Though I wasn't above defending myself in a cat-fight, I didn't like the idea of striking a pregnant woman. As I clutched her to me, I had a strange realization. Connie Peters's stomach was a little pudgy, as in overindulgent, and soft. Nothing like the taut, ripe belly of a woman with child.

She wasn't pregnant!

But that didn't mean she wasn't homicidal. After escaping death at the hands of Virgie Carrington, a far better bred killer, I was going to be pummeled to death by an insane wife who'd pretended pregnancy to keep her husband from divorcing her.

"I'm going to kill you!" Connie brought both fists down on my back with enough force to make me lose my grip on her. She broke free and did some kind of karate spin while kicking sideways. I stepped back and avoided her foot.

When she had to put both feet down or fall, I grabbed her ankles and tugged. Her feet came out from under her, and she went down hard, striking the floor with sufficient force to knock the wind from her lungs.

Because I had no choice, I straddled Connie and pinned her arms to the floor. I found myself staring into her furious eyes. I couldn't tell if she was really insane, or if she was simply so angry she'd lost her ability to reason. Whatever, I wasn't going to turn her loose until someone with authority was on the scene.

"Call security!" I screamed at the gawking gaggle of nurses. When none of them made a move to do anything, I resorted to the death threat of the medical profession. "If you don't call for some help, I'm going to sue!" That scattered them to five different telephones.

The door of Coleman's room opened, and he staggered into the hall. As he took in the scene, I saw his expression drop into weariness.

"Sarah Booth, Connie, break it up."

I wasn't about to let the tiger go free and risk a chance of being eaten before help arrived. I kept her arms pinned and her lungs deflated until I heard the squawking radios of help.

Security arrived, and I found myself strong-armed off Coleman's writhing wife. She took the opportunity to drive one into my gut before the second security guard grabbed her. He wrested her to her feet and held her in a double-armed headlock.

I heard the staccato tapping of Tinkie's heels and her indrawn breath of disbelief. "What's going on here?" she asked. "Good lord, where did Connie come from? And Sarah Booth, why are you green?"

"I've come to dispense justice!" Connie said as she took a swipe at me with one foot.

I took a ragged breath, managing not to toss my cookies from the gut kick, and shifted my focus to Coleman, who swayed but remained standing. It was killing him not to be able to control the two women in his life.

"Are you okay?" Tinkie put an arm around my waist for support.

"I'm fine. The psycho over there tried to kill me. In case you haven't noticed, she isn't pregnant."

Tinkie assessed Connie's figure, her normally merry features settling into cold fury. "No, she isn't pregnant. Just a little flabby, with most of her ass shifting to her stomach. Isn't the term for that butt gut?"

Connie was unable to express her rage in actual words. She gave a howl and tried to hurl herself at Tinkie. The security officer, though slow on the move, was strong.

Coleman stepped forward. "Connie, what do you think you're doing?"

"I'm beating the shit out of the woman who wrecked our marriage and her insulting friend. We had a good marriage, Coleman. We had everything. Until you fell in love with her." She gave me a look that would have frozen hell over.

Coleman put his hand on the door frame for balance. "If that were true, Connie, you'd have a reason to be angry, but it isn't true. We never had a real marriage. I would have divorced you long ago, but I felt responsible for you. And then the whole pregnancy ruse." He looked at her with sadness. "It's over, Connie."

Connie at last quit struggling in the security guard's grip. It was as if the starch had gone out of her. She sagged. "That's all a lie. You wanted a baby, so I tried. I did all of it for you."

The moment was so awful, a few of the nurses slunk away to tend to other patients. Coleman looked from Connie to me. "We need to talk. All three of us. I've tiptoed around this issue for too long. Now it's going to get resolved." He looked at the security guards. "Turn them loose, please."

I thought perhaps the bullet had struck his brain. He wasn't the one Connie was going to jump as soon as she was free.

"Are you sure, Sheriff Peters?" one of the men had the good sense to ask.

Coleman nodded. "This isn't the time or place for this, but there's no helping it now. Sarah Booth, Connie, come into my room, please." The guards released us both and stepped back. Connie glared but made no move to strike me.

"I'll stand guard at the door," Tinkie volunteered. She was letting me know she wouldn't be far away if the fur started to fly.

I followed Coleman into the hospital room and closed the door. He sank onto the side of the bed. He was still pale, but he held himself with perfect posture. "Now, let's get this straight once and for all."

"We can't get anything straight as long as she's"— Connie pointed at me—"in the picture."

"That's where you're wrong, Connie." Coleman's voice was slow and deliberate. "Sarah Booth isn't the problem."

"What are you going to do?" Connie showed the first indication that she realized she'd made a terrible mistake. I had a revelation of my own: not only wasn't she pregnant, she wasn't nuts. She was perfectly capable of understanding what she'd done. Insanity was just her way of not facing the consequences of her actions.

"Coleman, what are you going to do?" she asked again.

I stood beside the door, waiting to hear Coleman's answer.

"Connie, whatever I've felt for Sarah Booth, I haven't acted on. She's not that kind of woman, and I'm not that kind of man. You need to know that. I've tried in every way I know to be the husband you wanted."

I could see the anger in her eyes. "How can you say

that? You never loved me. You married me because you couldn't shake me, but you never loved me."

He rubbed his eyebrow. "I tried to love you. A long time ago I convinced myself that I did. Even when I realized I didn't, I kept trying. Failing that, I tried to act as if I loved you. My thinking was that if I didn't love you, at least I could still be a good husband. That was a tragic mistake, and I see the error of it now."

I felt the tears gathering in my eyes. It's a hard thing for a man to look at the fabric of his life and see only the holes.

Connie grasped the footrest of the bed. "You can't divorce me. I'm sick."

Coleman took a deep breath. "I'm not buying that any longer, Connie. My first mistake was in staying married to a woman I didn't love. My second, more serious mistake was in turning my back on the woman I do love to accept a burden of responsibility. In doing that, I betrayed myself and Sarah Booth."

"Sarah Booth!" Connie practically spat my name. "What kind of woman goes after a married man? You speak of her like she's so wonderful. She's a tramp."

Coleman glanced at me, and the tiniest of smiles touched the corners of his lips. "Sarah Booth didn't go after me. In fact, she's done a lot to stay out of my path."

"Right. That's why she's always in the sheriff's office."

Coleman stood. It cost him, but he gained his feet. "Connie, you can have whatever you want financially. What you can't have is another minute of my time. Get a lawyer, because I intend to."

She stared at him, trying to calculate what his words were truly going to cost her. "I'm going to flay the hide off you in court."

"I doubt it. If I chose to fight you, Connie, I don't think there's a court in the world that would side with a woman who used the hope of a baby as a weapon against her husband. But I'm not going to fight. Take everything. There's not a thing I own worth fighting you about. Take it all. Take it and get out of my life."

Connie's breathing was hard. She turned to me. "You bitch. You're going to pay for this!" And then she was gone. She tried to slam the door, but the hydraulic release foiled her last attempt at drama. Coleman and I were alone in the room.

"Sarah Booth." He faltered, and I rushed to him, putting my arm around him for support.

"I don't know what to say," was my brilliant response.

"I sprang that on you kind of suddenly. I tried to talk to you before all of this—when I found out the pregnancy was a complete fabrication to keep me tied to her. The doctor in the mental institution finally told me the truth."

"It didn't occur to her that she'd have to produce a baby sometime in the future?"

He shook his head. "I think she thought she could seduce me and possibly get pregnant, but that kind of thing was over a long, long time ago for us. I tried to be a husband, but I didn't love her. Whatever intimacy we had was a sham, an attempt for me to cover the total lack of love I felt for her." He touched my cheek. "After years of dealing with liars and criminals, it honestly never occurred to me that Connie would lie about a baby."

With my urging, he sat on the edge of the bed, and I sat beside him. He slipped his arm around my shoulders and pulled me close. For a long moment we sat that way, with me listening to the beating of his heart.

"Are you sure this is what you want?" I asked him.

His smile was tired. "What I really want is to go back in time and undo the entire marriage." Something unpleasant touched the features of his face. "I've felt so guilty. For marrying her when I didn't love her. For not being able to love her."

"A Brillo pad would be more lovable, Coleman." The words were out of my mouth before I could stop them. "Part of the guilt rests on her."

"And part on me. I always knew, deep down, that I didn't love her the way I should. There is a special hell for half-measures."

I took his hand. "Love is earned. It isn't some magical thing that happens."

"It's magical with you." He leaned down and lightly kissed my lips. "See, that was magic."

I touched his stubbly cheek. "Are you certain this divorce is what you want?"

"Yes. I'm not going to live any longer in emotional limbo. I haven't asked you what your plans are, and I won't do that now. I have to make my own plans before I try to hook anyone else into them."

Sometimes Coleman was truly wise. I kissed him lightly on the lips. "Get some rest."

"There's nothing I'd like better." He sank back against the pillow and closed his eyes, asleep before I could exit the room.

Tinkie sat on my bed as I flipped through my closet for something to wear to Allison's gathering. Dr. Martin had decided to keep Coleman in the hospital another day, so Tinkie and I'd come home together. Sensing how turbulent my emotions were, she'd stayed with me.

"We solved another case. Allison is free—and rich. She lost the person she loved, but she has her whole life ahead of her." Tinkie rolled onto her back. "I can't imagine not being a private investigator."

"You could have been killed." I was still upset about the danger Tinkie had been in.

"But I wasn't. And neither were you. We put a serial killer in jail, Sarah Booth. We did it. We're developing quite a reputation."

I turned to look at her, caught by her innocence and strength. She was right. We had every reason in the world to celebrate. "I owe Humphrey an apology. He turned out to be a pretty good guy, and I never took him seriously."

"Bad timing on his part. Are you going to marry Coleman?"

"Aren't you jumping the gun a bit? He hasn't asked." I dug through the closet for my shoes to avoid looking at her.

"Aren't you hedging? You know he will. And I predict soon."

Tinkie was my partner and my best friend. I could be honest with her—which would force me to be honest with myself. "I don't know," I confessed. "My thoughts are one giant muddle. For so long Coleman has been out of reach—a married man. Now he's available. We can actually explore our feelings for each other." I plopped down beside her on the bed.

"And that thought terrifies you, doesn't it?"

She was good. She was damn good. I nodded slowly, my gaze on the heels I held in my hand.

"What do you want, Sarah Booth?"

"That's easy enough to ask but hard to answer." I went back to the closet and pulled out a red shirt with a deep V-neck and a side tie that was sexy and slimming. "This will go perfectly with my black jeans and those sexy heels. Red is Christmassy, and maybe it'll put me in the mood for the fast-approaching holiday."

"This sudden concern for fashion is interesting, but I recognize it as another dodge. Answer my question."

"That's a tough question," I hedged. "What do you want, Tinkie?"

"I want to put aside all the hurt and scar tissue I've been building against Oscar." She leaned on her elbow as she stretched out on the bed. "I want a child. A girl, specifically, but I'll settle for a boy. I want to sing and play with

my child in a garden filled with bright flowers and butter-
flies. I want to see you happy."

She had her wants down to very specific details. "I don't
know what I want."

"Because you're afraid of having it and then losing it."

Tinkie hadn't been to head-shrinking school, but she
was damn good at figuring people out. "Maybe."

"You're the bravest person I know, Sarah Booth. It doesn't
make sense that you'd be afraid to love someone."

"It makes perfect sense if you've lived my life."

"I've sometimes thought that you loved Coleman because you couldn't have him. It was safe to long for him—
far safer than the reality of having someone."

"Enough with the analysis!"

She got up and came over to me. She took my hands in
hers and held them to her chest. "Once I didn't run with
the opportunity given to me." She squeezed my hands
tightly. "It's the only thing I've ever regretted."

She held my gaze for a long moment before she released my hands and stepped back. "I'll pick you up in an
hour. I need to see Oscar and change my own clothes."

"Thank you, Tinkie, but there's no need to pick up
me." I called after her retreating back. "I'll see you both at
the party."

She was barely gone when Jitty appeared at my dressing
table, adjusting a truly unattractive mop cap fitted over
what looked to be unwashed curls. Her dress was a harsh
blue cloth, loosely fitted and covered with a dirty white
apron. "What the hell happened to you?" I asked. Jitty was
prone to numerous costume changes, but she always wore
elegant and attractive clothes.

"The revolution happened, that's what. Even a ghost
could lose her head if she showed up in too much finery."

"Sounds to me like you stayed at the ball too long." I
slipped into my black jeans.

"At least I had the courage to attend."

I stopped and turned to look at her. "What's that supposed to mean?"

"Tinkie was giving you some good advice. The only thing you ever regret is what you don't try."

"Tell that to Marie when her head rolls into a basket. She could have done without that 'let them eat cake' comment, and she might have lived to raise her children."

Jitty smiled. "You really aren't a student of history, are you?"

"Somehow I think I'm going to get the lecture no matter how I answer."

"Right. The monarchy of France was doomed not by the actions of Marie and her husband, but by the intrigues of men who lusted for power. The rabble was roused by those with an agenda. If you don't get history, take a look at what's happening in Washington D.C. today."

Politics was the furthest thing from my mind, and I was a little shocked that Jitty would take an interest in them. "Can I please get ready for this gathering without having to think about rabble and rousing and baskets filled with wigless heads?"

"Of course." She stood up. "I have an appointment, anyway. Just remember, Marie might not have paid attention to the warning signs, but when she goes to her death, she'll do so with courage." Jitty shimmered out of the room.

"I hate your freaking enigmatic last lines!" I threw a brush at the place where she'd been standing. She was gone, though, and no antics would bring her back. I slipped into my shirt and set to work on my make-up. I had a celebration to attend and an apology to give. I wanted to look my best no matter what the night—or the future—threw at me.